Critics adore Sara
romances . . . no
passion of frontie

HEARTS UNBOUND

A captivating Basque beauty sparks the desire of a hard-living Boise physician—but her father has chosen a man for her, also a Basque. Will the challenges of the lonely Idaho range force tradition to cross a daring boundary?

"Not your typical Eastern-lady-meets-frontier-doctor Western. . . . If you're looking to be transported somewhere unusual, and if you enjoy family/cultural conflict, I recommend *Hearts Unbound*. . . . A solid read."
—*All About Romance*

RIMFIRE BRIDE

A pretty and courageous schoolteacher comes to Bismarck and turns heads as a dress model in a shop window! And in the arms of the handsome single father who owns Rimfire Ranch, she discovers what home feels like. . . .

"Luck's devotion to historical accuracy shines again. . . . *Rimfire Bride* warms the heart."
—*RT Book Reviews*

"Exciting. . . . A must-read. Sara Luck is truly a talented storyteller. . . . You feel as if you are there in 1882."
—*My Book Addiction Reviews*

TALLIE'S HERO

A *Publishers Weekly* Top 10 Romance for Fall 2012

The dangerous American West is no place for a genteel British novelist fleeing a scandal . . . but one plucky lady embraces the spirit of Wyoming—and captures the heart of her new hero, a daring rancher with big dreams of his own.

"The Wild West retains its appeal in *Tallie's Hero*."
                                        —*Publishers Weekly*

"Steamy Western romance."

                                        —*Fresh Fiction*

CLAIMING THE HEART

As the Texas and Pacific Railroad expands across the wild frontier, a spirited young woman experiences the triumphs and tumult of building a part of history . . . and loving a track man bound to a politically powerful family.

"Terrific. . . . An enjoyable nineteenth-century Americana tale."

                                        —*Genre Go Round Reviews*

"Luck captures the true essence of the Texas frontier. . . . A fast-paced story with plenty of action and engaging characters."

                                        —*Romantic Times*

SUSANNA'S CHOICE

Sara Luck's "promising debut"
(*Romance Reviews Today*)!

*In a dusty Nevada mining town, an aspiring
newspaperwoman crosses paths with a wealthy
entrepreneur from San Francisco, and everything
changes—including her own uncertain destiny.*

"An exciting read . . . A passionate, adventure-filled historical romance."

—Romance Junkies

"Heartwarming. . . . Sensual. . . . This one's a keeper!"

—Night Owl Reviews
(5 stars, a Night Owl Top Pick)

"A solid story line with a just-right soupçon of romantic tension."

—Publishers Weekly

"Everything a historical romance reader could want. . . . An exciting story with strong characters and vivid descriptions of Americana history."

—My Book Addiction Reviews

"Luck is an author to watch."

—RT Book Reviews

ALSO BY SARA LUCK

HEARTS AFIRE

SARA LUCK

Pocket Books

New York   London   Toronto   Sydney   New Delhi

Pocket Books
A Division of Simon & Schuster, Inc.
1230 Avenue of the Americas
New York, NY 10020

This book is a work of fiction. Any references to historical events, real people, or real places are used fictitiously. Other names, characters, places, and events are products of the author's imagination, and any resemblance to actual events or places or persons, living or dead, is entirely coincidental.

First Pocket Books paperback edition May 2014

POCKET and colophon are registered trademarks of Simon & Schuster, Inc.

For information about special discounts for bulk purchases, please contact Simon & Schuster Special Sales at 1-866-506-1949 or business@simonandschuster.com.

The Simon & Schuster Speakers Bureau can bring authors to your live event. For more information or to book an event, contact the Simon & Schuster Speakers Bureau at 1-866-248-3049 or visit our website at www.simonspeakers.com.

Cover illustration by Aleta Rafton

Manufactured in the United States of America

10 9 8 7 6 5 4 3 2 1

ISBN 978-1-4767-5377-5
ISBN 978-1-4767-5379-9 (ebook)

HEARTS
AFIRE

ONE

New York Chronicle—December 1893

BRILLIANT PERFORMANCE

Miss Sabrina Chadwick continues to amaze New York theatergoers with her brilliant performances. Her portrayal of Lily Fontaine in the Lyle Ketterman production A Young Woman's Travail is perhaps the best performance of the season. She brings to the role all the nuances envisaged for the character by the playwright, Ethan Springer, beautifully displaying all the extremes: naïve to urbane, shy to assertive, victim to triumphant. From the moment she emerges from the wings she owns the stage, and hers is the brightest star in the firmament, the other players but pale lights in her luster.

The Ketterman Production Company's husband-and-wife team, Lyle and the former Bella Chase, have once again combined with their most talented actress to bring excitement to the boards. This writer cannot speak highly enough of this wonderful play.

Sabrina Chadwick was the name Victoria Drumm had chosen for the stage. At the moment Tori, as she preferred to be called, was already in makeup and costume, waiting in the wings for the curtains to open for tonight's production. She sat on a high stool and looked at the other players, smiling when she saw the nervousness of some of the newer cast members who were moving their lips as they silently went over their lines.

Robert Walker, the director, and Keith Collins, the stage manager, were busy with last-minute instructions. Tori looked around for the producer, but she didn't see him. For as long as she had known Lyle Ketterman, he had never missed a curtain opening.

"Bob, have you seen Lyle?"

"No," Walker replied. "But I'm sure he'll be here. He's always here."

"I'm a little worried about him."

"Don't worry. If ever there was somebody who could take care of himself in just about any situation, it's Lyle."

Collins approached the two. "Bob, if you don't have any objections, I'm going to go ahead and fly those tree flats between the second and third act. We don't need them and it gives us a little more room for the window flats if the trees are out of the way."

"Good idea," Bob said. Then, seeing one of the other players, he called out to her, "Julie, no, no, I want you to have the sprinkling can in your hand when the curtains open." Walker and Collins hurried away, leaving Tori alone.

Tori looked around, but still no Lyle.

"Good luck, Miss Chadwick," one of the newer young actors said.

"No!" an older cast member said, admonishing the offending party. "Never say good luck! Are you crazy? Do you want to jinx this production?" The older cast member pointed to a side door. "Go outside, turn around three times . . . spit, curse, then knock on the door and ask to be readmitted."

"What?" the young actor said.

"Just do it, or by damn, you'll never be in another production as long as you live!"

Tori smiled. She knew all the theater superstitions and traditions. Her uncle, Harold Freeman, owned this theater, and he and her aunt Frances had a flat on the second floor. Tori had lived with them from the time she was twelve years old until just a couple of years ago, when she had moved to her own apartment.

The stage of the Freeman was well illuminated by electric footlights. It had two spotlights, which, with gels and lenses, could widen or narrow focus, helping to establish the mood the actors wished to project.

"Curtain," Collins called, and Tori could hear the applause as the curtains drew open. Julie was onstage with the sprinkling can.

"Oh, these are such lovely flowers. Miss Fontaine does keep a beautiful garden."

The first act went off without a hitch, and every time Tori left the stage, she looked for Lyle.

He wasn't to be found, and she was growing more and more concerned.

Then, just before the close of the second act, Tori,

in character as Lily Fontaine, stepped downstage right. Reaching her mark, she stepped into the glow of a soft-focus blue spotlight. She lifted her hand to her cheek, tilted her head, then spoke her lines loudly enough to be heard throughout the theater, though with just the right tone in her voice to express the concern of the moment.

"Oh, am I to marry Simon McGraw? No, I cannot, for I will not be trapped in a loveless marriage. But if I don't marry him, Mother and Father will be turned out of their home. Oh, what am I to do? What am I to do?"

The curtains closed to the applause of the theater audience.

Tori hurried offstage, then into her dressing room, where she would change costumes for the next act. Hannah Inman, her makeup and wardrobe assistant, was waiting for her.

"You are the most wonderful actress, Miss Chadwick," Hannah said as she laid out everything Tori would need to freshen her face. "I've seen this play dozens of times, but every time I hear you deliver your lines, I cry."

"That's very sweet of you to say." Tori picked up a powder puff and began dabbing at her makeup. "Has Mr. Ketterman still not shown up? I'm beginning to worry that something may have happened to him."

"It's not Mr. Ketterman—it's Mrs. Ketterman."

"Bella? Has something happened to Bella?"

"Mr. Ketterman's coachman just came in. He had to rush Mrs. Ketterman to the hospital this afternoon. He said she was in a terrible state—crying and in such pain," Hannah said. "Poor dear, I so feel for her. You know how much she wanted this baby—why, that's all she's been talking about—and now the coachman says he's sure she's lost it. It must have been just terrible."

"Bella? Bella was expecting a child?" Tori asked weakly.

"Oh, yes. Didn't you notice she's been green around the gills lately? This baby's been makin' her awful sick."

"I hadn't noticed." Tori laid the powder puff on the dressing table.

The door opened and Mrs. McKenzie brought in the dress Tori would need for the third act.

"Here's your costume, dear. Be extra careful when you put it on. I took in the waist a bit so it fits a little better."

"Thank you," Tori said, so quietly the words were barely audible.

"Have you heard about poor Mrs. Ketterman?" Mrs. McKenzie asked. "The coachman said Mr. Ketterman is just beside himself. They both are devastated."

"I know he was excited about the prospect of becoming a father," Hannah said. "What man tells everyone he knows when his wife is with child?"

Mrs. McKenzie sighed. "What a wonderful husband he is. Mrs. Ketterman is so lucky to have a man who adores her like he does."

"Five minutes!" Walker shouted from just outside the door. "Five minutes till curtain."

"I have to get Mr. Crites's costume to him," Mrs. McKenzie said, hurrying out of the dressing room.

"You'd better hurry, Miss Chadwick," Hannah said. "You haven't even begun to change."

"I . . . I have three minutes after the curtain rises before I'm onstage again."

"Can you dress yourself? I promised Mr. Collins I'd help move some of the props for him."

"Yes, go ahead."

Hannah hurried out of Tori's dressing room, and Tori whispered to herself, "A baby? How could that possibly be?" She sat for a long moment, staring at her reflection in the mirror as tears began welling in her eyes.

A short knock on the door caused Tori to jump.

"Sabrina, are you ready?" Walker called.

"Uh, yes."

"Then get in your place quickly, my dear. The curtain has just opened for the third act."

Tori looked over at the costume she should be wearing for her next stage appearance. She hadn't even begun to change, and she knew that even if she started now, she couldn't possibly be dressed in time. She left the dressing room and walked out to the wings.

Some of the others who were waiting to go onstage saw that she hadn't changed, and they looked at her in shock.

"Oh, Miss Chadwick, your costume!"

Tori stood there, tears streaming down her cheeks, as she listened to the dialogue coming from the stage. The words that she had heard every night since the season opened tended to blur.

"Are you all right?" one of the bit-part actors asked.

Tori wiped her tears, but didn't answer. Her cue was delivered:

"You should watch what you say, Jason. Lily would not be pleased by such words, and I hear her coming now."

Tori stood frozen, making no move go onstage.

"Did I hear her? I am sure I did," the actor said, now ad-libbing in an attempt to save the moment. He put his hand to his ear. "Yes . . . *I hear her coming now.*"

"Miss Chadwick, your cue, your cue!" the bit-part actor said.

Tori stepped onstage.

"I trust, my dear Lily, that you did not mishear my words, for surely it was not my intent to be indecorous," the actor portraying the role of Jason said.

Tori had a line, but she didn't respond as the tears continued to stream.

"I say, it was not my intent to be indecorous," the actor repeated.

Tori stood but a second longer, then she turned and rushed off the stage without saying a word. The two actors looked at each other for a long, speechless interlude.

"Sabrina! Sabrina, what is it? Where are you going? What just happened out there?" Walker questioned.

Tori didn't answer. Instead, she hurried past the cast and crew, who looked on in shock and confusion.

As the silence lengthened, the audience began to get restless.

"Go on!" someone shouted.

"Say something!" another audience member shouted.

The two actors fled the stage, and the curtains closed.

"Bob, do you want to tell me what this is all about?" the actor who was playing Jason asked angrily. "How dare that woman leave us standing naked onstage like that!"

Walker shrugged his shoulders. "You tell me what happened. You know as much about it as I do."

"She was crying before she went onstage," Julie said. "I saw her."

"What caused that? She's usually so composed."

"I don't know, but she was visibly upset and she was crying."

"I saw it, too," said the young actor who had wished her luck. "Oh, I hope I didn't . . ."

The older actor who had admonished him earlier put his hand on the young man's shoulder and said reassuringly, "It wasn't because of you."

By now the house was beginning to grow angry and the boos and catcalls grew louder and louder.

"Bob, you'd better get out there," Keith Collins said.

"Me? Why should I face that crowd?"

"Because you're the director, and the producer's not here."

"All right, all right, bring up the houselights, and I'll do what I can to get us out of this."

As soon as the houselights came up, Walker stepped before the curtain and stilled the boos by holding up his arms to call for quiet.

"Ladies and gentlemen, as the director of *A Young Woman's Travail*, I beg your indulgence. We have had a medical emergency here tonight, and this performance is concluded."

"We want our money back!" someone yelled.

"If you will stop by the ticket booth, you will be issued rain checks for a future performance. The Ketterman Production Company apologizes for any inconvenience this may have caused. Good evening." Walker turned and disappeared behind the curtains as the yells and booing began again.

With an angry expression on his face, Bob Walker strode past the cast and crew, who were now standing in shocked silence. When he reached Tori's dressing room, he banged on the door.

"Sabrina?" he called. "I want an explanation of just what happened out there! Are you sick?"

There was nothing but silence from the other side of the door, and Walker knocked again.

"Miss Chadwick?" he said again, a bit louder.

When she still didn't answer, he banged on the door so loudly that it could be heard all over backstage. Now his concern had given way to anger.

"You'd better have a good excuse, young woman!" Walker shouted. "Do you hear me? You'd better have a damn good excuse! Now, you open this door!" He tried the doorknob again but still got no response. "All right, missy, if this is how you want to play, I can play this game, too. I'll see to it that every penny of the returned receipts comes from your paycheck, unless you have some plausible reason for this petulant behavior! Good night, Miss Chadwick." He turned from the door and stormed back to the stage wings, where everyone else was anxiously waiting.

"What's her story? What happened?" Collins asked.

"Who knows? I need a drink."

"Me, too. I'm coming with you."

Cripple Creek, Colorado

"Buchannan, you're nothin' but a damn trouble-maker! What makes you think you got a right to be stickin' your nose in somebody else's business?" The speaker was holding a knife in the way of someone who knew how to use it. It was low and horizontal, the blade coming out from the thumb side of the hand, which gave him more flexibility.

"I caught you red-handed, Landry. You were high-grading from the Isabella, and you know it, and when you're stealing gold from J. J. Hagerman, you're stealing from me, too," Link Buchannan said. "I don't like to see my dividends walk out the door when the likes of you and your cohorts steal ore by the buckets full."

Lincoln Seward Buchannan, called Link by all who knew him, was standing in the middle of Myers Avenue on a cold and dreary afternoon. He was unarmed and facing an angry, knife-wielding hulk of a man named Gorran Landry.

Such confrontations were familiar for the booming gold-mining town; this was unusual only in that a miner was calling out a "socialite." Because of that, a crowd began to gather.

Landry's smile was menacing as he moved toward Link. "I don't care how blue your blood is, when I cut out your gizzard, you'll bleed red just like the rest of us."

"You've had too much to drink, Landry. Now, just go on home and sleep it off," Link said. "And besides, if you did cut me up, you'd have a long stay in the state pen. Is that what you want? Just take a look at all these people watching us."

"Them's not people. Them's whores and their johns gatherin' round to watch me take out a fine Philadelphia bastard."

Link looked toward the small crowd lining the street. Most of the onlookers were women, and most of them were residents of the many bordellos that lined Myers Avenue. "They make good witnesses."

"Course they do, 'cause they're all your friends." Landry moved toward Link.

"All right, Landry. If you're hell-bent on doing this, give it a try." Link spread his feet about shoulder width, bent slightly at the waist, and let his arms hang loosely in front of him.

An evil smile spread across Landry's face as he began nodding his head. "I'm gonna enjoy this a whole lot, and these folks is gonna back me up all the way. You're askin' for it, slicker."

Landry lunged toward Link, thrusting his knife before him. Link moved to one side as gracefully as a bullfighter avoiding the horns. The knife thrust found only empty space, and because of his lunge, Landry was left off-balance. Link reached out and grabbed the knife hand by the wrist. He jerked his attacker forward, using his own momentum, then, sweeping his leg against Landry's, threw him down.

Now, with Landry belly down on the ground, Link put his knee in the middle of his back and twisted his would-be assailant's arm behind him.

Landry yelped in pain.

"Drop the knife or I'll break your arm!"

Landry opened his hand and let the knife fall.

Link picked it up, then held the point against Landry's neck. "Can you give me one good reason why I shouldn't slit your throat?"

Landry said nothing, but spit in the dust.

Link kicked the man in the ribs. "Get up."

Landry got up, rubbing his arm. "You coulda broke my arm, you bastard. Now give me my knife."

Link threw the knife at the top of a light pole, burying the blade a quarter of the way into it. "Go get it. Don't you ever come around me again, and if I catch you in any mine I'm connected with, I'll see to it you have a long vacation."

With a hangdog expression, Landry walked away, chased by the laughter and chiding of the assembled crowd.

Stepping up onto the boardwalk, Link heard slow, deliberate clapping from a man leaning against the light pole.

"I'm glad you were aiming high," the man said as he extended his hand to Link.

"Speck, have you been here all along?" Link asked, addressing his friend Spenser Penrose.

"Uh-huh. Just watching to see if you needed me to step in and give Landry a swift right hook. I'm afraid

I wouldn't have been as generous as you were. I would have taken him out."

"Sure you would have," Link said, laughing with his friend.

Link, Speck Penrose, and Speck's business partner, Charles Tutt, had grown up as childhood friends, all living within a few blocks of each other in Philadelphia. They had competed against one another as they swam across the Delaware River or rowed on the Schuylkill. Everything the boys did was a contest—who could catch the biggest fish off the bridge, or who could skate the fastest on the ice—and this friendly competition had continued into adulthood.

Charles Tutt had been the first of the three to come to Colorado. Initially, he had tried his hand at raising cattle near Colorado Springs, but when that operation didn't succeed, he began selling real estate and insurance.

When an unseemly fraternity prank forced Link to give up his plans to attend law school, Albert Buchannan demanded that his son take a position in his bank. Link did everything he could to force his father to fire him, so when Charles Tutt invited Link to join him in Colorado Springs, Link left Philadelphia with his father's blessing.

That was five years ago, and Colorado had been good to Link. His gregarious personality along with his rugged good looks had enabled him to succeed, and when Speck, who was down to his last $100, joined the pair, Link decided it was time to open his own office, setting up the old competitive spirit that the three had enjoyed since childhood.

"I don't know about you, but I could use a drink about now," Link said.

"That's what I want to hear. I was on my way to the Topic to see how my girls are doing," Speck said. "Would you care to join me?"

"Sounds good to me."

The Topic, a dance hall on Bennett Avenue, was located in a building owned by Tutt and Penrose, and he considered the "girls" to be his employees as well as his friends. Because the miners worked around the clock, the dance halls never closed. The girls served as dancing partners for the men at any hour of the day or night, but their main job was to sell liquor. Each girl was paid a commission for every drink she sold.

While the traffic in prostitution was heavy in Cripple Creek, the girls at the Topic were not hired for that. Most of the brothels were located one block south on the 300 block of Myers Avenue. Here, the more elegant parlors were intermixed with several one-woman cribs.

"Hello, Mr. Penrose, Mr. Buchannan," one of the girls said, meeting the two men just inside the door.

"Ah, here's my Kate," Speck said as he gave the attractive woman a hug. "Can you put my friend and me in the meeting room?"

Kate's eyebrows lifted. "Do you want company?"

Speck laughed. "Not this evening, honey. Hennessy is the only company we'll need."

Kate smiled as she led Link and Speck into a small room off the dance floor. "For you, I'll find the best cognac in the house."

"You're a good girl, Kate, and I won't forget it," Speck said.

"Is that a promise?" Kate brushed an errant curl off Speck's forehead with a smile as she left the two men.

Once they were comfortably seated and the brandy delivered, Speck proposed a toast "To us," he said as he handed a glass to Link. "Two of the best-looking scalawags ever to leave Philadelphia."

"Ha! It wasn't me Kate was fawning over," Link said.

"It's my black hair. You know, Link, you should think about covering up that gray you've got showing."

"I've worked hard to grow every one of these gray hairs."

"Speaking of which, how's business?"

"It's good. I've got a few prospects dangling on the hook."

"Oh, do you? Would I happen to know these prospects?"

"There you go, Speck Penrose. I'm not telling you a damned thing." Link shook his head. "I'll be meeting my people in Colorado Springs as soon as I can get everything put together."

"I guess you'll see Charles?"

"Of course. If I play my cards right, Josephine may invite me for Christmas dinner."

"I'll miss being there," Speck said. "I love those kids just like they were my own, especially little Charles."

A broad smiled crossed Link's face. "Do you mean that the way it sounds? Are you looking to get some of your own?"

"You read too much into things, my friend. All

I'm saying is that I like my partner's kids. Nothing more."

"I'll bet the Amazon has something else to say about that. Everybody knows you're in love with Sally Halthusen."

"I'll have to admit, I enjoy her company, but it's because she's done such a good job training my horses," Speck said. "It has nothing to do with anything else."

"Sure, it's the horses. I think that big woman's got it in her mind that she's going to marry you, and you're not going to have one word to say about it."

"There could be worse things," Speck said. "How about you? Don't you think it's about time you found someone and settled down?"

"Listen to this drivel—coming from the biggest womanizer in Colorado. We're the same age, Speck. I'd see you getting hitched to Sally long before you find me getting snagged by one woman. Cripple Creek, and now Gillette, even Colorado Springs—these towns are a bachelor's paradise. Why would I want to mess that up by settling down?"

"You just wait. I'll wager a bet—say, five thousand dollars—that you'll be married long before I am. After all, you're an old man, at least six months older than I am, sir."

"I'll take that bet, but no more acting as your cowcatcher," Link teased. "You know you push me out in front of you just to fend off all the women around here. I don't mind the working girls you send my way. The ones that bother me are the self-righteous ones, the ones who wouldn't step foot on Myers Avenue for fear it would ruin their holier-than-thou reputations. They're just standing in line waiting to marry any fool who's either ambitious or lucky enough to take a fortune out of these mountains."

Speck laughed out loud. "You've got that right, my friend. You have indeed."

New York

Tori's apartment was in the Gerlach Hotel, between Broadway and Sixth on West Twenty-Seventh Street. Several members of the Twelfth Night Club, the recently formed club for professional women of the theater, lived there as well. As Tori stood at the window, she looked out over the twinkling lights of the city. Even at this early-morning hour, the street below was active, as several horse-drawn hacks made their way beneath the swags of Christmas greenery that crisscrossed the street.

Christmas. She had been invited to an open house at the apartment of Frank Leslie, another resident of the Gerlach. Frank was now the legal name of Miriam Leslie, the widow of the founder of *Frank Leslie's Illustrated Newspaper*. She had changed her name for business reasons, so she wouldn't have to change the masthead of the newspaper. Tori enjoyed her acquaintance with Mrs. Leslie, who held receptions every Thursday. Through them, Tori had become friends with contemporary Broadway stars such as May Robson, Clara Lipman, and Maude Adams, as well as other representative artists, musicians, and literary folk. Tori was certain the Christmas celebration would be an extension of those gatherings, even including Frank's recently divorced fourth husband, William Wilde, and his famous brother, Oscar.

Because of her actions tonight, though, that world would be closed to her forever. She had been approached by Charles Frohman to play the lead role in Clyde Fitch's *Masked Ball*, but because of her loyalty and devotion to Lyle Ketterman, she had turned him down, and Frohman had chosen Maude Adams to play opposite John Drew instead. Now Maude was the most financially successful actress on Broadway—not Sabrina Chadwick.

But it didn't matter.

Tori's stomach grumbled loudly to remind her that she hadn't eaten since morning. Most of the time the cast of the play took their dinner together after the last show, and she was sure that's where they were now. She also realized she would be the topic of conversation, and every one of them would be angry with her for what she had done. And they had a right to be.

Turning from the window, Tori went to her bed. Fully dressed, she lay there, staring into the darkness.

By the time the morning light streamed in through her window, Tori had made a decision. She would go to the hospital to confront Lyle Ketterman. He had, no doubt, heard what had happened the night before, and she wanted to make certain he understood his role in her calamitous performance. But when she got to the hospital and found where Bella was, Lyle was nowhere to be seen.

She stepped into the room. Bella, with her eyes closed, looked so small and innocent, so pale. Tori stood beside the bed, too emotional to speak. She stared at this woman—someone who had befriended her, someone whose money had made her a star, and yet Tori had betrayed her in the most unimaginable way—and in that moment, she knew what she had to do. She turned and as quietly as possible stepped to the door.

"Sabrina? Is that you?" Bella called out quietly.

Tori wanted to rush out of this room, but she stopped.

"I'm so glad you came. You missed Lyle, poor dear. He's been by my side all night, and he just stepped out for a bite to eat. He's taking this so hard, but I told him there's plenty of time to have another baby."

Tori turned to face Bella.

"I'm sorry, I'm so sorry." Tears welled in Tori's eyes.

"Thank you, dear." Bella reached for Tori's hand and took it in her own. "I want you to know how much I have enjoyed our friendship. You are very special to me, and to Lyle, too."

She doesn't know, Tori thought. She doesn't have the slightest idea.

"I'm sorry," Tori said again. "Please, forgive me."

"Forgive you?"

Tori turned and hurried from the room.

TWO

Cripple Creek

Link Buchannan stepped out of his office on the west side of Second Street and entered the next door.

"How's my girl?" Link asked as he stepped behind a paper-strewn table and encountered a frazzled young woman.

The woman tilted her head and lifted her chin as she accepted the chaste kiss Link placed on her cheek. She never let her eyes stray from the paper that was lying on the desk as her fingers continued to beat the keys on the typewriter.

"I'm sorry, Link, I don't have your prospectus ready yet," Mollie O'Bryan said, "but you said you weren't leaving for a couple more days. If you'll give me a few more hours, I'll have everything done."

"Look at this place, Mollie." Link took in the cramped little room. "You need help. Surely there's some nice young woman in this town who can use a typewriter, or at least someone you can teach. It can't be that hard to do what you do."

With that comment, Mollie stopped typing and

looked up. "Oh? Why don't I teach you if it's so easy?"

"Just maybe I'll let you do that, if it means I get to spend more time with you."

Mollie laughed. "You're not fooling anybody, Link Buchannan. You just want to find out all the inside news I get without my having to tell you. Isn't that right?"

"It could be." Link looked down at the paper lying beside the typewriter. "Hmmmm . . . what's this?"

"It doesn't concern you. Nobody's made a big strike that you don't already know about."

Link picked up the paper and began reading.

"Who brought this to you, Mollie?"

"Jimmie Burns. He's just sending the minutes of a meeting some mine owners had. There's nothing important that I can see."

"If I read this right, the Portland is agreeing to a nine-hour workday and paying three dollars. Who all is getting this letter?"

"It's going to Hagerman, Moffat, Howbert, and Lennox," Mollie said as she looked through her stack of papers. "I don't know who else right now, but I do know twelve mine owners are signing on to this work schedule. Is that important information to know?"

"Everything is important in my business." Link kissed the top of her head. "Just get my pamphlet ready when you can. I want to get it over to the *Crusher* to have it printed."

"You'll have it by tomorrow, I promise, even if I have to stay here all night."

"Don't do that, Mollie. I don't like it when you

stay so late. Some hothead will come stumbling out of Crapper Jack's feeling too much of his peach schnapps and he'll think you're Bilious Bessie or Greasy Gertie."

Mollie laughed. "As long as he doesn't get me mixed up with Dirty Neck Nell, I'll be fine."

"I'm not teasing. I mean it. Don't stay late."

"All right, I won't. Thanks, Link, for caring."

Just then the door opened and the bell tinkled. An attractive, well-dressed auburn-haired woman stepped into the stenographer's office.

"Miss de Vere," Link said as he dipped his head. "I am pleased to be in the company of two of the most beautiful women in Cripple Creek."

"Two of the hardest working, you mean," Pearl de Vere said, "and I hope Mollie takes that as a compliment."

"I do, Pearl. This office wouldn't be the business it is if you hadn't sent some of your best customers to me," Mollie said.

Pearl's eyebrows lifted. "I'm glad it's only Link who heard you say that, my friend, lest the rumors start flying up and down Myers Avenue. As it is, everybody questions how you, a twenty-year-old single woman, can make it in this town without going to work for the likes of me, unless"—Pearl turned her attention to Link—"unless some good man wants to marry our Mollie."

"I'm sure there's such a man in Cripple Creek," Link said.

"But it's not you. Is that what you're telling me?" Mollie asked.

"It's the *good* man part I'm talking about," Link

said, enjoying the banter. "I don't think I can qualify for that."

"Oh, yes," Pearl said, "that is if I can take the word of any one of my girls. You're one of their favorite customers."

"Shhhh." Link put his fingers to his lips. "Don't let Mollie hear you say that. I've got her convinced she's my only girl."

"Get out of here," Mollie said. "We both know what you want from us."

"You probably do, at that." Link headed for the door. "And I can stand right here and tell you from the bottom of my heart, I admire and love you both."

The two women rolled their eyes and shook their heads as they watched the handsome man step out of the office, the little bell tinkling as he closed the door.

New York

Sitting in the cavernous waiting room at Grand Central Terminal, Tori Drumm took a deep breath as she leaned back against the hard bench. Had it been only a week since she'd walked out on *A Young Woman's Travail*?

Tori had to laugh. *A Young Woman's Travail*. What an apt description of her present state.

The last six days were a blur as she had gone about getting her personal belongings out of the Gerlach. During it all, her aunt Frances had been her bulwark, never once asking her to explain what could, honestly, be construed as her irrational behavior. The one consequence that Tori had not reckoned on was the financial toll her uncle would experience upon having the lead actress replaced by an unknown understudy. Someday, somehow, she would make it up to him.

Her biggest regret was the falsehood she had told when her aunt questioned where she planned to go. Tori had said Chicago, and as she looked at her ticket to check her schedule, her first stop was indeed Chicago, so technically it wasn't a lie.

"Tori? Is that you?" a woman asked as she approached Tori.

Tori didn't look up. She had gone to great pains to make herself unrecognizable. Her curvaceous shape, normally accented by costumes, was underplayed by the nondescript steel-gray cloak she had chosen for her traveling apparel. The long, dark hair that some reviewers described as her signature trait was now pulled back into an austere bun and concealed beneath a jet bonnet. Her brown eyes, which when onstage seemed to gleam, set off as they were by theatrical makeup, were now but augmentations of a pleasing, if not striking, face.

"We missed you last night."

The woman who had spoken sat on the bench and reached for Tori's hand.

"Oh, Mrs. Leslie, you shouldn't have come," Tori said, recognizing her neighbor.

"And why not? You're a Gerlach girl. Were you going to leave without saying good-bye to all your friends, or will you be back for my Christmas open house?"

Tori lowered her gaze. "I've forgotten my manners.

I should have sent my regrets. Can you forgive me?"

"I can forgive you, but that's not the important part. Clara Lipman told me what happened at the theater, and my question to you is: Can you forgive yourself?"

Tori looked directly at Mrs. Leslie. The question she had posed was far more consequential than she realized, and tears began to well in Tori's eyes. Tori opened her mouth to speak, but no words came.

"My poor dear," Mrs. Leslie said, pulling Tori into her arms. "Let me tell you, from one who has walked in your shoes, no man is worth it."

Tori stiffened and pulled back. What did Mrs. Leslie know?

"I don't suppose you've had time to read this." Mrs. Leslie pulled out a newspaper from her bag and handed it to Tori. "Lyle Ketterman is an ass. Put him out of your life."

The paper was folded to expose a woodcut drawing of Tori taken from one of the billboards that advertised *A Young Woman's Travail*.

She began reading:

ACTRESS LEAVES STAGE
IN MIDDLE OF PERFORMANCE

Miss Sabrina Chadwick left the stage during the performance of A Young Woman's Travail, *at the Freeman Theater Saturday evening, last. Recently regarded as one of the brightest luminaries in New York theater, her strange action shocked not only the audience in attendance, but the entire cast and company of the production.*

The star's reason for walking out in the middle of the play remains a mystery, as are her whereabouts. Ketterman says that the actress is in violation of her contract, and if she does not make good on her bond, she will likely be finished in the theater.

When questioned further, Ketterman added, "I can't believe Miss Chadwick would do this to me. I expected more loyalty to the one who has made her a star. And instead of offering comfort to my beloved wife, who is in hospital, and who has been nothing but a helpful friend to her, Miss Chadwick chose to turn her back on us, as well as the entire production company."

Mr. Ketterman went on to say he believes Miss Agnes Burkhart, who is being prepared for the role abandoned by Miss Chadwick, will make an even more convincing Lily Fontaine.

"I believe in the long run," Ketterman continued, "the theatergoers will find the unexpected departure of Miss Chadwick to have been a blessing in disguise. And I say, good riddance."

"I've really made a mess of things," Tori said as she handed the paper back to Mrs. Leslie. "He hates me."

"Right now, you think you've lost someone for whom you cared deeply, but believe me, Lyle Ketterman is not worth it. I think it's wise that you're leaving Gotham for a while. Do you know where you are going?"

"Chicago." Then Tori continued with the truth: "I

change trains there on my way to Colorado Springs. I'm going to visit my brother."

"A very wise choice. The climate, the people, the atmosphere—it won't be long until you've forgotten all your troubles. Will you write to me?"

"Oh, Mrs. Leslie, I would love to."

"Good, I'm going to hold you to it, and I promise you, I will write back. Wonderful! And now I have a gift for you. I planned to give it to you for Christmas, but I think it will serve you well on your trip to the Springs." Mrs. Leslie handed a package to Tori. "I think it is most appropriate under the circumstances. Open it, if you will."

Tori opened the package and found two books: *California: A Pleasure Trip from Gotham to the Golden Gate* by Mrs. Frank Leslie, and *The One Fair Woman* by Joaquin Miller.

"Oh, this is your book," Tori said when she saw the author's name.

"Humph. Actually, you could say they are both my books. You see, Joaquin and I started an affair shortly after Frank and I were married. You might recognize me as his main character." Mrs. Leslie embraced Tori. "I must get back now, but I do want you to keep in touch with me. Tell an old woman everything you're doing. It will keep me young."

"I hardly think you're old. I can't tell you how much I appreciate your coming, and your gifts. Thank you."

"Enjoy them, and, Tori, may I offer you a word of advice? There is a line in Joaquin's book that I always thought he wrote especially for me. 'We will reform tomorrow.' It's a good line." With that, Miriam Leslie turned and left.

Cripple Creek

Link made his way to the Palace Hotel, which served as the unofficial trading spot for both personal and business information circulating in town. When he stepped into the lobby, the room was crowded with men of all descriptions.

"There he is—the man of the hour," Verner Reed said when he saw Link. "They tell me you're the one who put together the sale of the Mary Nevene."

"I did," Link said.

"Fifty thousand dollars for an unproven claim. That's some talking, I'd say."

"That's why we're in business. Everyone wants to take advantage of the Anaconda. Did you hear it's officially in bonanza ore?"

"I'd say. Milo Hoskins said he shipped twenty-five tons that had the largest amount of money ever returned on one carload of ore. The assay showed thirty ounces to the ton, and when Jimmie Doyle doubted the results, he had them assay it again. Do you know what they found the next time?"

"I haven't heard," Link said

"It was forty ounces to the ton. That makes twenty thousand dollars for one carload of ore. Can you just imagine how much money is going to be taken out of this old cow pasture?" Verner asked. "And now that the railroad's coming all the way to Midland, the freight costs will go down and the profits will go up."

Link smiled. "Let's not get ahead of ourselves just yet. Any number of things can happen along the way to us all becoming millionaires."

"Well, I say it's going to happen," Verner said. "You are coming to the banquet tomorrow night, aren't you?"

"Of course. I hear there are so many people coming in from Denver and Pueblo, they had to put an extra car on the excursion train."

"I guess everybody wants to be on the first train into Midland, but little do they know that last eight miles by coach will be the most exciting, especially if Eddie Fromm lays the whip to the horses"

"Eddie wouldn't do that to those folks," Link said, "unless old 'Bloody Bridles' is in his coach. Then he may give our Populist bastard governor a run he won't soon forget."

"You know Governor Waite's not going to show his face in Cripple Creek. Not since he's thrown in with the Western Federation of Miners," Verner said. "Do you think the WFM will try to organize here?"

"I think they already have," Link said. "Peter Hettig told me John Calderwood and Manny Drumm have organized a union up at Altman, and they're calling it the Free Coinage Number Nineteen."

"What a surprise! With a name like that the mine owners had better look out. I wouldn't put it past the governor to join himself."

"I don't think the union will have much power— not with so many men pouring in every day looking for work. They wouldn't dare strike."

"You're probably right. We'll just see if anything is said tomorrow night."

The next night the Palace Hotel was filled with mine owners, businessmen and businesswomen of the city, as well as those from Colorado Springs, Denver, and Pueblo. James Parker, who was president of the Chamber of Commerce, stood at the door, greeting everyone who entered the lobby:

"Welcome, welcome to Cripple Creek. Glad you could come. Just step on into the dining room."

Link did as he was told. As he was making his way through the crowd, he saw Speck conversing with Pearl. The pair stood near the immense fireplace where logs were roaring on this crisp December evening. Link smiled as he watched Speck shriek with laughter at something Pearl said.

"Link! Link, my boy, over here!" Speck called, raising his drink by way of invitation. "Pearl's just been filling me in on the . . . shall we call them *shortcomings*? . . . of some of our more distinguished Denver guests."

"Pearl! Don't tell me you spread stories out of school?"

Pearl reached over and patted Link on the cheek. "Don't worry, darlin', if I told anything on you, it would only make you into a hero."

"Hey, what about me?" Speck asked.

"The same goes for both of you." Pearl locked arms with the two men.

"Let's get her to a seat before someone comes and steals her away from us," Link said.

The threesome found seats at a table near the back of the dining room.

"By golly, ole Jimmy's done himself proud tonight," Link said as he picked up the program that lay beside each plate and began reading the menu:

"Blue points on the half shell, whitefish, tenderloin with mushrooms, terrapin patties, asparagus, and lettuce with Roquefort and blue cheese. Why, tonight there won't be a finer table set in all of America."

"Let me see that thing." Speck grabbed the program from Link. "Here's the most important part: 'Diners may have their choice of these fine wines: Pontet Canet or Veuve Clicquot.'"

"Listen to the Harvard man speak that French," Pearl said.

"You just wait. By the end of the evening, I'll be speaking French, German, Latin—you name it, and if you've had enough to drink, you won't be able to tell the difference."

"Speck, have you ever seen me drunk?"

"No, Pearl, I don't think I ever have."

"That's what I thought. Say, are the Tutts in town tonight?" Pearl asked.

"Josephine wouldn't let Charles come. She says it's too close to Christmas, and besides, he doesn't want to listen to these windbags anyway," Link said.

"Who says we have to listen? I'm just here to eat and drink," Speck said.

At that moment, John Calderwood and Emanuel Drumm approached the table.

"Gentlemen," Link said, rising from his seat. "Won't you join us?"

"That is if you'll sit with the opposition," Speck said. "The rumor is you've started a union. Is that true?"

"It's true, and I'm here recruiting a few good men to help with the cause. Do you know Manny Drumm?" Calderwood asked.

"Of course we know Manny. Does that surprise you?" Link asked. "Here in Cripple Creek, we work together, we drink together, and we . . ."

"Fight together?" Manny finished the statement as a grin crossed his face.

Link grimaced as he rubbed his chin. "I wouldn't call that a fight. It was just a disagreement over who Lucy Dawes was going to dance with."

"My Lucy Dawes," Pearl de Vere said. "Where was she?"

"Now, Pearl, calm down," Speck said. "I took her up to the Topic and she earned a few coins. It wasn't anything."

Pearl shook her head as Manny and John joined their table.

The meal was delivered and eaten with gusto as everyone joined in a lively conversation. Then, after the dessert had been served, they heard the ringing sound of a spoon being tapped against a glass, and looking toward the head table, they saw James Parker standing behind the podium.

"Distinguished guests, our former congressman Mr. Tom Patterson—who, I might add, should be our governor—the Honorable Judge R. R. Eddy, attorney Harry Lee, ladies and gentlemen from Denver, Pueblo, Colorado Springs, and all those from right here in Cripple Creek."

"I was wondering when you were going to get around to the home folk," someone shouted, and all laughed heartily when they recognized Bob

Womack, the man who'd first discovered gold in the district.

"There is no mystery as to why we are gathered here," Parker continued.

"Food and wine!" Speck called out, and again there was laughter.

"To be sure, Speck," Parker replied good-naturedly. "And now that the railroad has reached Midland, a mere eight miles from our fair city, such viands—and drink, I might add—will be much more readily available."

Again there was laughter.

"But"—Parker held up a finger to emphasize his point—"the most significant change will be the reduction of freight tariffs associated with the shipping of ore. In short, ladies and gentlemen, the railroad will be to the district what the arteries and veins are to the human body. It will be our lifeblood!

"This day, December sixteenth, 1893, will be a memorable one in the annals of history for both the city and the state, and when the railroad rolls into this city in the spring, you can rest assured it will be the cause of the greatest celebration ever seen in Cripple Creek."

Parker picked up a glass of wine and held it forth. "Ladies and gentlemen . . . to the completion of the railroad to the Midland terminal!"

When the speeches were concluded, the talk turned to politics.

"Calderwood," Speck said, "I guess you and Governor Waite are pretty tight."

"I know him."

"Of course you do," Link said. "Waite was involved with the Aspen Knights of Labor, wasn't he?"

"He was."

"And you were the president of that union?" Link continued.

"I was."

"For an organizer, you don't have much to say," Speck said. "Senator Penrose, who happens to be my brother, tells me they had to call out Pennsylvania's muskets and bayonets before the Lehigh Valley strike ended. Now, tell me you don't plan anything like that out here."

"I can say miners are not the same as railroad workers. And right now, nothing is planned for the district, but things can happen," Calderwood said. "You called me an organizer and that's what I am. With good men like Manny Drumm at my side, I intend to stand up for the rights of miners."

"And how do you plan on going about that?" Link asked.

"To start with, I'm taking a few men to Denver to meet with Governor Waite. Then we're going on up to Butte to listen to what the WFM has to say. One thing's for sure, there won't be any Pinkerton men infiltrating our union like what happened at Coeur d'Alene."

"Manny, I know you're a good man," Speck said as he put his arm around the young man. "You were a good shift leader at the C.O.D. Mine. When you're in Montana meeting with the union, I hope somebody tells you what it was like in Idaho when the riots broke out. Some good men were killed on both sides. Then the military came in and rounded up six hundred men and held them in bull pens like a pack of wild dogs. Now, we don't want that to happen in Cripple Creek, do we?"

Manny replied seriously, "Mr. Penrose, Mr. Buchannan, there comes a time when no matter what the consequences, a man has to stand up for the things he believes in."

Colorado Springs

Link stepped down from the train, his satchel stuffed with all the information he would need to conduct his business the following day. His growing wealth was built on his reputation for being an honest broker, and he was sure this would be a successful trip.

Catching a hansom cab at the depot, he directed the driver to a Tudor-style house on Weber Street. Smoke curled from the chimney of the dimly lit house.

Link stamped his feet on the porch before he opened the door and stepped inside. "Otto?" he called. "Hulda? Anybody home?"

"Link? Is that you?" a barrel-chested man said as he hurried to the foyer with a lantern. "We thought you might be coming in today."

Link shook his old friend's hand. "Is the electricity out? Let's have a little light." Link pushed the button on the wall, and the chandelier burst into a warm glow, its hanging crystals casting prisms on the wall.

"Hulda," Otto Birk said, shaking his head. "She thinks it's wasteful to use the electricity."

"Well, you tell her I said to use it. Light up the whole house, because we don't want my neighbors to think I can't afford it."

Otto and Hulda Birk were both in their midseventies, and Link paid them to live in his house while he spent most of his time in Cripple Creek. Otto had been one of the early prospectors in the district and had located a claim that he could not afford to work. He sold it to Link for less than $300, and after putting a couple of thousand dollars into the claim, Link subsequently sold it for twenty times that amount. He had tried to share the money with Otto, but Otto was proud and wouldn't accept what he considered a handout. He did, however, agree to take a job as a caretaker.

"Have you eaten? Hulda has potato soup on the stove. Go on back to the kitchen while I take your satchel to your room," Otto said.

"Take it to the library. I'll need to do some work tonight."

"Work, work, work, that's all you do. Don't you know it's almost Christmas?"

"I know, I know." Link stepped through the swinging door that led to the kitchen.

"*Guten Abend*, Link," said a jovial-looking woman who was half the size of her husband. She placed a bowl of soup on the kitchen table. "I've got *Schwarzbrot* for you to have with your *Kartoffelsuppe*." She laid a loaf of black bread down beside the soup. "If we had known you were coming today, Ot and I would have waited to eat with you."

"It doesn't matter; it's just good to get some of your home cooking."

"Danke schön." Hulda gave Link a hug.

Otto had come to America several years before his wife, and as a result his command of English was better. Hulda still spoke with a heavy accent, and she often sprinkled German words in with her English. She took pride in keeping Link's house, and even though he spent little time there, she carefully went over every piece of furniture every week.

When Link finished his soup, he went into the library, his favorite room in the house. Otto had lit the fire, and the flames now cast shadows on the bird's-eye maple that paneled the walls. His satchel sat beside a tufted, brown-leather wing chair.

Link picked up the satchel and withdrew the brochures he'd picked up from the *Crusher* office that very morning. He hadn't had time to go over them, but knew that with Mollie preparing the draft, all his figures and arguments would be correct.

> *The World's Desire lies on the east slope of Battle Mountain, which is proving to have a rich network of valuable veins. The capital stock of this company is $500,000, and the treasury stock has wisely been fixed at the large proportion of $200,000. . . .*

Link put the paper down and lay his head back on the chair. Why was he doing this? Everybody he knew was caught up in making money. Most were making their money from peripheral businesses. Charlie MacNeill had a chlorination mill, Bert Carleton supplied coal, Verner Reed sold real estate, as did Speck and Charles Tutt. Of all the "socialites"— the young men from Ivy League schools who'd come out West to make their fortunes—only Larry Leonard worked as a miner. For an instant, Link felt a twinge of guilt.

Maybe John Calderwood was right. The miners worked for $3 a day. Whether they worked an eight-, nine-, or ten-hour day, it didn't matter. They all made the same $3.

A log snapped in the fireplace and brought Link out of his reverie. He put everything back in his satchel and went upstairs.

For a long time, Link lay in bed, his arms folded behind his head as he stared at the ceiling. The Christmas season was always difficult for him.

Link's mother had written to tell him that his father was ill, and that perhaps it was time for him and his only child to reconcile, but Christmas was not the time to do that. Link knew he was being selfish, that his mother's hurt at this time of year was every bit as great as his own, but the cause of her pain was Link's fault.

"Please let me go, please let me go," Della Buchannan had begged.

"No," Link had insisted. "Girls can't go sledding on Lemon Hill. It's too dangerous."

"Aw, let her come," Speck had said. "Nothing's going to happen."

That conversation had taken place nearly twenty years ago this very day, yet it was as fresh in Link's mind as if it had happened yesterday. He did take his six-year-old sister with him, and on their first trip down Lemon Hill, Link hit something—a rock, a log, he never knew. He was thrown off the sled with a deep cut on his forehead and a broken collarbone. Sissy, however, continued down the hill until the sled collided with a tree. Her neck was broken instantly.

With blood from his cut running down his face, Link cradled his lifeless sister in his arms while Speck ran back the mile to get his father and Link's mother. When Pricilla Buchannan saw her daughter, she began to scream hysterically as Dr. Penrose tried to comfort her.

Never once did she approach Link to try to comfort him.

After Sissy's body was removed from his arms, Link watched as the carriage pulled away. Dr. Penrose treated the cut on Link's forehead, and not until then did he feel the pain in his shoulder.

The cut left a light scar on his forehead, and the broken collarbone left a bulge where the bones had fused together. He felt for it now as he lay in the dark.

No. He couldn't go home. Not at Christmas.

THREE

On the Union Pacific

Tori closed *The One Fair Woman*, the book she had been reading as she traveled across the country. She assumed Joaquin Miller had modeled Countess Edna after Mrs. Leslie, and Tori had expected that she would identify with that character. But she didn't. She identified more with Murietta, the hero of the book, and with one particular line that she had just read:

He had never come to the forks of the road where the choice of the right way depended on his own judgment, but what he took the wrong one.

How that line resonated with her.

She had no doubt that she had encountered many "forks in the road" in her life, and if she would admit it to herself, she had taken the wrong one every time.

What about the fork in the road she was on right now?

She was on her way to Colorado to be with her little brother, Manny, whom she hadn't seen since she was twelve. Her mother had told her he was in

Colorado Springs. But over the last couple of years, Tori had been reluctant to even correspond with her mother.

All she knew was that Emanuel Drumm was twenty-four years old and not expecting a wayward sister to land on his doorstep.

She laid her head against the back of the seat and closed her eyes. Perhaps she should have gone to Cedar Rapids to be with her parents. When she'd changed trains in St. Louis, she'd considered going to be with them. Surely any transgression she may have committed would be forgiven by now. But no, she thought. She had chosen her path a long time ago. There was no going back now.

Not knowing what she would find in the depot in Denver, she made her way to the dining car to get a bite to eat. Finding a table, she sat down, and when the waiter approached her, she automatically requested a cup of coffee and a piece of fruit.

"Wait," she said as the waiter started to leave. "I want a stack of buckwheat cakes, two eggs, and a rasher of bacon."

"Yes, ma'am. Do you still want the fruit?"

"Yes, yes, I do." She thrust out her chin in defiance. Lyle Ketterman had badgered her about her weight from the time she had first appeared on the stage. She never had to think about that again.

"The little lady must be hungry," an elderly gentleman said as he approached her table. "This seems to be the only vacant seat. Would you mind if I joined you?"

"Please do."

"Is this your first trip out West?"

"Yes, it is."

"Then take a look out this window. You're in for a treat."

When Tori looked out, she thought she was looking at a distant cloud bank, then she realized she was looking at a towering chain of snowcapped mountains. She was smiling enthusiastically as she turned her attention back to her breakfast companion.

"Yes, my dear, the Rocky Mountains."

She was glad the old gentleman had joined her, as the conversation made the last hour of the trip go quickly. More important, she was forced to forget about the trepidation she knew she would experience when she got to Colorado Springs.

Saying good-bye to her newfound friend, she went into the depot to inquire about her transfer to the Denver and Rio Grande, which would take her south to Colorado Springs.

"Eight thirty this evening, miss," the ticket agent said, responding to her question as to what time her train would arrive in Colorado Springs.

"Thank you." Tori took out Aunt Frances's letter and read the return address. It said Hattie Drumm—no town, no place, no address, but the postmark was from Davenport, Iowa. Tori withdrew the paper and reread the paragraph in her mother's hand that had brought her this far.

I am pleased to report that I have at last heard from Emanuel. He sent word through an old friend, the Reverend Vivian Bentley

*(Sister, you may well remember him—he
lived just across the north forty from the
old home place). Anyway, the Reverend tells
me he found Emanuel in Colorado Springs,
enjoying the altitude and the fine weather.
He says he visited with Emanuel at his
abode in the Union Block on Tejon Street. I
am so happy to have corresponded with my
son and I hope to get a return post as soon
as Nathan will allow us to lite for a spell.*

Tori checked the date of the letter one more time.
May 20, 1893. That was only six months ago. From
the beginning she had questioned the syntax of
her mother's sentence. Did *abode* mean Manny's
abode, or did it mean Reverend Bentley's abode?
Tori couldn't think about that now. She was now
less than seventy miles from Colorado Springs. She
had come this far and she would find out when she
got there.

Link had awakened that morning with light
streaming through his bedroom window. He listened as the clock in the downstairs entrance hall
struck nine—much later than he normally arose.

The steam radiator was pushing out a comfortable blanket of heat, which meant that Otto had
tended to the furnace long ago. Getting out of bed,
Link padded barefoot over to the window and stood
there for a moment. He had a magnificent view of
Pike's Peak from his bedroom window, and he never
tired of watching the changing patterns of light that
played on the mountain. The view had been one of

the motivating reasons for his buying this house, but in hindsight, he knew it wasn't the only one.

Link bought the house—a house that was far too big for one person—because he wanted to impress his father. But that was a foolish reason for owning a house, especially since the likelihood of his father's ever setting foot in it was nil.

In the beginning, when Link began to make significant amounts of money, he sent drafts back to Philadelphia to be deposited in his father's bank. But never once did he get any response from Albert Buchannan.

After Della's death, Albert had become a driven man, spending more and more time at the bank, and when he came home, he sat in solitude, taking comfort from a bottle of whiskey. He ignored not only his son but his wife as well.

Within a year Link's mother's bedroom door was locked to his father. As an eight-year-old boy, Link did not realize the significance of that action, but as a twenty-eight-year-old man, he understood it all too well.

No wonder his father hated him.

He turned away from the window and, going into the small room that served as his dressing chamber, chose his suit for the day.

As he stepped out into the hallway, he smiled. The smell of fresh-baked bread was wafting up from the kitchen.

"Are they prune or apricot?" Link called as he descended the steps, grabbing his chesterfield from the hall tree.

"Just what makes you think I've made kolaches?" Hulda asked.

"Because you know how much I like them." Link grabbed a couple of the sweet rolls on his way through the kitchen. "I'm a little late today. Do you think Otto could take me down to Charles Tutt's office?"

"Of course he can. Ot works for you. If you want him to take you somewhere, that's what he'll do."

Link smiled as he picked up two more sweet rolls. "I'm taking these for Otto."

It was a short buggy ride from Link's house on Weber Street down to Tutt's office on Pike's Peak Avenue.

"Shall I wait for you?" Otto asked when he brought the horse to a stop.

"No, from here I'm going to the El Paso Club so I'll just walk," Link said. "And I didn't tell Hulda, but more than likely I'll be late tonight, so tell her not to cook for me."

"I'll tell her, but that doesn't mean she'll listen. You know how these German girls are. If you don't eat their cooking, they'll just make more."

"All right, I'll check the kitchen before I go to bed." Link got out of the buggy. He smiled as he made his way to the Tutt and Penrose Insurance and Real Estate Office. He thought it was endearing that Otto still thought of Hulda as a girl.

"Get in here out of the cold," Charles invited when he opened the door for Link. "Speck called to warn me you'd be in town. Said something about you wanting to wrangle an invitation for Christmas."

"He shouldn't have told you that," Link said as he stepped into the office.

"It doesn't matter. Josephine wants you to join us. Shall I tell her you will?"

"Are you sure she doesn't mind?"

"Of course it's all right." Charles poured a cup of coffee from a blue pot sitting on top of a small pot-bellied stove. "Here, this'll take the chill out of your bones."

"Thanks." Link accepted the cup and took a sip before he spoke. "How much do you think you could get for my house?"

Charles furrowed his brow. "That question sure came out of nowhere. What are you talking about?"

"I want to sell my house."

"Are you sure? I remember how proud you were when you were building it."

"Do you think it would sell?"

"Of course. It's a beautiful house, and since Winfield Stratton was the builder, that makes it even more in demand. But why would you want to get rid of it?" Then Charles smiled. "I get it—you want to build a bigger house, maybe over on Cascade Avenue."

"No, that's not the reason. You know I spend almost all my time in Cripple Creek now."

"In a house one-fourth the size."

"And that's the problem." Link chuckled ruefully. "Do you have any idea how lonesome one person can get in a house that big?"

"What about Otto and Hulda? If you sell the house, where will they go?"

"I'll need someplace to be when I do come to the Springs, so I'll want you to find me a smaller place where they can live. Hulda's getting too old to keep this one up, and she won't let me hire anyone to help her."

"Only you would try to hire a housekeeper for the housekeeper. You know you aren't responsible for those two."

"I feel an obligation to take care of the Birks."

"Because you made so much money off his claim?"

"That's a big part of it."

"That was straight-up business," Charles said. "A lot of people got out of Cripple Creek way too early. You did nothing illegal, or even immoral. You bought a man's claim and you turned it for a profit."

"A big profit. I owe Otto Birk and it's more than money."

"All right." Charles exhaled loudly. "I'll find somebody to buy your house, but I'm not going to even try until you go back to Cripple Creek. You know with all the new money pouring in, it won't take long. We can talk more about it when you come over for Christmas."

"Thanks, Charles, and I do appreciate the invitation. I know what a melancholy time this is for you and Josephine, and I hope I'm not intruding."

"There's no doubt we'll always grieve for our little Christmas baby, but now with a nine-month-old in the house, Josephine is feeling much better." Charles clasped Link's shoulder. "You in particular can empathize."

"I can. It's good to have you and Speck as friends. You both know all my skeletons."

"Link, Della's death is not your skeleton. It was an accident. I don't blame anybody for our little Russell's death, and you should stop blaming yourself for Della. It happened a long time ago."

"I know, but try to tell that to my father. Thanks, Charles, and thanks for sharing your family with me for Christmas."

"Good evening, Mr. Buchannan. We've missed you," Clarence Doubleday said as Link arrived at the El Paso Club. "Welcome to the city."

"Thank you, Clarence." Link set his satchel on the floor beside him. He stripped out of his greatcoat and handed it to the doorman. "There seems to be a lot of activity here tonight. Anything going on that I should know about?"

Clarence smiled. "Mr. Rope is challenging Mr. Otis for the championship cue tonight. Mr. Otis has won it three times, and if he can win tonight's game, he'll only have to win one more time before the cue is his. Will you be in the billiard room, sir?"

"As much as I'd like to see William Otis get beaten, I'm afraid I'm here strictly for business. Is there a room open that I might use for my meeting?"

"Yes, sir. Shall I reserve room number three for you?"

"That would be good. These are the men I am expecting to meet." Link took a piece of paper from his breast pocket and handed it to Clarence. "I'll be in the East Room."

"Very well, sir." Clarence took the list from Link. "Shall I send Julius to the pantry to fetch your usual libation?"

"Of course, and will you have Julius set up a decanter in my meeting room? I'll need four tumblers."

Link sat in the East Room for quite some time watching as one group of men after another made their connections and found their way to other parts of the club. He was beginning to think his potential clients were not going to appear, but at last three men approached him.

"Mr. Lincoln Buchannan?" one man said as he extended his hand.

"Yes." Link rose and shook hands. "But please, I'm not sure I know how to act when someone calls me Lincoln. I'm Link."

"All right, Link it is. I'm George Cramer, and these are my cohorts, Mr. Dodge and Mr. Andrews."

"Very good. Shall we make our way to the private room I have reserved?" Link led the way to the stairway. "Are you staying at the Antlers?"

"Yes, but unfortunately, my wife has accompanied me on this trip, and this morning she insisted we take a tour of Colorado Springs. If my business with you goes well, who's to say we won't be ready to leave Denver and move to this fine city."

"It is a fine city, and I know just the person to sell you a house. Gentlemen, shall we get down to business?" Link ushered then into the meeting room, and when they were seated, he withdrew several brochures from his satchel. "I have two offerings for you—the World's Desire and the Estelline."

"What about the Morning Glory? I thought you said it might be available," Jonah Andrews said.

"I'm sorry. The offer has been withdrawn. Just this morning I received word that the current lessee opened a cut in the side of the hill and disclosed a vein showing free gold that's ten to twelve inches wide and is estimated to run a thousand feet."

"Oh, dear, are we too late?" Mr. Dodge asked.

Link smiled. "I hardly think so. Let me tell you about the Estelline. It's on Prospect Hill, but the best thing about it is that it adjoins the Washington on the south."

"And that's still part of the Stratton group?"

"Indeed it is. The Estelline could certainly have a part of the Independence or Washington veins passing through it from end line to end line."

"Mr. Buchannan, that's good enough for me. If Winfield Scott Stratton is the first millionaire to come out of Cripple Creek, and my claim is next to his, I could damn near be the next one," Cramer said. "We'll take the Estelline."

"Perfect, I just happen to have the paperwork ready for your signature." Link picked up the decanter of liquor and filled the four tumblers. "Shall we drink to the transaction?"

As the train began its descent from the lofty heights, the snow cover lessened and Tori could see some vegetation. Then the train rolled into a region of buttes surrounded on both sides by rock formations that resembled castles and needlelike shafts and Corinthian pillars.

In the entire time of her travel across the country, Tori decided she had seen the most magnificent scenery in the last three hours. The conductor came through the car as the train—which had picked up speed as it came down from the summit—began to slow.

"Colorado Springs!" he called. "Next stop is Colorado Springs!"

Tori felt a quick surge of excitement, then apprehension. She was about to discover if she had taken the right or the wrong fork in the road.

Link and his guests stayed at the El Paso Club for some time, enjoying a cordial dinner and several drinks. When they left, Link intended to return to his own house, but he noticed George Cramer was having a difficult time with Mr. Andrews.

"Let me go with you," Link offered. "We can take the Rapid Transit down Tejon to Pike's Peak, and then we can walk the rest of the way to the hotel."

"I'd appreciate that. Jonah has just come back from Boulder, where he's been taking the Keeley treatment, and I'm afraid his wife won't be too pleased with me if I've gotten him drunk."

"If he's had the injections, that may be a good harbinger for the Estelline," Link said as he boosted the man onto the trolley.

Cramer laughed. "You're right. My partner can say he's got gold in his blood and he's actually telling the truth."

⌒∞⌒

Link and the three men made their way up to the Antlers. Its turrets and balconies as well as the broad piazzas were illuminated with diffused lighting, making the hotel the most imposing bit of architecture in Colorado Springs.

The men tried to enter as discreetly as they could, hoping to get the inebriated Mr. Andrews to his suite as quickly as possible. They were just entering the tower, with its spiral stairway to the upper floors, when a woman approached them.

"Oh, George, there you are," the older woman said. "My friend has a terrible problem, and I told her you'd be able to help her."

"How is that, my dear?" George Cramer asked.

"She just arrived, and unfortunately she doesn't have a reservation here at the Antlers, and with the holidays and all the wintering guests, Mr. Barnett can't find her a room in any of the respectable hotels. I told her you would take care of her."

"Elizabeth, what do you expect me to do?" George Cramer asked. "If there aren't any available rooms—"

At just that moment, Jonah Andrews collapsed onto the floor.

"Oh, my goodness!" Elizabeth exclaimed. "Has Jonah died?"

"No, no, but we've got to get him to his room." George and Mr. Dodge struggled to get Andrews on his feet while several onlookers gathered around. As an afterthought, Cramer turned to Link. "Oh, will you see to my wife's friend?"

"Of course."

For the first time, Link noticed a woman dressed in a conservative gray traveling cloak, her head lowered, a jet bonnet obscuring her face. She was standing apart from the commotion that Mr. Andrews's collapse had created.

"Are you Mrs. Cramer's friend?" Link asked.

"I am the woman who doesn't have a room." Tori looked up and met Link's gaze.

Something in the woman's face . . . maybe the depth of her dark eyes or the tilt of her chin . . . caused Link to catch his breath.

"I suppose I should have wired ahead, but I had no idea such a thing would be necessary," Tori said.

Perhaps it was her voice, so well modulated, and with a touch of sophistication, that held Link's attention.

"What's going on here?" Elliott Barnett, the manager of the hotel, said as he approached the group. "The Antlers expects its guests to behave with absolute decorum at all times."

"I think Mr. Cramer has the situation well in hand," Link said. "Are you absolutely certain there's not a single bed available for this young woman?"

"I'm sorry. With our winter residents and our Christmas guests, we have nothing," Barnett said. "I called the Alamo, the Alta Vista, and the Elk, and every hotel has a full house. Of course, I did not check the Spalding, but I don't think a lady of her station would care to stay at that facility."

Link turned to the woman, intending to ask if she would want Mr. Barnett to call the offending hotel, but he was unable to summon as much as one word.

What was it about this woman that so affected him? She was attractive, yes, but he wouldn't call her striking.

"I suppose I could go to my brother's place. He lives here in Colorado Springs, but it's so late. I didn't want to disturb him until tomorrow, but now I suppose I have no recourse."

Link cleared his throat before he spoke. "You say your brother lives here?"

"Yes," Tori said, her voice breaking.

"Well, that's the answer. I'll take you to his house. Do you know where he lives?"

"All I know is the Union Block on Tejon Street."

"The Union Block? That's almost all businesses, isn't it?" Link asked.

"I believe there are some rooms to let," Mr. Barnett said. "I know Frank Atherton lives over Jackson's Drug Store, but that's not too safe anymore. Frank was robbed by some masked men a few nights ago. Why, they tore up his sheet and bound him—tied him to the bed and left him there—but Frank worked his way free. He ran in here about six o'clock in the morning, and we called the police out." Barnett shook his head. "I hope your brother's expecting you. A knock on the door in the middle of the night in the Union Block is not a very good idea. All I can say is, yell good and loud before he opens that door, or he could be sending a bullet right through you."

"Thank you, Mr. Barnett. I think you've given us ample directions." Smiling what he hoped was a disarming smile, Link took Tori's arm and guided her down the hallway and out onto a balcony that lined the western side of the building. When they had descended the stairway, they maneuvered through a series of masonry terraces and eventually reached the street.

"This doesn't seem to have been a very positive impression for your first night in Colorado Springs. I'm afraid our reputation as the Saratoga of the West has a little tarnish on it. I'm Link Buchannan." Link bowed his head, but didn't drop his hold on her arm.

"I'm afraid I've caused you a lot of trouble, Mr. Buchannan."

"Think nothing of it. I'm going that way anyway. We'll find your brother and you'll be safe and secure for the night."

"Thank you, I appreciate it."

When Link and Tori reached the Union Block, Link tried the door for the stairway beside the drugstore. When he found it was locked, he felt Tori shiver beside him.

"Don't worry, we'll find him. There has to be a stairway in the alley that will lead upstairs."

Link led Tori down a narrow passageway that led to the back of the Union Block. He noticed that she instinctively pressed her body closer to his, and he put his arm around her and drew her tight against him. When they reached the back stairway, he turned and asked, "Shall we do this, or shall we wait until tomorrow?"

Tori wanted to say wait, but she had no choice. It was approaching midnight, and if she didn't find Manny, where would she go?

As an answer to the question, she placed her

foot on the first step and carefully made her way to the top, with Link following behind her. When they reached the door, it was locked.

"I guess this is the place to yell," Link said. "Let's hope your brother hears us. What's his name?"

"Emanuel Drumm."

Link swung around from the door. "Emanuel Drumm? A man in his early twenties? Goes by the name of Manny?"

"Yes, yes! He's twenty-four and he does go by Manny. Do you know him?"

"I know a Manny Drumm, but he doesn't live here—at least not that I know of. About a week ago he sat at my table at a banquet in Cripple Creek."

"Cripple Creek? Is that near here?"

"It's close but you can't get there tonight."

Just then, Link heard from behind the door the distinct sound of a hammer being cocked. "Frank? Frank Atherton? Is that you?"

"Who wants to know?"

"It's Link Buchannan, from up on Weber Street. I'm looking for Manny Drumm. Do you know if he still lives here?"

"Hell, no. He left last summer. Went to Cripple Creek like every other fool out to get rich."

"Thanks, Frank, we'll leave you alone."

Link led Tori back down the stairs and was surprised to feel a surge of tenderness for this woman. She had to be dead tired, in a place where she didn't know a soul or what she would do. If she had any belongings, they certainly weren't with her now. When he got to the streetlight, he turned and saw that tears were brimming in her eyes.

"I have a suggestion," he said. "If you don't think it's too presumptuous of me, I have a bed you can sleep in."

He felt Tori stiffen immediately.

"No, no, no—not with me. I mean I have a house with four bedrooms and I live there alone except for Otto and Hulda. They're my caretakers and they live there, too, while I live most of the time at Cripple Creek."

Hearing those words, Tori collapsed against him in tears, her body as limp as a rag doll's.

He held her against him, trying to comfort her as he would a child.

"I've made a terrible mistake," she said as she sobbed uncontrollably. "I shouldn't have come, and you don't even know my name."

Link pulled his head back, and pushing her hat aside, he smiled. "That's easy enough to rectify. What is your name?"

"It's Sa—Tori."

"Satori. That's a pretty name—not one that I've ever heard, but it's pretty."

"It's actually Victoria Drumm, but my friends call me Tori."

"If your friends call you Tori, I would consider it a privilege if you allowed me to call you by that name."

"Mr. Buchannan, I would be honored."

"And my friends call me Link."

FOUR

My house is at least a mile from here," Link said, "but it's too late for the trolley. Perhaps we should go back to the Antlers, where I can hire a hack."

"I would appreciate that," Tori said. "With all the excitement, I forgot my valise and I'm sure to need it."

Tori was filled with apprehension as Link helped her into the carriage. She couldn't believe what she was about to do. As refined as the people of Colorado Springs seemed to be, and more to the point this man in particular, the hotel manager had revealed a seedier side to the community.

What kind of place was Link taking her to? What would this man try to do to her? If something terrible happened, who knew where she was? Would she ever find her brother?

All these troubling questions tumbled through her mind as they rode the short distance in silence.

"Here you are, safe and sound," the driver said as he brought the hack to a stop.

"Thanks, Pug, I'm glad you still had your team hitched up," Link said as he opened the door and stepped down. He withdrew a handful of bills from his pocket. "Here's a little extra. Buy those kids something special for Christmas."

"You don't have to do that, Mr. Buchannan."

"I insist. Take it. Without you I would have been lugging the lady's valise all the way from the Antlers."

"All right, when you put it like that, I'll take it, and you and your lady friend have a merry Christmas, too. Say hello to Otto for me."

"I will. I'm surprised he's not waiting up for me," Link said as he helped Tori from the hack.

The exchange with the driver put Tori's mind at ease. First, it verified that there was an Otto, and second, the charity Link had shown to the man was admirable.

When the coach pulled away, Tori looked toward the house in the moonlight. The two-story house had a sweeping front porch, with numerous gables sheltering dormer windows across the front.

"This is your house?" Tori asked as she hesitated to move up the sidewalk.

"Yes, it is, at least for a while."

"And you live here all alone."

"No, as I said, Otto and Hulda Birk live here with me. Actually, they live here more than I do."

"It surprises me that you don't have a wife. Any woman would be proud to be the mistress of this house." Then Tori felt her cheeks flame. "I'm sorry, Mr. Buchannan, that comment was very rude of me."

Link laughed as he steered Tori up the walk.

"Maybe a woman would want the house—just not the man that goes with it."

Tori stopped and turned toward Link. "I don't believe that. You've been most gracious to me, and I sincerely appreciate it. I don't know what I would have done without you tonight."

Link made no response as he opened the unlocked door and stepped into the front hall, where he set Tori's valise beside the open stairway. He shivered as he pushed the button to light the foyer pendant that hung from the tall ceiling.

"I think Otto let the fire go out." Link stepped to the fireplace, which contained a coal inset. "It doesn't matter. The kitchen will be warm. I'll bet you haven't eaten a bite. Come with me."

Taking her hand, Link led Tori through the darkened house, not turning on a light until he stepped through the swinging door and entered the kitchen. This room was indeed warm as Link stepped over to the Home Comfort range, which was still putting out heat. On the shelf above the oven was a pan of bread dough that had been set to proof.

The smell of fermenting yeast immediately brought to mind the cramped wagon that had been Tori's home as a child. On many days as her family traveled from one small town to another, the only food that her father would allow was the fresh bread that her mother would bake in the Dutch oven as it hung over a campfire.

"Would you like to take off your hat and coat?" Link asked as he was removing his own coat.

Tori looked toward him as if she hadn't heard him.

"Your coat? Do you want to take it off?"

"Oh, yes, of course." Tori quickly removed her cloak.

"I'm not much of a cook, but let me see what I can rustle up." Link stepped into a small room off the kitchen and returned with several eggs, a partial roll of summer sausage, and a cast-iron skillet. Setting the skillet on the stove, he reached for an enamel pan, causing several others to come crashing to the floor.

Link smiled knowingly. "That's all it'll take."

Not a minute later, a small woman dressed in a long flannel nightgown with a nightcap came through the swinging door.

"Link Buchannan, what are you doing in my kitch . . . ?" Hulda stopped when she saw Tori. "And just who do you think you are? In my kitchen at this hour? Don't you know decent folk visit in the daytime?"

"Hulda, I want you to meet Tori Drumm. I met her this evening coming from . . . I guess I don't know where you came from."

"I came from Denver today." Tori felt a twinge of guilt as she evaded the question she knew Link was asking. "I'm afraid I didn't think I would have such a problem finding a hotel room, and when Mr. Buchannan took me to the address I had for my brother, we found he has moved to Cripple Creek."

"So this one took you in, huh?" Hulda asked, her voice softening as she inclined her head toward Link.

"I did, and now we are both starved to death. I

was going to fix us some eggs, but now that you are up anyway . . ."

"Summer sausage! You were going to give this girl summer sausage? She deserves ham. Now you two just sit there and I'll take care of you." Hulda disappeared into the pantry.

"And now you've met Hulda Birk," Link said. "You can rest assured your reputation will be kept intact."

The next morning, Tori awakened to find the sun streaming through the venetian shade and smiled.

Her rooms at the Gerlach had been tastefully decorated in a dark palette of deep blues, maroons, and hunter greens, all colors that were fashionable in the city. Ornately carved, massive pieces in oak and mahogany lined the walls, while the chairs and couch had been upholstered in heavy damask. Hanging fringe, tasseled pillows, or velvet throw blankets were on every available surface, and Tori enjoyed living in such opulence.

This room was totally different. The walls were painted a sunny yellow, and the furniture was made to be functional. The bureau and clothespress were sturdy. But Tori admired most the bell-topped canopy bed with its feather mattress and bolsters. Its hand-forged black iron was intentionally left exposed. A brown-and-yellow counterpoint taffeta quilt was the only exception to the otherwise unadorned furnishings. Everything about the room looked clean and simple.

Reluctantly, Tori threw back the quilt and slid out of bed. The view she had was unbelievably beautiful, the irregular snowcapped summits rimming the town all appearing to pale in comparison to the towering majesty of Pike's Peak.

Tori stood for a long moment drinking in the grandeur and quiet beauty of the scene. Could this place help her rebuild, help her forget where she had been and what she'd done? She recalled Link's words last night.

You can rest assured your reputation will be kept intact.

"No, Link, my reputation is in shambles, and it has nothing to do with where I just spent the night. And I have nobody to blame but myself," Tori said aloud.

She turned from the window to begin dressing for the day. She chose a sensible traveling suit, as she would need to make her way to Cripple Creek. After gathering her hair into the tight bun she had worn on the train, she made the bed and tidied the room. Picking up her valise, a knot formed in her throat.

Why was she emotional?

Because the likelihood of her ever having anything like this as her own was forever gone. Any man who would accept her as she was was not the kind of man she wanted in her life.

She might disguise her looks when she needed to, but she could never disguise her lack of virginity.

How could she ever have fallen in love with Lyle Ketterman? How could she have let him dupe her so completely?

In an act of rebellion—her first attempt at liberation from her past—she pulled the pins from her bun, letting her wavy nut-brown hair fall down her back.

"Tori Drumm, you're on your own. Even though you're not onstage, you're still an actress, and you can pick yourself up." Tori took a deep breath, grabbed her valise, and stepped out of the comfortable room.

"I was beginning to think I should send Hulda up to check on you," Link said when Tori reached the bottom of the stairs. He hadn't realized how attractive she was, and a smile crossed his face.

"Oh, dear." Tori searched for her timepiece. "My clock seems to have stopped. What time is it?"

"You haven't missed lunch yet."

"You must think I'm most ungrateful for your hospitality. I'm sorry, but the bed was so comfortable, and—"

"You were tired. Let's face it, last night was a trying experience for you. I can't believe Manny didn't tell you he'd moved to Cripple Creek. From what I know of him, he's quite dependable."

"I'm glad to hear that's your opinion of my brother." Tori hesitated for a moment. "You may find this hard to believe, but I hardly know Manny. When I got the idea to come to see him, the move was quite spontaneous. I'm afraid I had no way of letting him know I was coming."

"Well, I'm sure Manny will welcome you. And it's always nice to have new people move into Cripple Creek. It is rapidly becoming one of Colorado's most dynamic cities."

"I'm glad to hear that. If it's possible, I want to get there today." Tori set down her valise. "I'd like to spend Christmas with my brother."

"I'm sure he would be happy to have you, but I think there are some things for you to consider. First of all, the train doesn't go all the way to Cripple Creek yet, so you have to take a coach the last eight miles, and those eight miles are, shall we say, interesting."

"What does that mean?"

"If you haven't ridden a coach in the mountains, you're in for some excitement, but that's not the only thing you should think about. I told you Manny had shared my table at a banquet not long ago. If I recall, he said he was going to Denver. Why don't you stay here until we can find out if he's back yet?"

"Oh, Mr. Buchannan, I couldn't do that."

"Why, not? You said the bed was comfortable."

"It's . . . it's too close to Christmas, and I wouldn't want to intrude at a time when you'll be enjoying your family."

Link directed his gaze away from Tori before he spoke. "My family—that is, my mother and father—are back East, and we don't celebrate holidays together. And Otto and Hulda get together with a bunch of Germans and do whatever Germans do for Christmas, so you won't be imposing at all. I've been invited to have Christmas dinner with friends, and I'm sure Josephine would enjoy having another woman around."

"Josephine? Is she your fiancée?"

"Oh, no. She's the wife of my partner, or rather my ex-partner, Charles Tutt. They're both dear friends whom I have known since childhood. If you'll take a seat, I'll give Charles a ring and tell him I'm bringing a guest."

After stepping out to place the call, Link returned and sat on the bench beside Tori. He reached over and picked up her hand. "I can't wait to hear what Charles is going to say when he hears I'm bringing a woman to Christmas dinner."

"Is there phone service to Cripple Creek?"

"Yes, as a matter of fact, it's brand-new. They just established a copper metallic circuit between the camp and the Springs this month. Why do you ask?"

"Is there any way I could find out if Manny is there?"

Link withdrew his hand. "I'm sorry. Of course you're anxious to see your brother, and you would want to get there as quickly as possible. When I hear from Charles, I'll have him put in a call to Speck Penrose, and Speck can chase down whether Manny is in town or not."

Link's voice was flat, and Tori was sorry she had mentioned her brother. "I just want to know if he's there. I'm not sure Manny would want me just yet. Do you know, does he have a wife?"

"You really don't know him, do you?"

Tori shook her head.

The telephone rang before she could say anything, and Link stepped to the phone.

After exchanging a few words with Charles, Link hung up and turned to Tori. "We'll know by this afternoon if Manny is in Cripple Creek. In the meantime, you have an invitation to the Tutts' for Christmas, should you want to go."

"Thank you. If Manny is not in residence, I'd be grateful to accept."

After lunch, Link led Tori into his library. "This is my favorite room in this whole house." He put a piece of wood on the fire. "Otto wanted to convert this fireplace to a coal-burning one, but I wouldn't let him. I love to watch the flames dance and listen to the wood crack, even though I guess it's not very heat efficient."

"There's nothing more romantic than a fireplace," Tori said as she sat in one of the two leather chairs. Then her cheeks flamed. "I mean, in books . . . people who are in love always lie in front of a fireplace."

"Hmmm, that's interesting."

"Are you making fun of me?"

Link was surprised by Tori's direct question. He was used to women who were either more coy about their comments or else so coarse they didn't pretend to listen to what a man was saying

"No, I'm not. I'm sorry."

Just then Hulda came into the library carrying a tray with two cups of coffee and some cookies. "Would you like a lebkuchen? I just took them out of the oven, so they haven't hardened yet, but they taste good." Hulda set the tray on the table between the two leather chairs.

Link took a bite of one of the soft gingerbread cookies and offered the plate to Tori. "Thanks, Hulda, you brought these in at just the right time.

Sitting in front of a fireplace is a good place to eat cookies, too."

When Hulda had left, the two sat in silence for several minutes, watching the flames and eating the cookies. Once again, they were interrupted by the ringing of the phone.

"Excuse me, that has to be Charles."

Sitting in the library, Tori saw several photographs on the walls and rose from her chair to examine a couple. One was of Link and two other men—she guessed Mr. Tutt and Mr. Penrose. One man, sporting a well-trimmed mustache, was exceptionally handsome, so much so that he could easily have been on the stage. He was wearing high-topped English riding boots and a Western hat. The other man, who was taller than both Link and the heartthrob, seemed to be the more studious with his glasses and beard. He was wearing a suit with a high collar and a wide tie.

She studied the picture, concentrating on Link. His looks weren't exactly aesthetic, at least not in the way of the leading men with whom she had appeared onstage. Most of the men she knew and had associated with, including Lyle Ketterman, could only be described as classically handsome. But that didn't mean that Link Buchannan wasn't good-looking—he had a ruggedness about him that she found appealing. He had a scar on his forehead—nothing disfiguring, just noticeable enough to add interest to his face.

She wondered about Manny. What did he look like now? She remembered him as a freckled, tow-headed child with an infectious grin. If he walked into this room, would she recognize him? Would he recognize her?

"That was Charles," Link said, coming back into the room. "He's spoken with Speck, and he says Manny's not in Cripple Creek. No one knows for sure when he'll be back, but the man he's with isn't expected until after New Year's, so it's my guess Manny won't come back until then either."

"This was not a good idea. I should never have come. What's the old adage? You should look before you leap? I'm afraid I didn't follow that advice."

"Don't be so hard on yourself. After all, you've only been here one night."

"How much worse can it be? I have a brother who isn't home, and who won't be home for who knows how long, and who probably wouldn't recognize me if he walked through that door. You were kind enough to provide a room for me, but now I think the best course of action would be for me to get on the next train going east."

"That doesn't make sense. You came out here to see your brother, right?"

"I did."

"And now, as the crow flies, you're less than twenty miles from him and you don't want to wait and see him?"

"I don't know. It's been fourteen years since I last saw him, and I can say we definitely don't know one another."

"Then that's all the more reason you should stay. You have to be a little curious about the man your brother has become. I know if I had a sister, I'd want to know all about her." Link's hand went to the scar near his hairline, and he began absently running his finger over it.

"I suppose when you put it like that, I am curious to know what happened after I left. And what it was that brought him to Colorado."

"If it's been fourteen years since you last saw him, you both had to be quite young."

"He was ten, but even then, my father expected a day's work out of him—and me, too, for that matter. I was twelve when I was sent to live with my aunt and uncle, and I've not had much contact with anybody in my family since then. It was only by coincidence that my mother wrote that she had heard from Manny and that he was living in Colorado Springs."

"I can relate to that. Things happen that drive wedges between those we love, and someone has to make the first move before anything can be resolved. Maybe for you, going to see Manny will change things."

Tori did not answer, but her wistful look was telling.

Link realized that much was left unsaid. He also knew that, whatever it was, it represented a painful part of Tori's past, and he made no effort to probe any further.

"We have a lot of people who started out living in Colorado Springs, then moved to Cripple Creek when gold was discovered," Link said, purposely changing the direction of the conversation. "I'm a prime example. I have this house here, but I consider myself a resident of Cripple Creek."

"Then it was just happenstance that you were in Colorado Springs. It was my good fortune that I ran into you."

"It was fortunate for me as well."

"For you?"

"Yes, for me. It gave me the opportunity to meet a beautiful young woman; not only to meet her, but to be able to be of some assistance to her. And since you don't know your brother, I'll take great delight in introducing the two of you."

"You're being most kind. And I'm very grateful. After all, you did come to my rescue."

"Are you an actress?"

"What?" Tori gasped. "Why do you ask that?"

"Because if you were an actress, this would be the perfect time for you to clasp your hands over your heart and declare before all that I am your hero."

Tori smiled as she wondered what Link would think if he knew just how many times she had delivered that very line from onstage. She put both hands over her heart, then turned her head three-quarters to the left and slightly elevated. "'All the world's a stage, and all the men and women merely players. They have their exits and their entrances; and one man in his time plays many parts.' In this, your entrance, you are my hero!"

"That . . . that was very good!" Link said, surprised at her reaction. "That's Shakespeare, isn't it?"

"You know Shakespeare?"

"I was introduced to him at college. That was, what, *Hamlet*?"

"*As You Like It.* Although the 'in this, your entrance, you are my hero' was my own addition."

"And I think the Great Bard would approve of having his lines 'so nobly spoken' and amended by such a lovely young lady."

Tori laughed. "'So nobly spoken'? You're a bit of the ham yourself, Link Buchannan."

"'Ham'?"

"Yes, an actor who overplays his role."

"I don't think I ever heard the word used that way."

Tori realized that she might have opened a window that, for the moment at least, she wanted to keep closed. "I've seen it in some of the things I've read. It comes from the theater."

"I'm impressed. I think you would look terrific on the stage. Your dark hair and your eyes—I can just see you in a play. Have you ever thought about trying out for a role? They have several little theater groups here in Colorado Springs, and I know they're always looking for new people to join them."

"Thank you, but if I stay, I'll be in Cripple Creek. I don't think you mentioned how you know my brother. You said he'd attended some sort of a banquet with you. What does he do?"

"The banquet was to mark the occasion of the railroad getting within eight miles of town, and just about everybody came to celebrate. About Manny. I know him, but I can't say that I know him well. I've had a drink with him and we've played a game or two of cards. Even had a scuffle or two with him, but I can't say I really know what he's up to now."

"What do you mean by that?"

"Well, everybody in Cripple Creek has something to do with gold mining. Either you're prospecting for gold, or you own a mine and you're shipping gold, or you're working for somebody else mining gold, or you're supplying a service to the miners. It's all tied together."

"And which of those do you do?"

"Sometimes I wonder. I suppose you could say I supply a service, because when an owner needs to raise capital to continue working his claim, I find people who are willing to risk their money to keep it going. Everybody thinks gold mining is the way to strike it rich, and for a few that's true, but right now, at the end of '93, of all the thousands of people who have poured into the district, only fifty-nine claims have shipped any ore or even had gold in sight."

"Is my brother one of those?"

"No, he's not. I'm sure he's a prospector because everybody's always looking to be the next Winfield Stratton or Jimmie Burns or somebody like them, but right now, I'm not sure what Manny is up to. He's working with a man named John Calderwood, and Calderwood's trying to organize a union."

"Is that good or bad?" Tori thought about the unions that controlled the theater back in New York. She remembered when flats were delivered for a production, and they had to sit in the rain and were ruined because the proper union worker wasn't there to bring them inside.

"It depends on what side of the fence you're on. There's nobody who works harder than a miner, and when you're working at such a high altitude, you're expending more energy just by breathing, so

I can appreciate that they would want more money, but if it's your claim that's being worked and you feel it in your bones that there's gold just a few feet away and you've run out of money, then every penny counts. It's a dilemma, and I have a feeling we'll soon see how it plays out."

FIVE

Tori had no alternative but to accept Link's hospitality and stay in Colorado Springs. He assured her that Speck would send word as soon as Manny returned to Cripple Creek, but she secretly hoped he wouldn't come back until after Christmas.

The holiday season had always been a busy time for those in the New York theater. With all the visitors to the city, there were days with three and four performances, not all played by leading members, but Uncle Harold's theater was definitely in use. And even after becoming Sabrina Chadwick, Tori helped her aunt and uncle with the housekeeping. When the Christmas season ended, they were always relieved. Here in this household, Christmas was a time of anticipation, a time of preparation. The cherry branches, which had been cut on St. Barbara's Day, were on the window seat, and the first chore of the morning was to carefully refill their water, then rotate the containers so that each branch might catch the sun's rays, in hopes that the buds would swell and bloom on Christmas Day. The Advent calendar, with its twenty-four candles, was kept, and every day the appropriate candle was lit as Hulda counted down the days. She seemed to have a different cookie—or *Weihnachtsplätzchen*, as she called them—that had to be baked on each day, with names Tori had never heard: *Springerle*, which had to be made on the first day of Advent, *Spritzgebäck*, *Engelsaugen*, *Haselnussplätzchen*, lebkuchen, and dozens more.

And Tori was enjoying the activity with the enthusiasm of a child, even when Hulda issued commands with the authority of a drill sergeant— "Grind me some more hazelnuts, make some vanilla butter, decorate the gingerbread."

Tori especially liked when Link joined them in the kitchen.

"What do you have for me to sample?" he asked as he picked up a hot cookie off a tray that had just been brought from the oven.

"No, no," Hulda said as she slapped at his hand. "You know these are going to the sanitarium."

"Not all of them, I hope." He picked up another hot cookie and ate it.

"If you're going to do that, you can make yourself useful. Here, crack some of these hazelnuts, and don't break the meat."

"Yes, ma'am." Link gave a mock salute. "Why do I love this woman so?"

"Because she takes such good care of you," Tori said as she put chocolate glaze and then a nut on each of the cookies. "I don't believe I've ever seen so many cookies come out of one kitchen. Why do you need so many?"

"You heard her. A lot of them go to the lungers."

"The 'lungers'?"

"Yes. The Sisters of Charity run the Glockner Sanitarium for tuberculosis sufferers. It seems several people who think they know about those things have decided the altitude and the climate here is just right for consumptives. A group of women like Hulda make certain the patients have a never-ending supply of Christmas cookies."

"Speaking of which, would you mind delivering these today?" Hulda asked as she stepped out of the pantry carrying a large basket.

"I'll do it, but only if you'll let your scullery maid go with me—that is, if she wants to," Link said.

"I'd love to go," Tori replied.

"Good. I'll have Otto hitch Buster to the buggy, and we'll leave right away."

With the buggy loaded with the basket of cookies, Link turned the horse onto Tejon Street, where they rode for almost twenty blocks before reaching the sanitarium.

"If the climate here really does cure tuberculosis, you'd think every consumptive in the country would come," Tori said when they pulled up to the building with its parklike grounds and magnificent view of Pike's Peak.

"That's just it. Maybe it doesn't," Link said. "But a little sunshine, clean air, and good food does a lot for their frame of mind." He stepped down from the buggy, then helped Tori out. "Do you see how this building is designed?"

"I'd say it's sort of unusual." Tori stood there looking at the Y-shaped building.

"Mrs. Glockner wanted each room to have a little bit of sunshine every day." Link took out the cookie basket just as a woman dressed in a black habit came down the path to meet him.

She was rather plump, with a smiling face beneath her white hood. "Mr. Buchannan," she said as she approached Link. "I thought you might pay us a visit today."

"Tori, I want you to meet Sister Basilia," Link said. "She is the mother superior and keeps everyone in line here. I'm told she wields a whip when it's necessary."

Sister Basilia laughed. "Mr. Buchannan, you do carry on."

"I made this basket of cookies for you," Link said, offering the basket.

Sister Basilia stared at him suspiciously. "You made them, did you?"

"Well, sort of. I had to taste a lot of them just to make sure they were good enough to serve."

"And I'm sure that was a very important part of the process." Sister Basilia smiled.

"I'm glad you recognize that."

She took the cookies. "I thank you and Dr. Anderson thanks you, but most of all, the patients do. It's a bit early, but I'll say merry Christmas to you, and to you, young lady. And especially to my good friend Mrs. Birk, who may have had a hand in this operation."

"Ahh, I've been found out," Link said with a big smile. "Merry Christmas to you, Sister."

"Yes," Tori said. "Merry Christmas."

As Sister Basilia, with basket in hand, turned and started toward the building, Link helped Tori into the buggy.

"And now, we're ready for a real job. Have you ever cut down a Christmas tree?" Link asked.

"No." Not only had Tori never cut a tree, she had never even had a Christmas tree.

"Well, that's what we're going to do now. We're going to find the perfect Christmas tree."

Link took a service road that went behind the sanitarium and then headed for the foothills of the mountains. Once there, he hopped down, retrieved a saw from under the seat, then pointed across an open area where the rise of the mountain began.

"You're going to saw it down? I would have thought you would chop it down."

"No, chopping knocks off too many of the needles." Link pointed toward the green conifers. "That's where we're going to find the perfect tree. Are you ready?"

"Lead the way." Tori fell in behind Link as they walked across an open field until they reached the trees.

"We want a small one, no higher than this." Link indicated about waist high. "But this one doesn't look good. It has to have a good shape."

"What's a good shape?"

Link turned to Tori as a wide smile crossed his face. His eyes took in her body as he fought to control what he wanted to say. "A good shape would have branches in all the right places. It has to be beautiful, even if it's not adorned, just like a beautiful woman. This one looks nice, but so does that one." He turned his attention to the trees. "We don't want any bare areas where the poor little thing has lost a limb."

"There are so many to choose from and they all look good to me."

"Then you pick one."

"You want me to choose?"

"Yes. If Hulda doesn't like her *Tannenbaum*, then I can blame you," Link teased.

Tori laughed. "You're awful. All right, I choose this one." She pointed to a fluffy spruce that grew in a perfect cone from its straight trunk.

"Why this one?"

"It spoke to me."

"Then that's the one we'll choose."

An hour later Link carried the little fir tree into his kitchen. "What do you think, Hulda?"

"Oh, ist der Weihnachtsbaum wunderbar!"

"Good. We have this one because the tree spoke to us, you know."

Tori chuckled, then hit Link playfully on his shoulder. She liked how Link was including her in everything.

"While you were gone, Mr. Tutt stopped by," Hulda said.

"I knew it. He can't stand not knowing who I'm bringing for Christmas. You didn't tell him about Tori, did you?"

"I didn't say anything, and he didn't ask anything.

He left a packet for you. It's on the table in the hall."

Walking into the entry hall, Link picked up an envelope and opened it. Inside was a note attached to a folded newspaper.

He read the note, then returned to the library, where Hulda was covering a table with cotton in preparation for the tree.

"You're not going to put the tree up tonight, are you?" Link asked.

"I am not. A tree gets put up on December twenty-fourth, and not a day sooner. I'm just getting the table ready."

"Good, because Tori and I don't want to miss helping you. It seems Charles had planned on taking Josephine out tonight, but she says he needs to entertain the children while she plays Mrs. Santa Claus." Link looked toward Tori. "How about it? Would you like to go with me to the Garden of the Gods this evening?"

"The Garden of the Gods?"

"Yes, that's what they call the opera house. A traveling theater group is in town and Charles sent us two tickets." Link handed Tori the newspaper clipping.

A DELIGHTFUL PRODUCTION

Coming to the opera house on December 23 is Hoyt's A Trip to Chinatown. *The engagement has special interest attached to it from the fact that this most successful of Hoyt's comedies comes to this city with the same company that presented it for 657 consecutive nights at*

Hoyt's Madison Square Theater in New York. The production will be identical with that which has had such success in the metropolis. The cast is the same, including Harry Conor in his original creation of Welland Strong, Anna Boyd as the Widow Guyer, Lottie Mortimer as Flirt, George A. Beane Jr. as Ben Gay, and Harry Gilfoil with his whistling specialties as the waiter. Bessie Clayton, the little dancer extraordinary, is a special feature of this engagement and will no doubt succeed in arousing the same enthusiasm here as has greeted her appearance elsewhere. The musical numbers with which this comedy is so liberally interspersed have become famous throughout the land. Among the more popular may be mentioned "On the Bowery," "You Gave Me Your Love," "The Girl I Left Behind Me," and "Do, Do, My Huckleberry, Do."

Tori started as she read the article. She had attended this very play at the Hoyt Theater. And she had met both Harry Conor and Anna Boyd, having seen them at one of Mrs. Leslie's salons. What if they were to see her and remember her? She frantically searched for some plausible excuse not to go.

"We can enjoy the play, then have a late supper afterward, and the best part—Hulda won't have to spend her time in the kitchen tonight."

As Tori thought about it, she realized that the chances of her being seen and recognized were remote. She knew from experience that the bright lights on the stage made it impossible to see the audience as anything more than a dark blur. In addition, her meeting with Harry Conor and Anna Boyd had been well over a year ago, and brief, and she had not been seated at their table.

If she had learned anything about show business, it was that most performers were narcissists, and if the conversation didn't revolve around their own performances, they tended not to listen. She decided that there was little danger of her coming into contact with either of the stars, and if by happenstance she did, no one would recognize her.

Tori smiled. "How thoughtful of Mr. Tutt. I'd love to go."

"Wonderful. But, Hulda, don't touch the tree. I'm sure it will tell Tori where to put the ornaments."

Tori didn't know what to expect of an opera house in such a remote location, but she was pleasantly surprised. It was as well-appointed as any theater she had ever played in in New York. A curved balcony followed the outer dome, and a beautiful chandelier hung from the artfully painted ceiling. Four elegant boxes draped with heavy, wine-colored velvet flanked each side of the stage, two on the upper floor and two just off from the orchestra pit. Gilt-edged banisters helped to conceal the elite occupants.

When they were ushered to their cast-iron seats, Tori was pleased that they were some distance from the stage, even though they were on the inside of the curving aisle that divided the seats into sections. The orchestra pit was lower but directly in front of them, and the cushioned seating was elevated from front to rear, giving everyone an unobstructed view of the stage.

The orchestra played the overture, and the lights in the theater dimmed. For just a moment, Tori put herself backstage, waiting for her entry as butterflies gathered in her stomach. Then the curtain rose to an empty stage.

Harry Conor stepped center stage and began to sing.

Even though Tori remembered the play, she laughed and applauded in all the appropriate places, doing so as enthusiastically as anyone else until the final curtain came down. The lights in the house went up, and for a moment she was apprehensive. She realized that during the curtain calls was when she would be most exposed. Tori made it a point to lower her head when Harry Conor and Anna Boyd stepped out for their curtain calls.

"Would you like to go backstage to meet the players?" Link asked. "I believe our tickets permit that."

"What? No!"

Tori realized she had said the words too forcefully. "It's just that you mentioned we would be dining, and I'm afraid I'm starving. I don't suppose that's very ladylike of me, is it?"

Link laughed. "How thoughtless of me. Of course you're hungry. You didn't eat all the cookies I did, and we missed lunch."

Tori breathed a sigh of relief. The faster they got out of this theater, the more at ease she would be.

"Would you care to eat at the Antlers? I know when you arrived, your experience there wasn't the best, but maybe I can make it up to you."

"I'd like that very much."

Link helped Tori put on her cloak; then, in a spontaneous and completely unexpected move, he put his arms around her and gave her a quick kiss on the forehead.

"What was that for?" Tori asked, surprised.

"I don't know," Link replied with an easy smile. "But if you'd rather I not have done that, I'll be glad to take it back."

Again, he kissed her on the forehead, and she tried to suppress a giggle. "I believe you said something about eating?"

Despite the lateness of the hour, the dining room was quite full, and looking around, Tori realized many of the patrons had come directly from the theater. The maître d' escorted them to a table off to the side of the dining room, then left them to peruse the large menu.

"This looks delicious, and the choice is quite extensive," Tori said as she examined the menu.

Link smiled. "Yes, not for nothing is the town called Little London. We have a few people who like to put on the dog around here, and since the Antlers is the place to be seen, where else would you expect to get"—Link picked up the menu and began to read—"scallops, sauce ravigote, or sweetbreads à l'Eugénie?"

Picking up her menu, Tori asked, "Who wouldn't want Malossol caviar or antipasto Lucullus?"

"Now you've done it. Leave old Lucullus out of this. I know him well."

"Aha—'Lucullus dines with Lucullus'!" Tori said,

reciting the famous line attributed to the Roman general.

"Well, the old guy was right. When you dine with yourself, you should do it right. But I'm curious: How did you know who Lucullus was?"

"Of course I know him. He was a fine patron of the arts."

"Speaking of which, look who just came in. That's Alice Bemis, and she is certainly a patron of the arts, at least here in Colorado Springs. And look who she has with her," Link said.

Tori turned toward a fairly large group of people who had just entered the dining room. It seemed to be the entire cast from *A Trip to Chinatown*. Tori saw Harry Conor standing beside the woman she assumed was Alice Bemis, because the lady was going from table to table introducing the star. She was glad the maître d' had seated Link and her at the edge of the dining room. Perhaps she could avoid an introduction.

"Good evening, sir," the waiter said as he approached the table. "Has the lady made a selection?"

"I believe she has." Link turned to Tori. "What will it be?"

"I'm not all that hungry. I'll start with some consommé and then I'll have the crabmeat salad."

"How can that be? You were starved when we left the theater, and now you're eating like a bird," Link said. "Bring the lady her dainties, but bring me a cup of potato soup, grilled sardines, and a toasted cream cheese sandwich. Oh, make that two cheese sandwiches. And when we're finished, please bring the patisseries around."

When Tori heard Link's choice, she was struck by his lack of pretension. If this had been an after-theater supper with Lyle, he would have ordered the most expensive thing on the menu—not because that was what he liked, but because he would have wanted to impress.

Impress with Bella's money.

Stop it. Stop it right now. You've come out here to start a new life. Forget New York, forget Lyle Ketterman.

Tori enjoyed the conversation and the simple fare, even accepting one of the points of Link's cheese sandwich. She knew the pleasure she was experiencing—being in Link's company, being in his home, being a part of his life—would soon be coming to an end. This was an honorable man, one who deserved an honorable woman.

"Are you ready?" Link asked as he took the last bite of his éclair.

"Yes, and thank you. I didn't think I wanted to go to the opera house, but this has been a most enjoyable evening." Link took Tori's hand as he helped her to her feet. "I'm going to amend that statement. This has been a most enjoyable day."

"It has been, hasn't it?"

With a light touch on Tori's waist, Link guided her through the maze of tables toward the exit. She waited while he settled the bill and went to retrieve their coats.

"Link—Link Buchannan! I knew that was you," an older woman, who was quite attractive, said.

"Mrs. Bemis," Link said, taking her hand. "I saw you enter with the theater entourage."

"Oh, yes, wasn't it a magnificent performance? Did you get to meet the stars? Here they come now. Let me introduce you." Mrs. Bemis pulled Link toward the group.

Link looked to Tori with a helpless expression on his face. He motioned for her to join him, but she shook her head no. Soon he was encircled by the cast of the play, and Tori chose that minute to step into the public room of the hotel. She busied herself looking at the lifelike paintings of animals and Indians that were hanging on the walls.

She felt rather than heard the approach of someone. Thinking it was Link, she turned.

"Pardon me, ma'am, for intruding on your privacy," the man said, "but I've been observing you in the dining room. Do I know you?"

"Mr. Conor," Tori said, hoping to defuse this conversation quickly, "your portrayal of Welland Strong was magnificent, and you are without doubt the star of the show. We in Colorado Springs are so fortunate that you've brought this fabulous production to us."

"Thank you, my dear. Six hundred fifty-seven performances. That's how long we ran on Broadway."

"Then that's why you were so marvelous. I would love to hear all about your exciting experiences in New York, but I seem to have lost my escort. Oh, there he is now."

Tori waved her hand and hurried toward Link. She knew the moment he saw her because his whole face spread into a dazzling smile.

"There she is. Mrs. Bemis, I would like you to meet my guest, Miss Drumm."

"Good evening, my dear. I see you've met Mr. Conor," Mrs. Bemis said. "This is Miss Boyd, Miss Mortimer, Mr. Beane, and I don't know where Mr. Gilfoil is. What was your name again?"

Tori swallowed before she answered. "Victoria Drumm."

"I'm pleased to meet you," Anna Boyd said, then turned to the other actors. "Who does she remind you of?"

"I don't know," one of the others said, "but she does look familiar."

"Well, look at her! This is Sabrina Chadwick, or at least she could be Sabrina Chadwick's twin sister," Anna said.

"I'm afraid I don't know her, but I'm most flattered," Tori said.

"Oh, honey, don't be flattered. Sabrina Chadwick is the kind of tramp who gives all of us in the theatrical profession a bad name," Miss Boyd said.

"It has been most enjoyable meeting you, and I hope you enjoy your stay in Colorado Springs," Link said, sensing Tori's discomfort. "And for you, Mrs. Bemis, I'll see what I can do to help you raise money for the college library. I know I can get the 'socialites' to dig into their pockets when I get back to Cripple Creek."

"Well, don't leave too soon. *The Laughing Girl* is scheduled to come to the opera house after the New Year, and according to the *New York Herald*, Clara Lipman enacts her part admirably," Mrs. Bemis said.

"No wonder she's so good. The New York gossip is that she's married the leading man," Anna Boyd said as she looked toward Harry Conor. "Now, that would make for a good performance."

"I hate to leave this scintillating repartee, but, ladies and gentlemen, it is now Christmas Eve and our Christmas tree is officially calling to us. Good night," Link said as he helped Tori into her coat.

Tori stared at the moonlight shadows of tree branches that were dancing on her bedroom wall. She had been in bed for more than an hour, but she couldn't sleep.

The meeting with the actors at the Antlers had been most unsettling.

Up to that hour, the day had been perfect.

Yet she was troubled. Was her past that big of an obstacle? Would Link Buchannan care if she was a virgin?

She didn't know the answer.

In New York, it probably wouldn't make any difference, at least not among theater people. Hadn't Anna Boyd mentioned that the rumor was that Clara Lipman had married her leading man? Clara was one of Tori's closest friends. She assumed that if Clara had really married, it would have been to Louis Mann. And had Clara engaged in any indecencies, Louis would certainly have known about it.

Morality.

Her whole life had been one morality play.

For the first twelve years of Tori's life she had traveled with her family across Middle America. Her father, Nathan Drumm, was a preacher whose church was a tent. She could still envision the sign painted on the side of the wagon, a gold cross alongside gilt-edged red letters:

REVEREND NATHAN L. DRUMM
SPREADING THE WORD OF GOD
SAVING SOULS FOR JESUS
BAPTISMS DAILY

When a revival was completed in one town, Victoria and her brother, Emanuel, as their father insisted upon calling them, would ride with their mother in the camp wagon that served as their home. The Reverend Drumm would drive the other wagon carrying the big tent and several dozen boards that could be fashioned into benches.

Nathan was what some called a charismatic preacher, and Tori's earliest memories were of him standing on the dirt in front of the gathered "sinners," his sleeves rolled up, his right arm lifted, his forefinger jabbing into the air, and sweat rolling down his face as he preached.

"The Lord will lift your burdens, he will wipe dry your tearful eyes, the sick shall be healed and the crooked made straight. Hearts, guilty with sin, will be cleansed and made holy. And the cold, worldly churches of brick and mortar shall be as nothing when compared to this tent tabernacle which rises, gleaming from the dust. With oil in your lamps and offerings in your hands you come to this meeting, not only to worship, but to donate generously so that, with your support, I can carry on the work of saving the souls of sinners."

Then, one day at a tent revival outside a small town in Missouri, twelve-year-old Victoria made the mistake of making eye contact, then actually holding hands, with a boy who was not more than fourteen years old. The Reverend Drumm became incensed. He sent the boy away, and then, after cutting a switch from a willow tree, he pulled Tori into the tent and whipped her until welts rose on her body.

No one—not her mother, not her father—ever told her what she had done wrong, but soon thereafter, her aunt Frances came to get her. From that day forward she had lived in New York City, never to see her family again.

If a father who preached brotherly love, and a mother who had rocked a child in her arms, could reject a twelve-year-old girl for what Tori considered an innocent transgression, what would a man do if he fell in love with a fallen woman?

She would never know. No man would ever toss her aside as her father had done. She decided she would leave Colorado Springs tomorrow, and when she got to Cripple Creek, she would find someone who knew her brother. Whenever he returned, his sister would be there whether he liked it or not.

She closed her eyes, willing herself to go to sleep, but her mind couldn't erase the smiling face of Link Buchannan.

"How do I get myself in such messes?"

After a fretful night, Tori awakened to the smell of baking bread. "I wonder if that woman ever sleeps," Tori said aloud as she rose from the bed.

It was December 24, and Tori had been looking

forward to the Christmas celebration, but after last night's near exposure, she knew she could not stay in Link's house another day.

Mrs. Bemis had said that *The Laughing Girl* was coming to the opera house. It was one thing to fool Harry Conor and Anna Boyd, but she could not fool Clara Lipman. Clara's flat had been on the same floor at the Gerlach as Tori's. Tori could not take the chance of running into her friend in Colorado Springs.

Reluctantly, Tori took out her valise and packed her belongings.

When she got to the bottom of the stairs, she set her bag down and took her coat from the hall tree. Her hand was on the doorknob when Hulda came into the front hall.

"There you are, my dear. I've been waiting for you. Let me put your valise away." Hulda took the case and did not question why Tori had it with her or why she had on her coat.

Tori watched as the woman walked away, having no recourse but to follow Hulda.

"Today is stollen day. I need you to cut up the citron and bitter orange. Make small pieces." Hulda set out the candied fruit and a knife and a cutting board. "Then when you have that done, you need to grind the cardamom seeds, but they have to be cool before you do it. Use the wooden mortar for the cardamom, but use the marble pestle. Then grind the almonds, but don't use the same mortar. Use the marble one."

Tori was standing in the middle of the room, still in her coat.

"Well?" Hulda looked directly at Tori, waiting for an answer.

"Wait till I put my coat away."

A smile crossed Hulda's face. "Link is a good boy. You've made the right choice."

Tori's mouth opened but no words came out.

As she walked back to the front hall, she thought about Hulda's words. First of all, Link Buchannan was certainly not a boy. He was one of the most virile men she had ever met.

And Tori hadn't made a choice—at least not one that involved Link. Her choice had been to get away from him—but then Hulda had taken charge. Was Tori so transparent that Hulda could see that Tori was attracted to Link? She knew, if her situation were different, she could fall in love with Link, but that could never be.

For the entire day, the house was filled with the delicious aroma of sweetbreads being baked. Link and Otto were in and out of the kitchen as they filled baskets with goodies and delivered them to neighbors and friends. At the same time, either Hulda or Tori was answering the door, accepting gifts of jams or jellies or honey or pickles or mincemeat or cured ham or a variety of other things, but not cookies. It was as if each person had been assigned a gift, and Hulda Birk was the designated cookie maker.

"That's it. We've delivered all the cookies," Link said as he came into the kitchen, then lifted the lid on the dough box. "At last this thing is empty, and I want you to quit. You'll fall asleep in church tonight."

"Church?" Tori asked.

"Oh, I guess I didn't tell you—or ask you," Link said. "I try to go to church at least one time a year, and Christmas seems to be the best time to do it. I just assumed you'd come with me."

Tori lowered her head. Memories of Christmas at her father's church were not pleasant.

"Tori, that was most presumptive of me. I'm sorry," Link said.

"No, I want to go."

"Well, you two aren't done yet," Hulda said. "What about the house? We've got a few things to do. Otto will hang the wreath and wrap the streetlamp with greens. Link, you decorate the stairway. Tori, you make red bows to tie up the greens, and then there's the tree to decorate."

"Yes, ma'am," Link said as he gave Hulda a mock salute. "Come on, Tori, we'd better get out of her way before she has us scrubbing floors." He grabbed Tori's hand and pulled her into the front hall, where Otto was making the evergreen roping.

For the next several hours Tori and Link worked side by side decorating the staircase, the doorframes, and the mantels of the various fireplaces. Tori had never spent a more enjoyable day, and she was thankful Hulda had stopped her from leaving.

The last thing to be done was to decorate the tree. Link stepped into a little room off from the library to get the glass ornaments that were special to Hulda. The *Glaskugeln* had been brought all the way from Germany, and each ornament had belonged to her when she was young.

But instead of the wooden crate that contained the silvery-lined fruits and nuts, Link brought out Tori's valise.

"Isn't this yours?"

"Yes," Tori said, her gaze meeting his.

"All your things are in here. Are you leaving?" Link's expression was crestfallen.

Tori's eyes cut away as she chewed her bottom lip. "I thought I should leave. I thought I should get to Cripple Creek."

"All right, if that's what you want, we'll catch the train tonight. The train will run on Christmas Eve, just like any other day."

"I didn't mean for you to go. What about your friends? You told the Tutts you would be there for Christmas and I don't want you to miss that on my account."

"Tori, do you have any idea what a mining camp is like? At the beginning of this year, Cripple Creek had about two thousand people, and now it's close to seven thousand. Take Victor. That's another settlement in the district. Last January it had one cabin, and now it has three thousand people living there. And most of these people are men—men who used to have jobs in the silver mines, but thanks to our president and our Congress, there's a serious depression in silver mining. These men are living off beans and salt side in the daytime, and then they booze all night. Every fleabag sack in Cripple Creek is full, sometimes with two or three men to the bed. Now, I know for certain Manny Drumm is not there. If you got to the camp—without me to help you— just what would you do? Where would you go?"

"I guess I didn't give it much thought," Tori said in a voice so low Link could barely hear her.

Link set the valise down and closed the distance between them. He took her in his arms and held her tight, and he was pleased when he felt her relax and her arms encircled his neck.

Taking in the scent of her, he detected a woodsy smell with a hint of ginger or anise, and he smiled when he remembered her morning chores. Instinctively, he drew her closer and kissed her head.

He pulled back and looked into her eyes. "Tori, I don't know what's going on in your life that brought you here. I would be lying if I said I hadn't wondered why a beautiful woman, one as educated and sophisticated as you obviously are, has come to visit her brother—one she hasn't heard from in years—but right now that's none of my business. I'm enjoying your company, and I'll get you get to Cripple Creek." He kissed her on the tip of her nose.

"Would you think I'm wishy-washy if I say I don't want to go?" Tori asked as her eyes filled with tears.

"No. I'd say you just can't resist my irresistible charms." He wiped a tear from her cheek. "Now, we'd better get that tree trimmed before we get in trouble."

Finally the decorating was finished, and Link and Tori walked through the house looking at their work.

"You have a beautiful home, Link. I know you're proud of it," Tori said.

"I am, but I'm thinking about selling it."

"Why?" Tori furrowed her forehead. "Why would you want to do that? Don't you need a house here?"

"Yes, but this one is too big for one person. Otto and Hulda won't always be with me, and then what would one person do in a house this big?"

"You could always get married and have a family."

"That's not as easy as you think. I told you about all the men who are pouring into Cripple Creek. Well, what I didn't tell you is that a lot of women are coming in, too, but they're mainly 'working girls' who follow the men, and they don't exactly make good wives." Link shook his head. "Good friends, maybe, but not good wives."

Tori turned and hurried to the kitchen, where she heard Hulda and Otto. She thought of what Link said. Good friends, but not good wives. A sadness came over her, one that all the Christmas cheer in the world couldn't erase.

"Didn't Ot do a wonderful job choosing just the right branches?" Hulda asked as she was arranging the carefully tended cherry branches, which were now in full blossom. "You know, my dear, according to St. Barbara, if they bloom on Christmas, it's a good sign for the future." She winked at Tori. "Don't forget to take these when you and Link go to the Tutts tomorrow."

"Won't you be here?" Tori asked.

"Oh, no. Ot and I are going up to Palmer Lake to spend Weihnachten with my sister, Gertie. She and Hiram are the caretakers for the Estemere, and we all have such fun getting that big old place cleaned in the middle of the winter."

"How . . . how long will you be gone?"

"As long as it takes. Link always does a good job closing up the house when he leaves, and with you here, too, I know nothing will be forgotten."

Tori nodded but didn't speak. This situation was soon going to get out of hand.

"I don't want to rush you, Hulda, but if you don't want to miss the train, we'd better be leaving," Link said, joining the two women in the kitchen. "Otto has Buster hitched to the buggy and he has everything loaded."

"I'll just be a minute. Your frankfurters and potato salad are in the warming oven. Now, don't forget to eat them," Hulda said as Link helped her into her coat.

Link laughed. "When have I forgotten to eat? Especially your traditional Heiligabend supper?"

Hulda patted Link on the cheek. "My boy, I'm going to make a good German out of you yet. Take care of him, Tori. And *frohe Weihnachten* to you both."

"Frohe Weihnachten," Tori said, and though she did not understand German, she knew the words were kind.

While Link was out of the house, Tori attended to her toilette. She took great pains with her hair, trying to control the waves that fell naturally. After several attempts, she settled on parting it in the middle, then making large curls at the sides; the rest she twisted into a high knot on the crown of her head. When she was finished, she smiled.

"Maybe not done as well as Hannah could do, but good enough for me."

Tori took out some of the makeup that Hannah had taught her to use. For the theater, Miss Inman had always applied it so heavily that Tori often thought she looked grotesque, but Hannah had coached her many times: subtlety—not so much that anyone knows you are wearing stage makeup, but just enough to make you look beautiful. Tonight, that was the effect Tori wanted to achieve.

When she was satisfied with her hair and makeup, she opened her valise and withdrew a royal-blue satin dress with a square-cut neck and an empire waist. With her hair and her makeup, she was pleased with the look. Withdrawing a pair of walking gloves, she pulled them on. Pushed down from the upper arm, they wrinkled comfortably.

"Perfect," she said as she looked into the mirror. And then it was as if she heard her father standing before her, quoting from the book of Proverbs: "'Behold, there met him a woman with the attire of a harlot.'"

"Behold the harlot," Tori said quietly.

She let out a sigh, removed the gloves and then the dress. Kneeling beside her valise, she took out a serviceable seal-brown walking suit. The bodice had the fashionable leg-of-mutton sleeves, while the skirt was slightly flared in front with a pleated fullness in the back. She slipped on the skirt, feeling the weight of the haircloth interfacing that held the pleats in place.

This outfit wasn't right either. It was Christmas Eve, and wasn't that supposed to be a merry time?

This time she pulled out a black serge skirt and a red waistcoat. She paired the red with a cream-white embroidered inset, and when she was dressed, she felt she had achieved the look she wanted.

This was the first time Tori had been alone in Link's house. As she stepped out into the hallway, she recalled his remark that he was trying to sell his home—that it was too big for one person.

Curiosity led her across the hall to his bedroom. She tried the door, and when she found it unlocked, she stepped into the room, which was now cast in shadows as the daylight was fading.

The room exuded masculinity, from the gentleman's chest with its shaving mirror pulled out, to the wishbone dresser with its pivoting mirror. Two boxes were separated by a slab of marble, and Tori lifted one of the lids. It was filled with carefully ironed handkerchiefs, and she smiled.

This was the work of Hulda Birk. There was little wonder why Link wasn't married. As long as he had Hulda, he didn't need a wife.

But then Tori turned to the bed. In keeping with much of the wood in the house, it was made of oak. The headboard with its detailed carvings stood well over six feet tall, while the footboard was low, allowing one to watch the flames of the fireplace if the fire was lit.

Tori moved to the bed, and running her hand over the velvet texture of the pieced quilt, she recognized a log-cabin pattern in shades of green and red, but this one was different. Instead of the familiar chimney and logs, this one had Christmas symbols in each block—a star, some candles, sprigs of holly, and a tree, among other things.

It had to be Hulda again.

Tori sat down on the bed, her hand resting on the footboard. Maybe Hulda could iron his handkerchiefs and make his bed, but Link Buchannan needed some things from a woman that a housekeeper couldn't provide.

How she would like to be that woman!

Abruptly, she rose from the bed and hurried from the room. How could she entertain a thought like that, especially on a night when she was going to a church service? A Jezebel. That's what her father would call her, and that's what she was.

Nature had helped decorate Colorado Springs with a fresh snowfall as Tori and Link left for the Christmas Eve service. With the wreaths, the colorful bows, and the candles in the windows, Weber Street looked like an artist's rendering of a Christmas village.

"Which church will we be attending?" Tori asked as she pulled her coat around her.

"Grace Episcopal," Link said. "It's only a block away, so I think it's easier to walk than to hitch up Buster again."

"You're not fooling me for one minute, Link Buchannan. You mean Otto isn't here to hitch up Buster."

"They do spoil me." Link took her hand. "I don't know if I've said this, but I'm glad you're here."

"Thank you." Tori felt a tremor of excitement as Link squeezed her hand.

"Mr. Buchannan," a man called as he came out of a neighboring house. "Please tell Hulda how much the children enjoyed her cookies. We love Zaltana, but she's never learned to bake, at least not Christmas cookies."

"I'll tell her when she comes back from Estemere," Link said. "Miss Drumm, I would like you to meet my esteemed neighbor Mr. William Jackson."

Tori and Mr. Jackson exchanged greetings and Link continued, "You may know of the book *Ramona*. His late wife was the author."

"Helen Hunt Jackson," Tori said excitedly. "I have a very good friend who knew your wife well."

"And who might that be?"

Tori was reluctant to say the name, but she could not avoid it without appearing to be a braggart. "Miriam Leslie."

"Oh, yes. I remember her visit well. I think she and Frank were on their way to California when they came to our cottage in the mountains," Mr. Jackson said. "That may have been the summer Grace Greenwood was in residence. Can you imagine three writers together? Those were wonderful days."

"Mrs. Leslie remembers them fondly," Tori said.

"Well, please give her my regards, and merry Christmas to you both. I just needed to step out in the fresh air for a moment." Mr. Jackson looked through the window of his own house. "You'd think Zaltana could corral those four little ones and get them to bed, but it's pure bedlam in there."

"Everyone is excited on Christmas Eve. Give our best to Mrs. Jackson," Link said, "and merry Christmas."

For the remainder of the walk to church, Tori and Link didn't speak. She was sorry William Sharpless Jackson had broken the spell.

Once they were seated in the church, Tori sat in awe, looking at the gold and white banners, the red poinsettias, the white altar cloth, and the many candles being lit by acolytes in red vestments. For as long as she could remember, this was the first church service she had attended in an actual building. She couldn't help but compare the beautiful stained-glass windows, the rich wood pews with the needlepoint kneelers, and a pipe organ that made the music sound as if it were coming from on high, to her father's "tent cathedral."

Bells began to ring, and then the procession started with the cross, followed by the red-robed choir, the lay readers, and the priest. The congregation, accompanied by a brass ensemble, began to sing "The First Noel," and they did it with such . . . joy, was the only way Tori could describe it, that she felt herself a part of it, and she sang with the others.

A lay reader gave the first lesson: "'And she brought forth her firstborn Son, and wrapped Him in swaddling clothes, and laid Him in a manger; because there was no room for them in the inn.'"

As the congregation continued to sing the carols and listen to the story of Christmas being read, she thought about how dissimilar this church was from her father's. The Reverend Nathan Drumm's sermons had always been confrontational, challenging, even angry, and the people who attended them were rife with guilt and confusion.

The biggest difference of all was that her father didn't believe in Christmas, calling it a "pagan ritual."

"You cannot have a doll," her father had told her

when she was five years old. "It is clearly stated in Exodus that 'thou shalt not make unto thee any graven image, or any likeness of anything that is in heaven above, or that is in the earth beneath.' And a doll is, clearly, a graven image."

As Nathan Drumm pointed out, when he forbade his family from celebrating, "There are no holy days except the Sabbath mentioned in Scripture. Christ was not born on December twenty-fifth, that is the date of an early Roman festival, and to celebrate it as the birth of Christ is paying homage to a pagan custom. I will not allow that blasphemy in my house."

Tori remembered reading Clement Moore's poem to Manny when they were children. Afterward, Manny had asked their father if Santa Claus knew about Tori and him. As an answer to his question, the boy was given a spanking and told that Santa Claus was the Antichrist.

When Tori moved to New York, her uncle Harold and aunt Frances did celebrate Christmas, but never in a religious sense. They celebrated by having a big dinner and by buying gifts. Over the last few years, as Tori became a successful actress, there were many parties—most noticeably the extravaganzas given by Miriam Leslie. But those parties were all secular, so while Tori wasn't denied the nonspiritual aspects of Christmas, she did sometimes envy those for whom Christmas was a meaningful day for family.

Even though she had known Link and the Birks for only a few days, she had been made to feel as if she belonged. Tori was looking forward to going to

Cripple Creek to reconnect with her brother in the hope that they could reestablish a familial connection. She didn't know what she was going to do, but she was resourceful enough to believe that she would be able to support herself in an honorable occupation. For the first time since leaving New York, she believed she was moving toward a new part of her life, rather than running away from an old.

SIX

The Christmas Eve service was over, and as the parishioners started home, many were still singing "Joy to the World." As Tori and Link walked, the words grew more and more distant until soon she could hear nothing but the sound of their footfalls in the light covering of snow. When they arrived at Link's home, it was dark, unlike other houses on the street.

"If you'll take care of Hulda's supper, I'll light the candles," Link said as he opened the door. "We don't want the Jacksons' house to outshine ours."

An innocent comment—"to outshine *ours*." But that comment filled Tori with emotion.

Tori headed for the kitchen and removed the food from the warming oven. The smell of the potato salad with its rye and vinegar dressing permeated the air, while the frankfurters were browned to perfection. She found some hard rolls in the breadbox, and when Link returned, the meal was ready.

"Shall we eat in the dining room?" Tori asked.

"No, I'd rather eat here, if you don't mind." Link

pulled up two stools and put one on each side of the butcher-block table. "I'll even put on a tablecloth so Hulda won't get mad if I drop a frank on her bread-board and leave a spot of grease." He took out a clean white cloth that had the imprint of Hellinger Feed Store stamped on it.

Link and Tori enjoyed dinner—a very different meal from the one she would have had if she were still in New York.

"This is a far cry from oyster stew," Link said. "That's what my family always had on Christmas Eve. What about yours?"

Tori struggled to know what to say. She finally remembered a dish Uncle Harold had always insisted upon.

"Bakaliaros."

"Where are you from? Don't try to tell me that's a traditional dish in Iowa?"

Tori was taken aback. What made Link say Iowa? She hadn't said a word about where she was from, yet Iowa was where she believed her parents were.

She tried to cover her discomfort with a laugh, but it sounded fake even to her own ears.

"Bakaliaros is fried salt cod, and it's very good, actually. But not as good as this." Tori reached across the table and wiped a drip of the salad dressing off the dishcloth.

She couldn't help but feel that eating as they were made the meal much more intimate. She knew that if this were her house, and if she and Link were mar-ried, they would eat many of their meals at this table.

She smiled at the idea of being married to Link. Where did that thought come from?

Had someone told her just five days ago that she would be spending Christmas Eve in a spacious house occupied by only one other person, and that person would be a man—a most attractive, single man—she wouldn't have believed it. But here she was, sitting in front of the fireplace, poking at the logs as she watched the flames curl around them.

Link lit the candles on the tree, and one by one the colorful glass ornaments reflected the light onto the gleaming Stoke-on-Trent tiles that faced the opening of the fireplace. The tree was a beautiful work of art—its aromatic perfume filling the room as it mixed with the scent of the candles and the essence of burning wood.

"This is nice, isn't it?" Link asked as he joined her on the rug in front of the fire.

"It's more than nice. It's beautiful!"

"Yes." Link captured one of the curls that hung beside her face. "Especially when the firelight is reflected in your hair." He began removing the pins from her topknot, and when her hair was free, he ran his fingers through it, smoothing the waves.

Tori watched him with a quizzical expression, then realized that Link was going to kiss her. She also knew that she wasn't going to resist; a kiss was exactly what she wanted.

Link pulled her face to his and kissed her. Though the kiss wasn't unexpected, her reaction to it was. The light and tender kiss, that gentle touch of his lips to hers, was enough to cause a quick-building heat to spread through her entire body.

The kiss ended much too soon, and as she stared

into his eyes, she saw a glint of doubt, of self-condemnation for what he must have perceived as having taken advantage of her.

No, she wanted to say. *You need have no doubt. You did nothing that I didn't want!* Though she screamed the words in her mind, they remained unspoken.

Link started to say something but the words caught, and he cleared his throat before he spoke.

"I've got a present for you." He stood and started toward the tree.

Tori shook her head. "Link, I can't accept a present from you. I'm taking advantage of your hospitality as it is, and I certainly don't expect a Christmas gift."

"Well, whether you expect it or not, you're getting one."

Reaching under the tree, Link removed a hastily wrapped package that was tied with a gold ribbon.

"But I didn't get you anything," Tori said. "I'm embarrassed."

"Oh, but you did give me something."

"And what would that be?"

"Your company. You've been by my side for the last few days, and to be in the company of a beautiful woman is a gift to any man."

Tori lowered her head. Even when she was on the stage, she had a hard time accepting compliments. "I don't know what to say."

"Well, then don't say anything. Just open the present. I wrapped it myself."

Tori unwrapped the package. She pulled out a

red hand-knit neck scarf. When she picked it up, she saw that one end had been beautifully embroidered with the name *Tori*. The white letters were surrounded with stylized snowflakes.

"Hulda made this for you, so it's from all of us."

"Oh," Tori said, her eyes shining brightly. "The scarf is beautiful."

"I picked out the yarn. I knew you'd like it."

"I do. Thank you." This time, Tori placed a light kiss on Link's lips. She withdrew immediately, realizing what she had done. "Oh, I'm sorry. I shouldn't have done that."

"And why not? I kissed you."

From the hall they heard the whir, then the chime of the clock. It struck two.

"Man," Link said. "I had no idea it was so late. It's Christmas morning already, and you've got to be rested before you meet the Tutt kids. I think it's time we went to bed."

Tori felt her heart jump, and a tingling sensation in the pit of her stomach. They were alone in this house. What would she say if he really wanted to go to bed—with her?

Link put the screen in front of the fire, then blew out the candles on the tree. He took her hand, ostensibly to help her up the darkened stairway, but the effect was to send shivers through her body.

Link walked Tori to her bedroom door and flipped the light switch. In the dim light, he turned toward her, exposing the hunger that was in his eyes.

She knew she was telegraphing the same desire. She licked her lips, then opened them slightly as he moved toward her. He kissed her, and the heat spread throughout her body. As he melded his body to hers, she could feel her arousal building, just as the physical proof of his own need was pressing against her.

Link broke off the kiss, but he continued to hold her until she felt his ardor subside. A part of her was disappointed when he stepped back, still holding her shoulders.

"My beautiful, beautiful Tori. You'll never know how hard it is to walk away from you." Link kissed her one last time. Then he left the room, shutting the door behind him.

Tori removed her clothing and laid her things across a chair. Putting on her gown, she moved to the window. The Christmas wonderland that had been Weber Street was now not unlike any other night on the Colorado plateau at the foot of the mountains.

Crawling into bed, Tori imagined Link just across the hall. In her mind's eye he had thrown back the Christmas quilt and was lying there naked, trying to put the thoughts of the woman he had just held in his arms out of his mind.

When Tori awakened on Christmas morning, the amount of light streaming in through the window told her that she had slept much later than she normally did. She wasn't surprised by that because it had taken her a long time to fall asleep. What did surprise her was the smell of frying bacon.

After getting dressed, Tori went down to the kitchen. When she walked in, she saw Link bending over the opened oven door, looking inside. He was wearing one of Hulda's aprons, and she noticed the butcher-block table was covered with flour.

Tori raised her eyebrows. "You're cooking breakfast?"

"I didn't see you down here at the crack of dawn, so I decided I'd better do it myself." Link closed the oven door . "I think it will take the biscuits at least another five minutes."

"I'm sorry. I should have come down earlier," Tori said, although she was not sure what she would have prepared. Cooking was definitely not one of her strengths.

"I'm teasing, Tori. When I'm in Cripple Creek, if anything gets cooked at home, I do it, and if I do say so myself, I'm pretty good at it. How do you like your eggs?"

"Any way you fix them will be fine with me."

"They'll be scrambled, with cheese."

"That sounds good."

"Then you just skedaddle into the dining room, and I'll bring your breakfast to you when it's ready. Would you like a cup of coffee?"

"Of course."

Taking her cup of coffee, she went into the dining room and waited beside the fireplace. This one did not have an open flame but had a coal-burning inset that was putting out heat. She stood in front of it as her body absorbed the warmth.

Link Buchannan was proving to be an enigma for Tori. She found him to be an appealing man with his hair graying before its time. He was taller, with a more athletic physique, than most of the men she had known before. There was something else about him, something she had noticed right away, though not until she began thinking about it did she understand what it was.

Link had tremendous self-confidence . . . not arrogant self-awareness, but a self-confidence that showed itself in his easygoing manner, the way he approached people, the way he had been with Mrs. Bemis after the play, dealing with this woman of obvious wealth and importance with patience and gentlemanly decorum.

She thought about his cooking breakfast. No other man in Tori's acquaintance would cook breakfast; most of them would think that to do so would be an affront to their manliness. Yet Link was so secure in his masculinity that he thought nothing of it. The funny thing was, Link was the most virile man that she had ever met.

Tori put her hand to her lips to smother a laugh. He was even wearing an apron, not giving it so much as a second thought. Yes, Link Buchannan was a confident man.

A few minutes later, Link came into the dining room carrying a plate in each hand. He set one of the plates at the end of the table, and the other in front of the chair to the right.

"Madam, your breakfast is served. I hope you find it to your liking on this Christmas morning."

"Oh, how could we have forgotten? Merry Christmas!"

Link seated Tori, then took the chair at the head of the table.

"Tori," he said, hesitating, "I want to apologize for last night. I don't want you to ever be disquieted by something that I might do or say. If any action of mine, even unknowingly, should ever make you feel uncomfortable, please tell me, and I'll stop whatever it is I'm doing."

Tori didn't respond. She could have said that he wasn't the cause of her discomfort last night. Her own body had betrayed her: her reaction to his kiss, the quick surge of heat, the tingling sensation, and, most damning thing of all, her willingness—no, her eagerness—to take him to her bed. It was she who should be apologizing to him. He thought she was an innocent, and she didn't have the courage to tell him the truth.

"Please forgive me," Link said.

"Link, believe me, there's nothing to forgive."

For several moments, they sat in silence, each waiting for the other to speak.

"Do you like children?"

The question caught Tori off guard, and for just a moment she didn't answer. "Yes, I like children," she replied, wondering why he had asked.

"Good, because you're going to meet two of the best kids I've ever known. Actually there are three, but little William doesn't count. He's not even a year old and you can't play with him."

"I'm afraid I've not been around many babies. How old are the other two?"

"Sophia's the big sister. She's almost seven, and I think Charley will be five."

Tori smiled. "That's the age difference between

Manny and me, and I'm the big sister. Do you have brothers or sisters?"

Link averted his gaze as his hand went to his forehead. He rubbed his scar absently. "No. There's no one." Link rose from his seat and started clearing the table. "I'll take care of these dishes while you get dressed. We'd better get over to the Tutts' soon because Josephine's curiosity will be getting the best of her. I know she's been racking her brain trying to figure out who I'm bringing to Christmas dinner."

Tori dressed in the same red waistcoat and black serge skirt that she had worn to church, but this time she paired it with a white tucked blouse rather than the inset. She hastily put up her hair, working finger waves on the sides and then capturing the rest in a French twist. She didn't feel her hair looked as chic as it had the night before, but today her main audience would be a little girl and her brother.

Before leaving the room, Tori grabbed the scarf Link had given her the night before. The red matched her waistcoat perfectly. She wrapped it around her neck, securing it with a casual knot, making sure her name could be seen.

When she reached the bottom of the stairs, Link was waiting for her, his chesterfield bringing out his graying hair and hazel eyes. "Oh, my, miss, I do like that scarf. Wherever might I find one for my lady friend?"

"I'm sorry, sir, she'll have to find her own," Tori replied, enjoying the playful banter. "I was given a handsomely wrapped package last evening, and when I pulled the ribbon, this scarf was what appeared. But the biggest coincidence of all—voilà!" Tori flipped the end of the scarf up. "It had my name on it."

"Then it surely belongs to you forever and ever." Link retrieved Tori's coat from the hall tree. "But we'd better hurry. Buster is getting impatient."

"I sense that it isn't just the horse that's ready to go."

When Link and Tori reached the Tutts' home, Josephine greeted them warmly. A small boy raced toward Link and wrapped his arms around his legs, making it almost impossible for him to move.

"I've missed seeing my Charley boy," Link said as he lifted the child into the air while Charley shrieked with glee.

"You'd better be careful, Link," a tall, thin man with reddish hair said as he came to the door. He had an adorable baby in his arms. "Your boy just got into the Whitman's Sampler, and I'm afraid he about ate the whole box of candy."

"What, you didn't save any for Miss Drumm?" Link asked the child.

Charles turned toward Tori. "Miss Drumm? I am assuming that would be you, ma'am, and I apologize for my friend's manners. I'm Charles Tutt, and welcome to our home."

"I'm Victoria Drumm and I do appreciate being included in your family's holiday. I hope it's not an imposition."

"Of course it's not," Josephine said. She took Link's hand, and a caring expression came over her face. "Christmas doesn't always mean happy memories for Link and me, and it's good to have you to bring him out of his melancholy."

Link put Charley down and embraced Josephine. Neither said anything as tears formed in Josephine's eyes.

Tori, noticing a little girl standing off to the side, approached and knelt down to talk to her. "I'll bet you're Sophia."

"How do you know my name?"

"Because Mr. Buchannan told me. He said you are a very good little girl."

"I'm not little. I'm going to have a birthday. What's your name?"

"My friends call me Tori. Will you call me that?"

Sophia nodded. "Did Santa Claus give you any presents?"

"Yes, he did. See this scarf? It even has my name on it."

When Tori looked up, she saw Link watching the exchange between her and the little girl. "You do that very well, Miss Drumm. You should be a mother."

"Uncle Link, aren't you her friend?" Sophia asked.

"I hope I'm her friend," Link said, his eyes darkening.

"Then why don't you call her Tori? If you don't know her name, it's on her scarf."

"I'll remember that. Tori." Link took both of Tori's hands in his and helped her to her feet. When she was standing, he did not drop his hold but held her hands, a sensuous gleam in his eyes.

"Ahem," Charles Tutt coughed. "We could stand

here all day, but perhaps Tori would like to take off her coat and stay awhile."

The comment embarrassed Tori, but Link chuckled.

"You did ask us for Christmas dinner, and I've not heard you say one thing about eating."

"Link! You just got here. I expect you and Charles to entertain the children while I put the finishing touches on Sally's meal," Josephine said. "Tori, would you like to help?"

"Of course," Tori said, hoping that she would not be asked to do something that required actual cooking.

"I let Sally have the day to spend with her family, but she insisted on fixing everything before she left." Josephine tied an apron around her waist and set out serving pieces for the food.

"That was very thoughtful of you," Tori said.

"You know, I can't stand it any longer." Josephine turned to Tori. "Where did Link find you? I've never seen him like this before. It's wonderful."

Tori was flabbergasted by the comment. "I guess . . . I guess you could say he really did find me. When I arrived a few days ago, I tried to get a room at the Antlers but it was full. Mr. Barnett called several of the other hotels, and, shall we say, there was no room at the inn, so Link took pity on me. He offered to take me to my brother's place, but when we got there, we found my brother had moved to Cripple Creek. At that point, it was either go back to the depot and wait for the next train, or accept Link's very kind offer to bring me home like a stray kitty cat."

"That's the most romantic story I've ever heard. It's kismet that he found you." Tears were shimmering in Josephine's eyes. "Charles and I have been saying for a long time that Link needs a good woman to love." She paused. "I hope you are that woman."

Tori felt a flush creep across her face as she lowered her chin.

"Oh, my, I'm so sorry, that was so gauche of me. Can you ever forgive me?"

Tori forced a smile but said nothing as she continued to arrange gherkins on a relish tray.

The side dishes were carried into the dining room and arrayed on the sideboard, while the turkey was placed in front of Charles. Tori watched as he sliced the meat with an expertise that comes from having been raised with the knowledge of proper etiquette.

For a moment the turkey reminded her of a guinea hen someone had once prepared for her family, feeling sorry for them because they lived in a traveling wagon. When her father saw the dark meat, he said it was unfit to eat and gave it to a stray dog. How had she and Manny ever survived that man? How could her mother still live with him?

Tori refocused her attention on the meal. The food was good and she enjoyed the conversation, which swung easily from topic to topic. They entertained her by telling her stories about some of the unique personalities who lived in either Colorado Springs or Cripple Creek. When the meal was over, she felt she knew Bob Womack and Winfield Stratton, and more particularly the founder of Colorado Springs, General William Jackson Palmer.

She particularly enjoyed the story of how Palmer met his wife, Queen, when they were on a railcar, and within weeks they were betrothed. Then Josephine retold the story of Link and Tori's meeting, and Charles quickly opined that by next Christmas they might have another equally romantic story to add to the local lore.

For the entire meal, every time Tori glanced at Link, she found him watching her, a boyish grin on his face. Even if she had chosen to avoid him, she couldn't. For this one day, she was enjoying herself immensely.

When the meal was over, Josephine engaged Tori and the children to help clear the table while Charles and Link stepped into the library.

Charles lit a cigar and turned to Link. "I like Tori."

"So do I."

"And that's a big surprise? Link, you've been mooning over that woman ever since you stepped foot in this house. What do you know about her?"

"I know that I like her."

"Well, that's all fine and dandy, but did Josephine say the night you met her you were taking her to her brother's house, and that he had moved to Cripple Creek?"

"That's right, and, Charles, I know what you're leading up to. Her brother is Manny Drumm."

"And that doesn't bother you at all? You know he's

thrown in with John Calderwood." Charles took a draw from his cigar. "Speck tells me this Free Coinage Union they formed up at Altman was accepted by the Federation, and now they've formed unions in Cripple Creek, Victor, and Anaconda. They've got about eight hundred members already."

"All right."

"No, it's not all right." Charles took another puff. "Whose side is Tori Drumm going to be on if it comes to a showdown between the miners and the mine owners? Or, more specifically, between her brother and you?"

"Tori's not a part of this. She hasn't even seen her brother for fourteen years."

"I'll accept that, but what's going to happen when she gets to Cripple Creek? You don't have to answer that because we both know what she'll do, and if you've fallen for this woman, you're the one who's going to get hurt. Just look at what's happening between Sally Halthusen and Speck. Old Doc Penrose doesn't think Sally's good enough for Speck, and come hell or high water, he'll separate those two. If you think training a few horses can come between a man and woman, what do you think a labor strike is going to do? All I'm saying is, don't fall too hard."

"You underestimate me, Charles. I'm not about to fall in love with Tori. Speck and I have a bet about who's going to get caught first, and I'm damn sure not going to pay him five thousand dollars."

Charles laughed. "I knew there was a bet, but I hadn't heard it was for that much. When are you going back to Cripple Creek?"

"Probably tomorrow. With the Birks gone, I don't think it's good for Tori to stay with me."

"If it bothers you, I'm sure Josephine would love to have her stay with us."

"Oh, no, we're fine, but I am taking her to Professor Stark's concert tonight. It's probably not a good idea to spend too much time alone."

"I understand, and I know you want to get back to the district, but would you consider staying another day? Herbert Locke has called a big meeting out at the Broadmoor tomorrow. He thinks if the miners are organizing, the owners ought to have some sort of a counter—or at least an idea what they're going to do if Calderwood and Drumm foment a strike. What do you think?"

"I suppose I could stay," Link said, "but I'm technically not an owner of any mine."

"Well, you're definitely not in the same category as Moffat or Burns or Hagerman, but what you do have is a cool head. Somebody's going to have to be a moderator between the owners and the miners, and that just might be the role you're chosen to play. What's one more day? Can you stay?"

"You say it's out at the casino?"

"Yes, the Broadmoor at ten a.m.," Charles said. "Now, we'd better go see what the ladies are up to."

At first Tori was reluctant to accept Link's suggestion that they attend a concert when they returned from the Tutts', but then she reconsidered. It would be far better to be out of the house than to be there without Hulda and Otto's mitigating presence.

Again she pulled out the royal-blue satin, and

when she was dressed, she realized that the gown fit a little more snugly than it had the last time she had worn it.

"Too much turkey, too many cookies," she said, but she didn't feel any of the anxiety that she might have experienced if she were still performing. She swept her hair away from her face, allowing waves to soften her cheeks as she put the hair into a bun and secured it with a matching blue ribbon. As an afterthought, she stuck in a white feather for a touch of whimsy. She wished she had been able to bring more of her wardrobe with her; her fur-lined cape would have been the perfect cover-up for her dress.

Tori turned from the mirror and sat down on the bed, burying her face in her hands.

"Stop it, stop it right now," she said with a forceful voice. "You chose to walk away from that life, now accept it."

Just then there was a light knock on the door. "Tori, I hate to intrude, but we should be leaving soon," Link said as diplomatically as possible.

"I'll be right there." Tori put some light coloring on her cheeks and lips. Then, grabbing her gloves, she stepped out into the hall and went down the stairs.

Link was waiting for Tori in the front hall and turned at her approach.

For just a moment, he couldn't breathe, then he found that he had to gasp for air. He knew that Tori was pretty, but the woman who was walking toward him—no, gliding toward him—was stunningly beautiful!

"Tori, I . . ."

Tori had seen the expression on his face, heard the wonder in his voice, and she suppressed a smile.

"Uh . . . Buster . . . he's hitched and ready." Link stammered, still not moving, his eyes drinking in the vision before him. "I guess . . . I guess we should go."

Tori flashed a broad smile. "Do you think I need a coat?"

Link lowered his head and an amused laugh escaped; then, looking up, he met her gaze with twinkling eyes. "If you ever so much as mention I reacted like a twelve-year-old kid, I'll deny it till the day I die. But, Victoria Drumm, you are one beautiful woman."

Taking her coat from the hook, he helped her into it.

Unlike the night of the play, when every seat was filled, the opera house was less than half-full.

"This is a shame," Link said when they reached their seats. "It took a lot of work, and probably quite a bit of money, to bring the Sobrinos here. You would think more people would have come out if for no other reason but to support Professor Stark. He does so much for the college."

"I would think that Christmas Day would not be a good time to plan such a performance," Tori said. "Generally, people are weary from so much activity."

"You're right. But it's still a shame."

Just then, the president of the college, William Slocum, stepped to the stage. "Ladies and gentleman, on behalf of Colorado College I welcome you this evening. We have the honor of presenting Senor Sobrino on the violin, Madame Sobrino, whose clear soprano voice will enrapture us, and our own Professor Stark, who will be entertaining us with the high standard we in Colorado Springs have come to expect from him. Let the concert begin."

The concert proved to be a delight, and when it was over, Link commented, "That was wonderful, but there should have been more people here to appreciate the music."

"We were here." Tori looked at him with a smile. "And we enjoyed it."

"Yes, we did." Taking her hand, Link lifted it to his lips, then kissed it gently. "And I couldn't possibly have asked for a more enjoyable companion. Thank you for coming with me."

They walked the short distance to where Buster stood stoically, tied to a hitching rail.

"How are you doing, Buster?" Link asked as he removed the blanket from the horse's back. "Are you glad to see us?"

The horse bobbed his head, and Tori chuckled. "He just said yes."

"Of course he did." Link folded the blanket and put it behind the buggy seat. "Buster's a smart horse; he talks to me all the time."

"Oh? And what does he say?"

"I can't tell you that. He shares secrets with me, and were I to betray his trust, why, Buster would never speak to me again."

Link helped Tori in, then hurried around to the other side and climbed in. He fit the robe around their legs, which brought them close together.

As they drove toward the house, few people were outside, due both to the hour and to the temperature. It was quite cold, and a cloud of vapor rose off Buster's flanks as he trotted down the street. Flakes glistened in the streetlamps as a light snow began to fall.

When they stopped in front of the house, Link stepped out of the buggy, then walked around to help Tori down.

"You go on inside," he said. "I'll take care of Buster."

"All right."

Link's hands were still on Tori, and he didn't let go. Instead, he stood there for a long moment, looking into her eyes as the snowflakes settled on her hair and coat.

Propriety would dictate that she turn now and start up the walkway to the house. That was what she should do, but she didn't move. She knew he was going to kiss her, and she also knew that she wasn't going to resist.

Link's lips brushed against hers, as gently as the touch of the falling snowflakes. Then, when he put his arms around her and drew her into an embrace, the kiss deepened, igniting the fire inside.

Tori matched his passion with an ardor of her own, taking his head in her hands and responding eagerly when his tongue pushed through her lips.

Then she felt him pull back and look at her with a disarming smile, her eyes shining brightly, reflecting the streetlight's glow. She raised her eyebrows as if to question if she had done something wrong.

"I don't want to put on more of a show for Mr. Jackson, and I don't think you do either."

Tori chuckled. "Well, if he saw it, I hope he enjoyed it as much as I did."

Link laughed. "You are a most fascinating woman." He kissed her on the tip of her nose. "Now, I'd better take care of Buster before he really gets mad at me."

Tori watched as Link led Buster and the buggy around to the back of the house, where the stable and the carriage house were; then she went inside.

She thought she would wait for him, but once inside the empty house, she was having second thoughts. The kiss outside had had to be limited. But what would happen now? She knew the two of them had a strong attraction, and given her reaction to Link last night, she wasn't prepared to get that close to the flame again. Turning quickly, she hurried up the stairs to her room. She locked the door even though she was sure he would never enter without an invitation.

As she stood there, staring at the door, she questioned whether the lock was for him or for her.

Back in the stable, Link was tending to Buster. He unhitched him from the buggy, then led him into his stall, where Link took off the harness and rubbed Buster down before putting a blanket over him. Link began talking to his horse.

"I hope this keeps you warm enough tonight." Link closed his hand around Buster's ear, rubbing gently. "You did a good job tonight, taking the lady and me to the concert, and I want you to know I appreciate it," he said soothingly.

Buster whickered and nodded.

"Tell me, Buster, what do you think of Miss Drumm? You weren't watching when I kissed her, were you?" Link chuckled. "It's all right if you were watching, I'm pretty sure that the entire neighborhood was. I hope I didn't embarrass her."

The stable was well insulated against the elements, but it wasn't heated because of the danger of fire. The water pipes were insulated, though, and that allowed him to draw water for Buster and give him some fresh hay.

That done, Link moved slowly back to the house, not knowing exactly what he would say or do when he saw Tori. When he stepped inside, one light was lit on the hall table, but the rest of the house was dark. He walked toward the library, his heart pounding. What would he do if Tori was waiting for him, sitting in the dark? He felt the quiver of arousal as he entered the room.

Empty. He let out a sigh as he exhaled the breath he was holding.

"Thank you," he said quietly. "I'm not sure I could have controlled myself, and we'd both be sorry in the morning."

SEVEN

Denver, December 1893

J ohn, you've known me for more than ten years, and you know I'm on the side of the miner," Davis Waite said. "I'll back whatever you decide to do up at Cripple."

"I know that, Governor. But these miners need to hear it from you," John Calderwood said. "Most of them voted for you, but they didn't really understand your union roots. Now these men can take your message back to camp, and when they get arrested, they'll know they won't be put in a pigsty of a prison like they had up at Coeur d'Alene."

"Tell them not to worry. You and I were there together in Leadville, when Pitkin declared martial law to stop a strike, but this governor's on the side of the miner. If the militia comes in, the military will support the union."

"That's good to know, because the battle's already begun. Manny, here, brought in a telegram that said about two hundred miners were able to shut down the Burns shaft this morning. Those sons of bitches are going to find out pretty quick, nobody's working a nine-hour day anymore," Calderwood said.

The governor laughed. "That's wonderful. The aristocrats thought I couldn't get women the right to vote, but I did it. Now they think I'm addlebrained to think a graduated income tax is fair. Or to think that a US senator should be voted on by the people of the state. I know, I may not get those things done, but an eight-hour workday for the men of Colorado? I damn sure will get that done.

"And we appreciate it," Manny Drumm said.

"Thank you. You keep up the good work," the governor said, "but now I've got to deal with this special session I've called for the legislature. I've heard they're going to adjourn as soon as they're gaveled to order. But you just watch me. I'll call another session this afternoon."

"That's why we voted for you, Governor Waite. You're a man of the people," Manny said.

Colorado Springs

Link met Charles Tutt at his office, and they took the trolley out to the casino for the meeting of the mine owners.

"Who's running the Broadmoor now that it's in receivership?" Link asked as they rode the car.

"The investors hired the count's manager, Duncan Chisholm, but it's not the same without Pourtales. It's a shame he couldn't hold it together. With the financial panic, he couldn't raise any more capital, and then his health failed. I think he's back in Prussia," Charles said. "Everybody misses him, but they miss the countess even more. Was there ever a more beautiful woman to walk the streets of Colorado Springs?"

Link smiled as he conjured up the image of Tori coming down the stairs last evening. "She was pretty, but . . ."

"I get it, you think Miss Drumm is prettier."

Link nodded. "Tori is a handsome woman."

"Ha! That woman's got her hooks in you so deep, you'll never get away. Has Speck met her yet? What am I thinking, of course he hasn't. All of this 'fondness' for this woman has happened in less than a week. I can't wait for you to take her to Cripple Creek. If Speck doesn't steal her away from you, I'll be mighty surprised."

"Does that leave me with the Amazon, then?" Link asked, a lopsided grin on his face.

Link enjoyed his friendship with Charles, and with Speck, too, although there was a grain of truth to what Charles was saying. Speck was the most debonair man in the county, and women, whether they were working girls or churchgoers, found him irresistible. Link wanted to keep Tori for himself.

"Oh, by the way, guess who's interested in your house? One of the Sinion brothers."

"The dairy farmer?"

"So? What's wrong with that?" Charles asked. "You do want to sell it, don't you?"

"No. I think I've changed my mind."

This time Charles laughed uproariously. "I'm telling you, she's got her hooks in you."

❧

As always, when Link stepped off the electric car at the gates of the casino park, he was struck with the beauty of the setting. The Broadmoor was at the foot of Cheyenne Mountain, on a mesa that gradually rose from the Fountain Valley. From this spot, he could see the prairie for endless miles, the mountain range, and Colorado Springs.

The casino itself was built on the dam of Cheyenne Lake, and a series of landscaped terraces flanked the steps that led to the colonial building. The word BROADMOOR was spelled out in carefully tended shrubs just below the wide veranda.

"Mr. Tutt, Mr. Buchannan," the uniformed porter greeted them as he threw open the door of the main entrance. "Your meeting will convene in the reading room that you will find to the south of the ballroom."

"Thank you, Absalom," Link said as he slipped a coin into the porter's hand. "I trust you had a good Christmas."

"Yes, sir. Thank you, sir," the porter said, a big grin covering his face as he helped the men out of their overcoats.

When Charles and Link entered the vestibule, a couple of the other mine owners, William Lennox and Ed De La Vergne, were just leaving the smoking room.

"Link, Charles," De La Vergne said. "Say, Link, you're more aware of what's going on at Cripple. Do you think there's anything to this strike talk, or does Moffat just have a bone to chew with somebody."

"I've been here in the Springs since the middle of

the month, but other than a lot of organizing, I can't say I was aware of any trouble," Link said. "I do know that John Calderwood—he's the one ginning up the miners—was in Aspen with Governor Waite when he was editor of the *Union Era.*"

"I guess that means we'll have to mind our p's and q's," William Lennox said.

"Why, William, I'm surprised at you. Wouldn't we do that anyway?" Charles asked.

All four men were laughing when they entered the reading room, where a cheery fire was blazing in the lava-stone-framed fireplace. The room was handsomely furnished with easy chairs and lounges, and most were occupied.

"Gentlemen," David Moffat of the Anaconda Mine began. "I'm glad to see you all here. I'm afraid we've got a problem that we're going to have to address. I'm sure you've all heard that the miners are organizing. Once we give in to them, it's over. Our only hope is to organize as well."

"Organize to do what?" Ed De La Vergne asked.

"Well, to begin with, we should present a unified front," Moffat said. "Right now we're all over the place. Some of us have a ten-hour workday, some have nine, and a few have an eight-hour workday, but we all pay the same thing—three dollars a day."

"As I understand it," Hagerman said, "the miners want an eight-hour, three-dollars-per-day schedule. If you recall, last summer my superintendent tried to put my men on a ten-hour shift, and that's when this union talk got started. They refused to work, so Mr. Locke backed down, and now they work an eight-hour day."

"Then maybe we should all go to eight hours," Charles Tutt said.

"No!" Moffat insisted. "That's the worst thing we could do."

"Why do you say that?" Link asked.

"Let's just let Jimmie Burns tell us the answer."

"You all know my manager, Frank Sanders," Burns said. "Well, he hired about a dozen men to work on a nine-hour shift. This morning about two hundred union men assembled at the shaft house and told my boys they wouldn't be allowed to work."

"What did Sanders do?" Lennox asked.

"What could he do? He locked up the shaft and telegraphed me for instructions," Burns said. "If he opens that mine on a nine-hour basis, there's sure to be trouble."

"Does that help you understand what we're up against?" Moffat asked. "We all know that up to now, for every dollar that's come out of any of our mines, there've been two or three poured in. Some of us are stout and can stand this loss until we hit a bonanza, but what about the little guy who's just hanging on to his claim by a shoestring? I say we push them—make it a ten-hour day. There are enough unemployed miners in Colorado, we won't have any trouble getting people to work for us."

"If you do that, don't you think you'll force the union's hand?" Link asked.

"Hell, yes," Moffat said, "but right now, we've got the upper hand. I don't know what the rest of you are going to do, but between James Hagerman, Eben Smith, and me, we hire a full one-third of all the miners working in Cripple Creek. I wired

Eben this morning, and he agrees. The three of us have made a pact—a ten-hour day starting February first. No exceptions. Now, how many of you are going along with us?"

Link watched as one by one the mine owners lifted their hands. He looked out at the peaceful lake behind the casino with swans swimming around its playing fountain. Did these men have any idea what they had just started?

When Tori came out of her bedroom, she overheard Link speaking on the telephone in the hall:

"Yes, I was at the meeting. I'll be interested in hearing what the other mine owners had to say when the news got back to Cripple Creek." After a moment of silence, Link said, "All right, I'll be on the train this afternoon."

Link hung up the phone, then saw Tori standing at the top of the stairs. "Good morning, or maybe I should say good afternoon." Link flashed a dazzling grin toward Tori. "I'm going back to Cripple Creek this afternoon, and you can come with me—or if you would rather stay here until I know for sure that Manny is there, you're welcome to do that."

Tori's eyes opened wide. "Stay in this house by myself?"

"I guess that is a daunting prospect. Even I don't like to rattle around here all by myself. If you'd like, I can ask Josephine if you can move over there."

"I think I would rather go with you."

"Good, that's what I was hoping you would say.

But you're going to have to hurry. The train leaves in about an hour or so."

"Oh, then I'd better get my bag packed."

Half an later Tori and Link were standing on the platform of the Atchison, Topeka, Santa Fe and Midland Railway depot. Tori thought the stone building with its red tile roof was quite attractive for a depot. It had a raised observation tower protruding from the roof, and she wished she had time to climb up and look around. She was sure she would be able to pick out Link's house and his church and the opera house. For sure she would recognize the Antlers Hotel because it was within walking distance of the station.

As the train rolled in, she was surprised by how gaily painted it was, with the cowcatcher, front, and smokestack a bright blue, then to the engineer's cabin it was gray. The tender was green, with the name of the line, COLORADO—MIDLAND, painted in gold.

"A pretty engine, isn't it?" Link commented when he saw Tori examining it.

"It really is. How far is it to Cripple Creek?"

"We don't go all the way by train. We only go to Midland, and that's about forty-five miles from here."

"Well then, this won't take long at all."

Link laughed. "It'll take longer than you think. We have to climb up Ute Pass, and the train can't go much over fifteen miles an hour on such a steep grade. In fact, we'll have to take on a helper engine just to make it over the top."

Unconsciously, Tori's brow furrowed. "What time do you think we'll get to Cripple Creek?"

"I can't tell you. Maybe where you come from the trains run on schedule, but out here, you get there when you get there. That said, I suspect we'll probably get there after dark."

And where do I go if Manny's not there? Tori did not voice her concern. She had learned to trust Link Buchannan. He would take care of her.

The conductor, dressed in a long blue uniform coat and a billed cap complete with a shining brass shield, stepped down from one of the cars and pulled out his pocket watch.

"Board!" he called in a singsong voice. "All aboard for Manitou Springs, Colorado City, Florissant, and Midland! Board!"

"That's us," Link said as he picked up Tori's bag. He offered her his other arm, and they joined the others in boarding the train.

They had just found their seats when the train started to move, first with a series of head-bobbing jerks, then it smoothed out and quickly left Colorado Springs behind.

"It seems like I've spent the last month on a train," Tori said.

Link chuckled. "You know, I've never asked you. Where did you come from?"

For an instant, Tori was reluctant to say, but she could think of no good reason to avoid the question.

"New York."

"The city or western New York?"

"The city."

"Well then, that explains things." An easy smile formed on Link's lips.

"What do you mean?"

"Well, I thought you were a farm girl from Iowa. Somewhere along the way, I got the impression that was where Manny Drumm was from, and I just thought you would be from there, too."

"I guess, technically, I am from Iowa. That's where I was born, but why did you say 'that explains things'? What did you mean?"

"I wondered how in the hell—I mean heck—a farm girl could make herself look so beautiful when she waltzed down the stairway the night of the concert."

"You don't think a farm girl could do that?"

"Not the way you looked, honey. Not the way you looked." He reached over and took her hand in his.

Tori liked the feel of his hand. It was possessive without being overly so. She knew right then she could fall in love with this man. She knew she could fall in love for all the right reasons.

Leaving the train at Midland, Tori and Link got into a coach for the last eight miles down to Cripple Creek. In the waning light, Tori could see that the district, as Link called the area, consisted of a series of rolling hills with a few stands of leafless aspens and scattered evergreens. After coming through snow-covered Ute Pass, she was surprised to see so little snow.

"Is it what you expected?" Link asked as the coach came to a stop to rest the horses.

"Not exactly. I thought it would be more like those mountains." She pointed toward snowcapped peaks to the south.

"The Sangre de Cristo. Those mountains are at least sixty or seventy miles away, and of course Pike's Peak is behind us, and it's only eight or nine miles from us. But every one of these hills has a name."

"And I suppose you know the names of all of them," Tori said, cocking her head as if defying him.

He began pointing. "That's Gold Hill, over here is Mineral Hill, that one up there is Bull Hill and beside it is Big Bull Mountain, back there is Battle Mountain, next to it is Raven Hill—"

"All right, all right," Tori said between giggles. "I should have known you'd know that."

"And furthermore, I've walked over just about every inch of these hills."

"Were you prospecting?"

"At first I did that, but then I realized there are only a very few who are going to get rich discovering gold. The real money comes from providing services to those who are trying."

"And that's what you do? Provide service?"

"Yes. I find people who are willing to bet their money that somebody else will find the gold. But right now I'm at your service, wouldn't you say?"

"You are."

"See that house with the red roof?" He pointed to a house that was well up the hill. "That's mine."

"Do you know where Manny lives?"

"Yes, my house is on Fourth Street. Manny's house is on Eaton, there—go that way from my house to the crossroad." Link pointed again. "That would be Eaton, then count four houses to the left, on the other side of the street. That's Manny's house."

"All right, folks, hang on! Here comes Tenderfoot Hill," the stage driver called from the box.

"'Hang on'? What does he mean, 'hang on'?"

"You'll see," Link replied with a chuckle. "Now, like Eddie said, you'd better hang on."

"Hang on to what?"

"To me!" Link put his arm around Tori.

"Heah!" Eddie shouted from the driver's seat, and Tori heard the snap of the whip.

The stage jerked forward and a moment later started down the long downgrade toward the town at a wild gallop. The coach bounced and lurched, sometimes even causing Tori and Link to rise from their seat. At Link's suggestion, Tori wrapped both her arms around him, and he wrapped his arms around her, pulling her tightly against him.

"We're going to turn over! We're going to crash!" Tori shouted in fear.

"No we aren't. Eddie knows what he's doing."

The horses continued to plummet down the grade at breakneck speed.

"Is that man crazy? This is scaring me to death! I—" Then Tori felt Link's lips close on hers. He kissed her, not hard and demanding, but firmly and possessively.

When he pulled his lips away from hers, she looked at him in disbelief. "Why . . . why did you do that?" she asked, her voice reflecting her astonishment.

"It isn't like we haven't kissed before." Link's eyes were twinkling in amusement.

"Yes, but not while I was bouncing around in a stagecoach that's about to go over the side of a mountain!"

"Look outside." Link offered a beguiling smile.

By now they were on the flat, and the brakes were squealing loudly as the coach began slowing down.

"We're almost home, and you're more concerned about the kiss than you were afraid we'd turn over."

Tori put her fingers to her lips, then returned his smile. "I must say, you do have an unusual way of calming my nerves."

The stagecoach squealed to a stop in front of the Palace Hotel, where several people were standing in front of the building, applauding the arrival.

"You must be quite the celebrity," Tori said.

"Why do you say that?"

"Look at all these people, and they're all clapping."

"They aren't clapping for me, it's the stage. Eddie brings it in every day at a gallop, and everyone gathers to watch the arrival. And now they're applauding because we're still alive. This time we didn't turn over."

"What?" Tori asked with a gasp.

Link laughed. "I'm teasing about the turning over. But they do enjoy watching the stage come in."

When Link and Tori stepped down from the coach, there was more wild applause as several people threw comments toward Link.

"Who's your new woman, Buchannan?"

"Don't keep her for yourself, now."

"I'll give a hundred for her."

Link maneuvered Tori through the crowd until

they got to a building next door to the hotel. Taking out a key, he unlocked the door, where in gold letters were the words LINCOLN SEWARD BUCHANMAN, REAL ESTATE AND INVESTMENTS.

Tori followed him inside, and Link set down the bags, then turned on the light. The office was sparsely furnished with a desk, a table, and a few chairs, a cold potbellied stove upon which sat a blue-steel coffeepot, and a coatrack. Spread all the way across the back wall was a map marked with dots that Tori supposed represented mines.

"Lincoln Seward—that must be you."

"It is. I was born at Independence Hall when President Lincoln's body was lying in state. They built a platform that went in one window and out the other so the public could pass by the bier.

"Even though my mother was confined, she and about three hundred thousand other people wanted to pay their respects, so she went. And while she was there, my mother announced her time had come. They took her into the tower stair hall, and I was born, April twenty-third, 1865, twenty feet from the spot where the nation was born. My father was embarrassed then, and I guess I've been embarrassing him ever since."

"I've never even seen Independence Hall, and here you were born there. That's impressive."

"Philadelphia is a wonderful place. I'll have to take you there someday."

Link's words *I'll have to take you there someday* caused Tori to feel a twinge of excitement. The thought of going on a trip, a real trip, with Link was exhilarating.

"Since it's getting late, would you like to go see if we can find Manny? I don't know if he's in town, but we won't know until we go look."

"I'd like that," she said, but only because she thought that was the response Link expected.

"Let me stow my bag here, and we'll go back to the Palace. If there's a hack still running, it will be waiting out front."

When they walked back to the hotel, a horse and cab was just pulling away.

"Junior, wait!" Link yelled, and the cab was pulled up.

"Yes, sir, Mr. Buchannan," a young boy hardly fourteen years old said. "Do you need a ride someplace? I was just about to take Hercules to the stable."

"I want to go to Manny Drumm's house. Do you know if he's in town?" Link asked.

"I ain't seen him, but he don't ride my cab much."

"Well then, take us up to Eaton Avenue." Link helped Tori into the cab, where a robe was lying across the seat. Link wrapped it around both of them, pulling Tori tight against him.

It took no more than five minutes to go from the hotel to the little house that Link had pointed out to Tori from the top of the pass.

"Wait here till we see if he's home," Link said to the driver. "Whether he is or isn't, I'll need a ride back."

"Yes, sir."

Link and Tori walked up to the darkened house, and Link knocked loudly.

"Manny? Manny Drumm, are you in there?"

He knocked again, this time lifting his eyebrows as he looked toward Tori.

"Manny?" he called, much louder this time.

Stepping down from the porch, Link walked around to peer in through the side window, but he saw no signs of recent occupancy.

"He's not here, and it doesn't look like he's been here for quite a while," Link said. "My guess is that he's still in Denver."

"What will I do now?" Tori let out a big sigh as her shoulders slumped.

"We'll go to the Union Hall. If anybody knows when he'll be back, it'll be somebody over there."

Link picked up her bag and walked back to the cab.

Tori followed, after taking a cursory look at the house. It looked to be a bungalow no more than ten to fifteen feet wide. How was she ever going to live with Manny? That is, if he would let her live with him.

"Junior, you're going to make lots of money tonight. Take us to the Union Hall, please."

"Yes, sir." The boy nodded and a big grin formed on his face.

Link and Tori climbed back into the hack, and Junior clicked to the horse. The Union Hall, like most of the other buildings in town, was constructed of wood. The white two-story building had the words WESTERN FEDERATION OF MINERS—ALTMAN—FREE COINAGE NUMBER 19 painted across the front

"Want me to wait for you, Mr. Buchannan?" the driver asked.

"Yes, I expect we'll only be a couple of minutes."

Link helped Tori down, and they went up the steps to the Union Hall.

"Why does it say 'Altman'?" Tori asked as she read the sign.

"There are about a half dozen mines on Bull Hill, so Sam Altman started a town up there so the miners didn't have to get up there every day. But now, just about everybody who lives there is a miner, so Manny's buddy John Calderwood decided it was a good place to start the union. Now all the men have joined together under the one charter, and I guess that's smart because it swells their numbers."

When they reached the door, Link stepped in front of Tori. "I'll go in first."

"What can I do for ya, mister? It's a little late . . ." a man said as he threw down a hand in the poker game he was playing. Then, seeing Link, the expression on his face grew hostile. "You can't come in here, Buchannan. Get out."

"Hello, Landry. I—that is, *we*—are looking for Manny Drumm."

"Well, he ain't here."

"Is he still in Denver?"

"You're a nosy son of a bitch. I wouldn't tell you even if I knowed."

"Would you tell his sister?" Link asked, stepping aside.

"His sister? Manny ain't got no sister. What you trying to pull on me?"

"Hello, Mr. Landry, I believe I heard Mr. Buchannan call you," Tori said as she moved forward. "I am

Victoria Drumm, and I've come to visit my brother. I thought he lived in Colorado Springs, but when I found he had moved, Mr. Buchannan was kind enough to see that I got here."

"I'm sure he did, miss. If you really are Manny's sister, he's gonna be fit to be tied when he finds out you let this polecat sniff around you. You know him and all his highfalutin, hard-drinkin', womanizin' friends from back East—why, they're our enemies, ma'am."

Tori smiled her most practiced smile, one she had used many times onstage. "Thank you for wanting to take care of me. I'm sure Manny will appreciate that. Now, can you tell me, is he here?"

"No, ma'am, he ain't. He did go to Denver like this bastard said—met with the governor, he did. And he ain't back yet, but we're expectin' him any day now. John and the boys need to get here 'fore we can start any fireworks. And Buchannan, you tell them other sons of bitches that we ain't going let 'em tell us what they're gonna pay. *We're* gonna tell *them*, and Governor Waite's gonna back us up. You got that?"

"I've got it, and I'll be sure to pass your message along. Would you tell Manny to stop by my office when he gets back?"

Landry squinted his eyes and looked at Tori and then at Link. "Don't you even think about touching Manny's sister, 'cause if you do, you'll have two hundred miners givin' you what for."

"Be that as it may, send Manny to my office. Let's go, Tori. Junior's waiting for us."

❧❧❧

When they were back in the hack and on the way to Link's office, Tori said, "Correct me if I'm wrong, but I sense some hostility between you and Mr. Landry."

"You got that, did you?" Link had an easy grin on his face.

"You don't feel that way about my brother, do you?"

"No, not at all. Your brother and I have a friendly relationship. I caught Landry high-grading ore from one of the mines I was brokering, and when I told the rest of the owners about it, he was fired. Landry thinks I should have stayed out of it." Link left out the part where Landry had come after him with a knife.

"I don't understand what high-grading is."

"It's pilfering, pure and simple. Miners carry out high-grade ore by slipping it in their lunch pails or their jackets or even in pockets sewn in their underwear. Then they take the rocks to some crooked smelter that breaks it down, and each party keeps half the gold. It doesn't sound like they could carry out that much, but on a good day, most of the high-graders could take out an extra dollar or more. If everybody does that, the owner loses a lot of money."

"Then if he was stealing, and you caught him, you were right to tell."

The coach came to a stop in front of the office, and Link sent Junior on his way.

"It seems like we've been here before," Link said as he opened the door for Tori. "It's late, and Manny's not here."

"I've been thinking about that. I heard what Mr. Landry said, and even if you asked me, I can't stay with you."

"I know, I'm not supposed to touch you." Link lifted Tori's chin. He lowered his mouth to hers, and this time, unlike the diversionary kiss in the coach, the kiss was slow and sensual. As his lips closed over hers, his tongue slipped into her mouth, and she recognized the taste that she now knew was uniquely his.

She knew she couldn't do this—she shouldn't do this, and she was going to end it, maybe not right now but soon. She felt his fingers in her hair and for a quick moment thought perhaps he was about to end it. But he didn't, and the kiss deepened. It went on for an eternity that was much too brief, before finally they separated and he looked at her with a curious smile on his face.

"Let Landry bring those two hundred men. I'm ready!"

"I'm sorry, Link, but we don't have a room," Erette McGibany, the clerk at the Palace Hotel, said. "It's past midnight, and every bed we have is committed."

"What about Joe Walsh over at the Continental?"

"You know before you ask. This town is full. Some of the boardinghouses are so crowded now that they are renting their beds by the hour, and that's just so a man can get a little sleep. They tell me the saloons are renting pool tables for a dollar a night. No, Link, you're not going to find any bed for this here lady. You'll just have to take her home with you."

"Oh," Tori said, growing more disturbed. "I can't believe this is happening again. What is it with me and hotel rooms? Do you know anyone—any woman—who might have a place for me to sleep? Just for the rest of the night?"

"I do have a suggestion," Link said. "You might not like it, but hear me out before you say no."

"I can't go home with you, Link. I shouldn't have gone with you in Colorado Springs, but at least Hulda and Otto were there. But in this town, everybody would know I spent the night with you."

Link chuckled. "You're right about that. Everybody knows everybody's business. Wouldn't you agree, Erette?"

"Yes, sir. I already know you're Manny Drumm's sister, miss. And I know you had a run-in with Gorran Landry at the Union Hall. No, sir, nothing gets by nobody—not in Cripple Creek."

"Junior?" Link asked.

McGibany laughed. "That boy's better than a telegram. Faster, too."

"Then he'll have plenty to gossip about tomorrow," Link said.

"Don't tell me you're going to take her to Pearl's?" McGibany asked.

"Do you have a better suggestion?"

"Can't say that I do. Ma'am, Pearl's a good-hearted woman. She'll do right by you."

❧

When Link and Tori left the hotel, they walked down to the next corner. Myers Avenue was every bit as lively as any street she might have seen in New York, but it held a seedy type of entertainment. As far as she could see, there were saloons with tall false fronts and dance halls with names such as the Great View and the Red Light. Several well-built houses were sandwiched in between the buildings. But the most depressing thing she saw were little, narrow tar-papered shacks with a door and a window. Some of the windows were covered with a drawn shade, while others had a woman dressed in the most provocative clothing, beckoning to the passing men.

"I would suspect you are taking me to the sporting district," Tori said.

"That's what Myers Avenue has become," Link said. "And, yes, I'm taking you to a parlor, but it's not just any parlor. Pearl de Vere is my friend."

"Oh?" Tori's eyebrows rose in question.

"Yes. She is my friend."

Link did not elaborate on what that meant, but Tori regretted that she had reacted as she had. Who was she to question anyone's morals?

A moment later they arrived at a two-story frame house that looked to be much more substantial than any of the others. No sign indicated what it was or who lived there.

Tori was surprised when Link opened the door without knocking. They walked through an attractive foyer with a Turkish carpet and tasteful wallpaper, into a drawing room where a beautiful red-haired woman was sitting behind a French escritoire. The desk door was dropped and she looked to be entering figures into a ledger.

"Link," the woman said, jumping from her chair and rushing toward him. "You've been gone much too long." The woman kissed him on the mouth, and Link pulled her to him, lifting the woman off her feet and swinging her around.

Tori's stomach began to tighten as she watched the greeting. She looked away, trying to take in her surroundings rather than concentrate on what she thought was an intimate moment between Link and the woman.

The room was unlike any other she had seen since leaving New York. It was decorated in what Mrs. Leslie would describe as the style of Marie Antoinette. The furniture was painted white and had a rich gilding that complemented the blue damask-patterned area rugs. The divan and the chairs were upholstered in shades of mauve, green, and blue.

"Tori?"

Tori turned to Link when she heard her name. He was looking at her as if he had called it several times.

"Oh, forgive me, Miss de Vere. You have a beautiful home," Tori said, refocusing her attention.

"Thank you, but as I'm sure Link has told you, it's a business. I'm happy to have you join us."

Tori shot a questioning glance toward Link.

An easy smile crossed his face. "She means join us in Cripple Creek. Pearl, Tori is Manny Drumm's sister, and she has nowhere to go tonight. Can you find a spare bed for her?"

"Manny. He's one of our favorites around here. Of course I can find a place for you," Pearl said. "Are you just here for a visit?"

"I'd like to stay for a while—that is, if I can find employment." Then Tori felt her cheeks begin to flush. She hoped that Pearl didn't think she was looking to work for her.

"I can help you with that. I know just about every businessman in town, and I can ask around and see who needs someone." Pearl laughed. "I'd even hire you myself, but I'm afraid you don't 'match' my other girls."

"Oh, I don't know," Link said. "She's about the right height, and you could put peroxide on her hair. All you'd have to do then is feed her a lot and she'd gain enough weight so your customers would want her."

Pearl hit Link on the arm. "That's awful. Just because you tease me all the time doesn't mean you should tease this lovely lady. Now, get out of here. You know Miss Drumm has to be exhausted."

Link smiled. "I knew I could count on you, Pearl, and, Tori, I'll see you tomorrow."

Link left, and Pearl turned her attention to Tori.

"Have you eaten anything, or did Link forget all about that?"

"I guess I haven't eaten since breakfast, but I hadn't noticed," Tori said.

"Well, come with me. Mrs. Fitzgerald has probably already retired, but I can rustle us up something." Pearl headed toward the back of the house.

When they reached the kitchen, Pearl took the teakettle off the stove and poured some water into the teapot. She took down a tin of Mazawattee tea and filled a diffuser, allowing it to steep.

"Where did you come from?" Pearl asked.

"From Colorado Springs."

"No. That's not the answer I wanted. If I'm going to help you, I have to know something about you. You don't seem to be a consumptive, so I am assuming you didn't come to Colorado in the middle of the winter for your health. If I were to guess, it's one of three things: you're running from the law, or you're running from a man, or you're flat broke. Now, was I right?"

"I've not done anything wrong and I do have some money," Tori said with a wistful smile.

"Then it's a man. Are you with child?"

"I'm not."

"That's good, because babies complicate things. Have you told Link about your man?"

"The subject hasn't come up."

"It will. You haven't asked for my advice, but if I were you, I'd get whatever happened out in the open as soon as possible. You'll find the men in Cripple Creek are pretty open-minded." Pearl laughed. "Can't say the same for the 'respectable' women, though."

Pearl took down two Dresden china cups and poured the tea. "Do you take milk?"

"Just sugar and a slice of lemon."

"My dear, you're in a mining camp. You'll skip the lemon." Pearl took out a loaf of bread and began carving off a couple slices. "But if you want some honey, here it is. About this job that you want: Can you sew?"

"Nothing more than sewing up a seam or putting on a button."

"All right. I don't suppose you want to work in a dance hall or a saloon."

"If I had to, I would, but I'd rather not."

"Well, you tell me. What can you do?"

Tori thought for a moment, trying to come up with some talent she had that might be marketable. "I can speak French."

Pearl burst out laughing. "I'm not sure there's much call for that skill here in Cripple Creek, but who knows who the cat might drag in."

A moment later a white-haired man, dressed in a black silk dressing robe, entered the kitchen.

"Addie thought she heard talking out here. I didn't know it was you," the man said as he turned to leave.

"No, no, come back, Mr. Fitzgerald. We're going to have a guest for a few days. Tori, this is my right hand—that is, he and his wife together. Hugh Fitzgerald."

"Good morning, ma'am."

"Oh, dear. It's past two," Pearl said, looking at a clock that sat on a shelf above the dough box. "I've got to get back to my desk. Mr. Fitzgerald, would you take the young lady's portmanteau up to Mindy's room? She's going to be with us for a while."

"Yes, ma'am. Shall I show her the room as well?"

"If you will, but let her finish her tea."

Mindy's room, like the others Tori had seen, was attractively furnished, with lace curtains on the window, and a floral Wilton carpet on the floor. The furniture was made of English oak, and Tori noticed the headboard had much more elaborate carvings than the simple design of the bed in her bedroom at Link's house.

"Would you like more steam?" Mr. Fitzgerald asked as he moved to the radiator and turned the valve without waiting for Tori's answer.

"Thank you," Tori said. "I hope I'm not imposing on Mindy by taking her room."

"You're not. I think she'll be away for a few months." Mr. Fitzgerald began turning back the quilt on the bed. "It can get pretty cold at this time of the year, but you have a quilt, and if you need more, there are some in the armoire. The bathing room at the end of the hall has hot and cold running water, but I wouldn't recommend using it tonight. I'll bring you a pitcher of warm water, and your chamber and washbowls are in the toilet table. Will there be anything else?"

"No, you've been most kind."

When Link got home, even though it was late, he couldn't go to sleep. He poured himself a shot of brandy and took a seat at the kitchen table. Swirling the brandy around in the snifter, he breathed in its aroma, then took a swallow.

Where else could he have taken Tori? The only other alternative was to bring her home with him. He had to admit that was the solution he would have preferred, but if he had done that, he wasn't sure how long he could have kept her innocent. It was strange how in hardly a week she had become a part of his psyche. He had never met anyone who could compare to Tori.

And now he had taken Tori to a whorehouse.

Pearl and her girls weren't like the other prostitutes. From the time Pearl had arrived in town, she had let it be known that she would tolerate no nonsense from her girls or from her customers. Consequently, few disturbances occurred at Pearl's place, whereas the deputy constantly had to go to other brothels, especially those run by Kitty Maxie or Jessie Armstrong or Blanche Burton.

Pearl was particular about whom she had working for her. The girls usually came from good decent families, and all could read and write. All seemed to have a sense of honor, in spite of their chosen profession. He didn't think anyone would say or do anything to offend Tori.

On the other hand, what if Tori decided to join Pearl? Link knew nothing about Tori's past, certainly nothing to give him a sure and certain knowledge that she wouldn't take the job. She came from New York, and from her demeanor and dress, he surmised that she had been exposed to money and culture. If money was her motivator, the girls who worked for Pearl were among the highest-paid employees in the whole city.

What if Tori did take the job? How bad would that be? He knew the answer immediately. He wouldn't like it—he wouldn't like it one little bit. A thought began to form in his mind. Men married women they didn't know all the time. The mail-order bride business was booming in the West. He would ask Victoria Drumm to marry him before he would let her work in a brothel.

Tori didn't know how long she had been asleep when she was awakened by sounds coming from the next room. The sounds, whatever they were, were quite audible.

At first she couldn't quite make it out, and she thought perhaps someone was in pain; then she realized that she was hearing a woman's cries of passion. Then she heard a low voice—a man's voice.

Then a muffled conversation between a man and a woman followed, though they were speaking so quietly that Tori couldn't make out the words. Then she heard the door open.

"You're a sweet girl, Maxine," a man said from the hallway.

"It's easy to be sweet around you, George. Good night, now."

Tori heard the door close, then the sound of water being poured into a basin. After that, complete silence.

Tori lay in the darkness, contemplating what she had just heard. She could well imagine what had just taken place in the room beside her. In her mind she, not Maxine, was murmuring the chords of pleasure, and it wasn't a George or a Lyle Ketterman who occupied her thoughts—it was . . . Link Buchannan!

EIGHT

Tori had no idea how long she had slept, nor did she have any idea of what time it might be. The room was bright with morning light, and the house was quiet, exceptionally quiet.

Tori sat up in bed, then swung her legs over the side. She had thought the floor might be cold, but it wasn't. She walked over to the window and looked outside, but the view, of the backs of the houses across the alley, wasn't appealing.

She was a little hungry, but she remembered that Pearl had said they wouldn't have breakfast until late, so she put the thought out of her mind. Then she recalled that Mr. Fitzgerald had mentioned a bathing room. Now, with the house so quiet, would be an ideal time to take a bath.

Grabbing her robe, she opened the door and looked out into the hallway. It was, as she had fully expected, completely empty.

Tori walked down to the end of the hall. She tapped lightly on the door to the bathing room and, getting no response, pushed the door open and looked inside. She had expected to see a bathtub and a lavatory little different from the bathing room at Link's house in Colorado Springs. But she saw much more than that.

Tori had thought that Miriam Leslie's bathroom was elegant, but not even it could compare to this. The tub and the lavatory were white porcelain, but the water faucets were sparkling brass. A huge mirror on one wall reflected the delicate pink rose pattern of the wallpaper. A glass shelf near the lavatory was lined with crystal bottles and jars. When Tori examined them, she found scented oils and bath solutions. She also saw various powders and perfumes, as well as pots of rouge for the cheeks, and mascara for the eyes. There were tubes of beeswax mixed with carmine, and Tori put a dab of the lip color on her finger, then ran it over her lips.

Not even Hannah, the makeup artist for the run of *A Young Woman's Travail*, had this much makeup.

The bathtub was inviting and she turned the knobs to draw the water. Steam gushed up as the water cascaded into the tub, and Tori, feeling experimental, poured some of the bath oil into the hot water. Then, taking off her robe and gown, she slipped into the water, and a moment later she felt a satiny sensation on her skin as she was enveloped by the scent of roses.

Tori luxuriated in the tub until the water began to cool. Not until then did she step out. Drying off with a large, fluffy white towel, Tori stood before the mirror, examining her body. Link had commented that Pearl would need to feed her so her customers would want her. She knew he was teasing, but was there some truth to what he had said? Was she not desirable?

Putting on her robe, she returned to her room. She took special care with her hair, making certain that all the waves and curls were securely captured in a tight bun. Then she withdrew her black serge skirt and a gray foulard blouse from her valise and was soon dressed.

"I may smell like a prostitute, but I'm not going to look like one," she said to herself.

Tori thought she heard someone downstairs, so she stepped out into the hallway and made her way to a stairway that led to the back of the house. When she reached the back hall, a motherly-looking woman stuck her head out.

"Good morning, my dear. You're up bright and early," the woman said. "You must be the girl in Mindy's room."

"I'm Tori Drumm."

"And I'm Addie Fitzgerald. Pearl told me you're Manny's sister. He's such a good boy. Everybody thinks he comes here to see our Lucy, but I know he comes to get some of my apple custard."

"Apple custard? I haven't thought about that for years, but our mama used to make it. Manny loved it."

"He still does." Addie went into the pantry. When she returned, she was holding a blue enameled pan. "It'll be at least another hour or so before anybody gets up around here. Would you like a scoop of custard to sort of tide you over?"

Tori's eyes were glistening as a knot formed in her throat. "Do you serve it with sweet cream?"

"Yes, ma'am."

Tori tasted the rich dessert, and thoughts of her childhood came rushing back. Her mother could make apple custard quickly over a campfire and it would keep for several days. For the first time in a long time, Tori wished she could see her mother.

But then, just as quickly, she put the thought out of her mind. She was sitting in the kitchen of a house of prostitution where her brother was a frequent visitor. What would her mother think if she could see what her children had become?

"Mrs. Fitzgerald, would you happen to have a pencil and paper? I think I would like to write a letter—just to let someone know where I am."

"Of course."

Tori took the pencil and paper back up to her room. She sat down and started the letter.

> *Dear Mama,*
> *I wanted to let you know, I am with*
> *Manny. . . .*

She stopped and erased the word *Mama*. She started again.

> *Dear Aunt Frances and Uncle Harold,*

Again she erased the greeting. She wanted to let someone know where she was, but who would that be?

For a long time she sat looking out at the dismal

back alley. She saw a drayman deliver a barrel of
beer to the saloon next door. A man who had obviously spent the night in a doorway stumbled to his
feet and moved out of her sight. Who would want to
know where she was?

Lyle Ketterman? No. He probably didn't give her
a passing thought. At last she picked up the pencil
and began to write.

Dear Mrs. Leslie,

*I trust that your Christmas was filled
with good cheer. While my holiday could not
compare to the excitement that is New York,
I had a most enjoyable season. On Christmas
Eve, I made the acquaintance of William
Sharpless Jackson, and he remembers you
fondly. Since the death of your friend Helen,
Mr. Jackson has taken Mrs. Jackson's niece
as his wife, and I believe he is enjoying
fatherhood.*

*I spent Christmas at the home of a
gentleman who was kind enough to take me
in when I discovered my brother no longer
lives in Colorado Springs. Emanuel has
moved to Cripple Creek, where he, like every
other able-bodied man, is chasing after gold.*

*My gentleman friend has brought me
to the "district," as everyone calls the gold
camp, but alas, my brother is in Denver
meeting with the governor.*

*Because so many people are pouring into
the camp, there are not enough hotel rooms*

*to go around. When I arrived last evening,
my friend offered to take me to his home,
but under the circumstances, I felt ill at ease
doing that. He found me a place to lay my
head, for only God knows how long, at the
home of a close friend of his. I must tell you,
his friend operates a very classy brothel,
and that is where I am currently domiciled.
At the present, I have not met anyone but
the madam, the butler, and the cook, but all
three seem to be personable.*

*Should you wish to correspond with me,
I will be forever grateful. I can receive mail
from general delivery at the Cripple Creek
post office.*

With kindest regards,
Tori Drumm

When Tori finished her letter, she went down the
back stairs hoping to find Mr. Fitzgerald to see if he
would post it for her.

"I didn't expect to see you so early," Pearl said
when Tori entered the kitchen. Pearl was dressed
in a tasteful willow-green suit that would have been
envy of any woman in New York.

"I guess I'm an early riser," Tori said. "What time
is it?"

"It's close to ten. If you can wait for breakfast, I
think I may have a solution for your problem."

Tori looked toward Mrs. Fitzgerald and smiled. "I
think I can hold on."

"Good. Get your coat, and I must say you couldn't
have chosen a better outfit for the job I have in

mind." Pearl put on a wide green velvet hat with several ostrich plumes. "Addie, we won't be gone long."

Pearl and Tori walked a short distance to Welty's Livery, where they picked up Pearl's open phaeton with shiny red wheels. It was pulled by a team of fine black horses. At first Tori didn't understand why Pearl would drive an open carriage in the winter, but she soon realized that Pearl's presence and attire was as effective an advertisement as any broadside she might have distributed.

As they rode along, the horses prancing proudly, men whistled and hooted, but Pearl never acknowledged their presence.

"We're going to see my friend Mollie O'Bryan. She's a stenographer who does work for a lot of the businesses in town, and I know for a fact she could use some help. Would you be willing to work for her?"

"Of course, but I'm not sure what I can do to help her."

"Believe me, if she takes you on, she'll teach you everything you need to know."

Fifteen minutes later, Pearl pushed open the door of a narrow brick building and stepped inside, pulling Tori with her. A young, attractive, but conservatively dressed auburn-haired woman was talking on the telephone, and she held her hand up and smiled in greeting.

"Yes, that is what I said. I want you to sell a thousand shares of Damon. . . . I know I just bought it, but it's doubled in price, hasn't it? . . . Then sell it."

Tori examined the small office, which was in total disarray. Papers were everywhere—on the counter, on an oversize desk in the center of the room, on a library table, even on top of the book cabinets that stood along one wall.

Two sturdy oak chairs were on the opposite side of the desk from where the woman was sitting in an office screw chair, and she motioned that Tori and Pearl should have a seat.

"No, that's it. Oh, but keep an eye out for the Zenobia, and let me know if there's movement in the Orpha May. . . . Mr. Miller, would I ever steer you wrong? Of course I have it on good authority. . . . All right, I'll be there."

She hung up the phone and smiled across the desk at Pearl and Tori. "Aren't you out a little early?"

"Mollie O'Bryan, I want you to meet Victoria Drumm."

"Miss O'Bryan," Tori said.

"If you're one of Pearl's girls, you're a friend of mine." Mollie rose from her chair and offered her hand to Tori.

"No, no." Pearl waved her finger back and forth. "Tori's not one of my girls. I'm rather hoping she'll become your girl."

"Oh?"

"You know you need help, Mollie. Just look around at all this mess."

"Can you type, Miss Drumm?"

"No."

"Can you take shorthand?"

"No."

Mollie sat back in her chair. "Then what can you do?"

"She can speak French," Pearl quipped with a smile.

"I do have one ability that may or may not be helpful," Tori said.

"And what might that be?"

Tori pointed to the book cabinet. "Choose a book, open it, and hand it to me."

"I don't know where this is going, but you have my attention."

Mollie walked over and pulled down a book with a brown leather cover. *"Colorado: Some Answers to Questions,"* she said, reading the title.

"Open it to a page, any page, and hand it to me," Tori said.

Mollie did so.

Tori looked at the book for no more than a minute, then handed it back to Mollie. "The second paragraph. Follow along as I recite it to you."

"What? Are you telling me you can memorize something that fast?"

Smiling, Tori began, "'The first known visit of civilized man to Colorado was in 1544, under Coronado, Spanish Viceroy of Mexico. During the years 1600 to 1762, the French explored, occupied, and claimed it. In 1746, the Spanish army invaded San Juan, and the southeast portion of the state was ceded to Spain in 1762. In 1800 the French regained possession. It was ceded to the United States in 1803 and then its history as a civilized community commenced.'"

"Did she do it?" Pearl asked.

"Amazing! Simply amazing! She didn't miss a word. Miss Drumm, with a talent like that, I'm absolutely certain I can use you. And I'll teach you how to type. How does fifteen dollars a week sound?"

Tori smiled. As an actress, she had earned as much as $250 a week. But for now, she needed a job. If it only paid $15 per week, so be it. "Thank you, I'll take it."

"Wait a minute," Pearl said, rising from her chair. "Tori can make three times that in one night working at my place. Let's find another job."

Tori wanted to stop Pearl, but she stood, trusting that Pearl had another position in mind.

"Pearl de Vere, you make me so mad. I'll give her five dollars a day, and that's two dollars more than any ten-hour miner makes."

"Yes, but can any of them speak French?" Pearl asked as she pursed her lips, suppressing a laugh.

"Can you start tomorrow?" Mollie asked, turning to Tori.

"Yes."

"I open the office at eight, and we work until five, with half an hour off for lunch. I'll see you tomorrow morning."

"Thank you, Miss O'Bryan."

"If we're going to work together, I think calling each other *Miss* is going to get awfully tedious. I'm just Mollie."

How did you learn to do that?" Pearl asked when they were settled into the rig. "I mean, read something and memorize it so quickly?"

"I don't know. It's just something I've always been able to do," Tori said, and to a degree, that was true. As a young girl, her father had insisted that she commit long Bible passages to memory. That talent had been further honed when she became an actress and had to memorize long passages of dialogue.

"Well, you certainly impressed me. And most importantly, you impressed Mollie."

"Thank you for introducing me to her, and thank you for getting me a bigger salary."

"I have a feeling you're going to be a big asset for her, and she'll be thanking me for bringing you to her. Now, what do you say we get back to the house? I'm famished."

When Pearl and Tori walked in, several girls were sitting in the drawing room. They were all attractively plump women with what looked to be natural blond hair. Tori smiled when she thought of Link's comment about her needing to be heavier.

"Addie said you're Manny's sister. I'm his Lucy," a pleasant young woman said. "Has he told you about me?"

"I'm afraid I've not seen my brother for a long time, but I'm pleased to meet you. I'm Tori."

"Lucy's a good girl," Pearl said as she casually draped her arm around Lucy. "Besides Lucy, we have Gala, Nellie, Katarina, and Maxine, and of course Mindy, but she's away." Pearl pointed to each of the girls as she called them by name.

Tori remembered the sounds she had heard from the room next to hers last night and remembered the man's parting words: *You're a sweet girl, Maxine.*

"None of us have last names," Lucy added with a laugh.

"Among friends, who needs a last name?" Tori asked.

The girls laughed.

"Pearl said you were a nice person who wouldn't be judgmental," Gala said. "And she was right."

An older woman wearing a black dress and a white pinafore came in. "Ladies, breakfast is served."

"Did Addie make pancakes this morning?" Maxine asked.

"Yes, ma'am, she did."

"Oh, wonderful! Tori, wait until you taste them. Nobody in the whole world can make pancakes like Mrs. Fitzgerald."

"I can't wait," Tori said, realizing that except for the apple custard that Mrs. Fitzgerald had shared with her earlier, and the honey and bread she had had with Pearl, she hadn't eaten for over twenty-four hours.

To Tori's surprise, the girls all held hands as Gala gave the blessing.

Nellie, perhaps sensing Tori's surprise, spoke up. "I guess you didn't expect to see whores praying, huh? But we say who needs the Lord more than we do?"

"I'm not sure he listens to us, though," Katarina said.

"Of course he does," Tori said.

"How do you know?" Lucy asked.

Tori thought of her father and realized that he would not only condemn these women, he would be equally condemning of her, just by association. But she also knew the answer to Lucy's question. "It's like Jesus said when they were about to stone a woman: Let him without sin cast the stone."

"I've heard that," Katarina said. "I never knew what it actually referred to, though. Why would they want to stone a woman?"

"Because she had committed adultery."

"You mean like we do," Maxine said.

"Yes." Tori nodded, including herself by implication if not by word.

The pancakes arrived, and everyone looked toward Tori to get her reaction. She took a bite, then smiled broadly. "Uhm, they are delicious."

"Is there a plate for me?" a man's asked.

Tori didn't even have to look around. She recognized Link's voice.

"Link! Oh, are you going to eat with us?" Gala asked.

"I sure am, if you have enough for me."

"We always have something for you, Link, you know that," Maxine said flirtatiously as she fluttered her eyelids at him.

Again, the words Tori heard last night came back to her: *You're a sweet girl, Maxine.*

She was trying to magnanimously accept her new acquaintances, but when Link was added to the mix, she had difficulty. Had he ever said those words to Maxine or any of the other women?

She was sure he probably had. So why could she be so accepting when she was told her brother often frequented this place—Lucy had even called herself "his Lucy"—but it made her angry when she thought of Link in the arms of one of these women?

She knew the answer: because she wanted to keep him for herself. But she also knew she wanted more than just a roll in the hay.

Link pulled a chair away from the wall and set it next to Tori. During the breakfast he watched her interact with the other girls, and while he was pleased that she didn't seem in the least judgmental, he also wondered why. Wouldn't an ordinary young woman who suddenly found herself in a group of prostitutes show some disapproval, even as she was openly accepting? What, in Tori's background, would allow her to be so receptive?

As he was thinking such thoughts, Link scolded himself. After all, he was the one who'd brought her here.

"Link, Tori's a working girl now," Pearl said.

"What?"

The way Link gasped the word made Pearl laugh. "I took her to see Mollie O'Bryan this morning. She starts work tomorrow morning."

"That's great," Link said almost too enthusiastically. "Mollie can use the help."

"I thought you'd approve," Pearl said.

"I'm looking forward to it," Tori said. "And I appreciate Pearl introducing me to her."

"To tell you the truth, I was thinking about taking you to see Mollie myself," Link said. "But it's probably better that Pearl took you. If I took you there, Mollie would probably think I wanted you there just to funnel information on to me."

"Information? What kind of information?"

"You'll find out soon enough," Link said. "Mollie's

in a unique position. She knows just about everything that goes on around here, and most of the
time her information is more valuable than gold."

"Hmmm. I'm not sure what you're talking about,
but I have a feeling my job is going to be interesting."

"I'm sure it will be," Link replied. "After breakfast, would you let me show you around the town?"

"I'd like that very much."

"Good. I've got a buggy outside."

After he helped Tori into the buggy, Link climbed
in and, snapping the reins, started the horse forward.

This was Tori's first real look at Cripple Creek
and Myers Avenue. Patches of snow were here
and there, interspersed with mud where the snow
was beginning to melt. She saw a mixture of tents
and scrabbled-together tar-paper-roofed buildings.
They passed a dozen saloons and several places
that Link said were parlor houses and one-girl
cribs as well as three or four dance halls. Tori's
spirits began to drop when she saw a livery with a
sign indicating the Grand Opera House was on the
second floor.

"It seems strange to see an opera house on this
street," Tori commented.

"Why? You've met Pearl. Wouldn't you say her
act is every bit as good as a prizefight or a minstrel
show?"

"Is that the only kind of performances you get
here?"

"No, a lot of times when a famous person is in

Colorado Springs, they want to come over here and see what they call the underbelly of the West. We've had everybody from Oscar Wilde to Susan B. Anthony come to see us."

"I know that Oscar spent quite a bit of time touring the West."

"Oscar? You call him Oscar?"

Tori felt her cheeks flame, and she forced a laugh. "I guess that did sound a bit familiar, didn't it? As if Oscar and I were great friends."

Tori and Oscar *were* good friends—he had often visited Miriam Leslie when she was married to his brother—but if Tori was going to make a complete break with her past, that wasn't information she wanted to share.

"Let's move off this street," Link said as he turned the horse. When they reached Bennett Avenue, the town began to change.

There were several more substantial buildings, many two stories, and others with high false fronts that rose almost regally above the lesser structures. Link pointed out some of the businesses: the banks, the hotels, the assay offices, the grocery stores, the mercantile stores, the livery, the blacksmiths, and the real estate offices. A new brick building was almost completed with the words TUTT AND PENROSE stamped across the front.

"Is that Charles's building?" Tori asked.

"Yes. He and Speck leased the C.O.D., that was their claim, and they came into quite a piece of change, so they're moving their offices into this building. I'll be moving there as well."

"When?"

"Soon, I hope."

"It is certainly an attractive building."

"Yes, it is." He moved his leg closer to Tori's as they sat under the robe.

"Is that a church?" Tori asked, trying to take her thoughts away from what the closeness of his leg was doing to her.

"It is. This one is St. Peter's Catholic Church. It has the highest steeple in the world."

Tori looked at the redbrick structure. It had a belfry, but it didn't seem to be anything out of the ordinary. "That's quite a distinction," Tori said, not wanting to contradict Link, "but I do believe New York's Trinity Church has a higher steeple."

"Is it nine thousand five hundred and sixty-eight feet high?"

"What?"

Link chuckled. "Well, the altitude for the church is nine thousand five hundred and eight feet; the church and steeple just add another sixty feet."

Tori laughed. "I guess you win that one."

They continued on down Bennett Street with Link pointing out all the businesses, then he took Tori out toward Globe Hill.

"This is where it all began, Poverty Gulch. And now the man who discovered this is flat broke," Link said.

"With all the gold, how could that be?"

"Bob Womack sold his claim for five hundred dollars and a bottle of liquor. That's the Gold King, and the C.O.D., and if you move up a little farther, there's the Mollie Kathleen."

"The C.O.D.? Isn't that the one you said Charles

and Mr. Penrose leased? If it's so close to where this man discovered the gold, why didn't they keep it for themselves?"

"It takes a lot of money to bring gold out of the ground. Just look around at all this activity."

From where they were, she could hear the sounds of the mines at work: rocks spilling over the dumps, the clanking of machinery, the occasional low, stomach-shaking thunder of underground detonations. Black smoke was belching from the huge smokestacks, and when the whistles blew as miners changed shifts, scores of dirty-faced men shuffled down from the hills and others took their places.

"It seems awfully busy," Tori said.

"Yes, and what you see is just a fraction of the mines. Right now there aren't more than sixty producing mines, but there have to be a thousand shafts and tunnels. Everybody's looking."

"What about you, Link?"

"Everybody looks, but there's more than one way to make a million dollars than by bringing gold out of the ground. Don't get me wrong, but when you start working for Mollie, you're going to find out what a 'gold mine' she has, and she never gets her hands dirty." He reached over and brushed an errant strand of hair off Tori's face. "We'd better get back to town."

As the carriage moved swiftly over the road, Tori was struck by the paucity of snow at such a high elevation. She could see a ribbon of frozen water than ran alongside the town, which Link said was the actual creek that gave the town its name. Drifts of snow were in a few gullies, and she saw children in bright-colored stocking hats building snowmen and pulling makeshift sleds. One went whipping in front of the horse on the ice-slick coating, causing the horse to turn.

"Those kids shouldn't be doing that," Link said as he got the horse under control.

A sheen of perspiration was on his brow and his cheek muscles twitched, and Tori could see that he was clearly disturbed.

"Clear the track!" someone shouted. Looking up the hill, Link and Tori saw a sled hurtling down the hill at breakneck speed, the sled bouncing and swaying, the runners sending off sparks. As it flashed by in front of the horse, they saw a young boy controlling the sled while a young girl sat in front of him. The boy was waving his arm much as he would if he were riding a bucking horse. His laughter echoed through the hills, but on the girl's face was a look of absolute terror. The horse reared, and Link fought to get it under control.

The sled finally came to rest some distance from them.

Link set the brake, got out of the buggy, and walked over to the sled just as the boy was getting up.

"Now, Flossie, you can't say that wasn't fun," the boy said, pulling the girl to her feet. Then he saw Link standing there and the smile left his face.

"Did we scare your horse?" the boy asked.

"It's not my horse I'm concerned about," Link said in a clipped voice. "It's the girl."

"My sister? What did she do?"

"It's what *you* did. If you want to slide down a

hill like a wild hellion and break your neck, then by all means do it. But you have no right to risk your sister's life like that."

"I told him I didn't want to, but he made me," the little girl said.

"Are you proud of yourself?" Link scolded.

"Aw, mister, nothing's going to happen. I'll take care of her."

"Something can happen just like that," Link said, snapping his finger. "If something happens to your sister, you'll live with it the rest of your life." Link turned abruptly and returned to the buggy.

He was too far away for Tori to hear what he had been saying, but she could tell by his demeanor he was clearly upset.

"Come on, let's get out of here." He offered no explanation for this scene, and Tori didn't ask.

NINE

When they came back into town, the first place they went was to a small log cabin located at the end of Prospect Street. A chimney protruding from a sod roof was pouring out a long rope of smoke.

Link stopped the buggy and sat for a long moment. He had not spoken since the incident with the children.

"You've heard me mention Speck Penrose. He and Charles Tutt are my oldest friends in the world," Link said. "And now you're going to get a chance to meet him."

"I'm looking forward to it," Tori said.

"No, that's not what I want to hear." A slow smile started to build on Link's face.

"Then why did you bring me here?"

"Because I'm testing you."

"You're testing me?"

"Uh-huh. Pearl and her girls tell me Speck's the most handsome man they've ever met. Now, if you're going to be my girl, I need to know if I can trust you around him."

Tori couldn't help but laugh. "What do you mean if I'm going to be your girl?"

"Well, I guess we're going to find that out, too."

Link helped Tori down from the buggy, and unconsciously she began smoothing her hair, trying to get her unruly curls under control.

"Speck? Speck, open the door!" Link yelled as he banged on the door. "You've got company!"

The door opened and a very handsome man indeed looked out. He was taller than Link, and he had raven hair, expressive eyebrows, and dark eyes. He wore a neatly trimmed mustache that contrasted with his sun-bronzed face. His broad smile beamed at Tori as he ignored Link altogether.

"Well, come in," he said invitingly. "I'm Spenser Penrose, my dear. My uncouth friend didn't provide me with your name."

"I'm Victoria Drumm." She extended her hand.

Instead of shaking her hand, Speck lifted it to his lips and kissed it. "Why haven't I met this lovely before now?" Speck asked, never taking his eyes off Tori.

"Because she's been staying with me in Colorado Springs," Link said possessively.

"That's interesting." Speck turned his attention to Link. "Are you building up your cash box?"

"Not yet, but it's never too early to start."

Both men laughed and shook hands heartily.

"I know I'm going to win," Speck said. "It's good you're back. When did you get here?"

"We came in yesterday."

"And where did Miss Drumm stay?" Speck's eyebrow lifted precipitously.

"She's staying with Pearl, but only until Manny Drumm gets back in town. He's her brother."

"Well, then your stay at Pearl's will soon be over," Speck said. "I think he came in from Cañon City this morning."

"Really!" Tori exclaimed with genuine excitement.

"How do you know Manny's here?" Link asked.

"My boy, don't I have my fingers on the pulse of this entire community? Is there anything I don't know?"

"Did you know Victoria was in town?"

"I guess I didn't, but I know she's here now. And I think I'm going to get to know her a lot better." Speck smiled a dazzling smile, showing his perfect teeth.

"Link, I hate to say anything, but I am anxious to find Manny. Should we go now?"

"I think that's a good idea, and I think you passed your test." Link took Tori by the hand and stepped toward the door. "Speck, I'll catch up with you later and fill you in on what happened in Colorado Springs."

As he drove away from Speck's house, Link chuckled. "Thanks for telling him your name was Victoria."

"You are thanking me for that?"

"Yes. Victoria is more formal. It tells Speck where he stands with you."

Now it was Tori's turn to laugh. "Should I call you Mr. Buchannan, or maybe Lincoln?"

"No, no, no . . . it's Link and Tori. That's much more intimate, don't you think?"

"I think you're beginning to make assumptions that aren't supported by fact."

"Oh? Have you or have you not kissed me several times already?"

"You kissed me!"

Link smiled at her. "Yes, that's what I just said."

"No, you said . . . oh . . . never mind." Tori shook her head. "Do you think we could go back to Pearl's to get my valise? I am anxious to see Manny."

"We're on our way."

"Back so soon?" Pearl asked when Link and Tori entered the house.

"Manny's in town," Tori said excitedly. "I've come to get my luggage."

"Then you're leaving us?"

"Yes. At least I plan to." Tori chuckled nervously. "I'm not sure how Manny will take this, though. I haven't seen him yet, and he has no idea I'm in town."

Pearl patted Tori on the arm. "I understand, and if it doesn't work out the way you want it to, you come right back here. You're welcome to stay here for as long as Mindy is gone, and that may be a while."

"Thank you. I can't tell you how much I appreciate what you did for me—putting me up when there was no place to stay—but most of all, thank you for introducing me to Mollie."

"I was happy to do it." Pearl's face softened. "Link, you take special care of this girl, you hear me?"

"I intend to," Link replied with a huge smile.

"Special care," **Link** said as he helped Tori into the carriage. "You heard what she said. I have to take special care of you."

"It would seem to me that you already have. But if Mr. Penrose is right, and Manny is here, I hope after today I won't be such a burden to you."

"Speck's right. If he says Manny's back in town, you can count on it." Then Link turned to look directly toward her. "And, Tori, I want you to know, you're anything but a burden."

She said nothing, turning her face away from Link. When they had gone a short distance, she said pensively, "Do you think he'll want to see me?"

"How could he not? Any man would be happy to see his own sister after so many years."

"Manny tried to write me a long time ago, and I was the one who didn't write back, so it was my fault we didn't keep in touch. Now here I am, coming hat in hand, needing his help. If he doesn't want me, I'll understand." She choked back tears.

"Tori, don't beat up on yourself. You're his sister, and men have a special affinity for their sisters. Manny will be overjoyed when he sees you."

"That's all well and good for you to say—you don't even have a sister."

A strange expression crept onto Link's face. "I had one once," he replied quietly. "She died."

"Oh, I'm so sorry."

"It was a long time ago." Link was quiet for a moment. "It was a sledding accident, and she was only six years old. She was riding on the sled with me when I hit a rock and lost control. I fell off, but Della didn't. The sled hit a tree and her neck was broken."

"Oh, Link." Tori reached over to touch his arm. She knew now why he had reacted the way he did when he saw the boy and the girl on the sled. "I'm so sorry."

He took Tori's hand and continued to hold it until they stopped in front of Manny's house.

"It looks like he's home—there's smoke coming from the chimney," Link said. He set the brake on the buggy, then hopped out and walked around to help Tori down.

"Well, this is it," Tori said as she shivered.

She had been to Manny's house before, but that had been at night. Now she saw its rough-sawn logs and tar-paper roof. The front was level with the ground, but from here she could see that the back was on stilts, lifting the house up off the hill. A set of steps climbed from the dirt to the back porch.

"Tori, don't be afraid. Manny's a good man."

Link led her up to the front of the house, then knocked rather loudly on the door. "Manny Drumm?" he called.

"Who is it?" a voice replied from inside.

"Link Buchannan."

The door opened. "Link, what are you . . . ?" Manny stopped when he saw Tori. "Who's this?"

"It's your sister, Tori."

"What?" Manny gasped, looking again at Tori. "My God, you're lying. My sister's in New York."

"I left, and now I've come to see you," Tori said.

"Well, come in, both of you. I just got home today, and it's pretty much a mess."

Tori stepped into the house, which looked to be about a twenty feet square. The walls were chinked logs, and the floor still had the smell of newly sawn lumber. The room had a handmade table with four chairs sitting around it and a cabinet with a door standing open, exposing a flour bin. A cast-iron pump was attached to a sink overflowing with dirty dishes.

On the other side of the room were two worn upholstered chairs and an iron-framed daybed. One of the two doors led to a room where Tori could see an unmade bed. She couldn't imagine what the other room might be.

Already she was having second thoughts about wanting to stay with Manny. In her mind, she saw the well-appointed room she had slept in the previous evening. Pearl had invited her to come back, and she was fighting with her conscience not to go back to the bordello.

She looked to Link, hoping he would help her decide. Even though she had only known him for just a week, he had been, during that time, her one contact with stability. And though it seemed strange, she felt less sure of herself with her own brother than she did with someone who had, but a short time before, been a complete stranger.

Manny looked at Tori quizzically. "So you say you're my sister?"

"I am your sister."

"How do I know that?"

"Do you doubt me?"

"Yes, as a matter of fact I do. I wouldn't put it past a few of these mine owners to try to pull something—send in some woman, someone they think I'd trust—just so they could spy on the union."

"Manny, believe me, except for Speck Penrose, whom Tori met not over an hour ago, I'm the only person she's talked to since she got here."

"You're lying. She was at the Union Hall last night. The boys told me some chippie was in there saying she was my sister. If that's the case, why weren't you at the stage depot when I got in this morning?"

"Because no one told us you were coming," Tori said with more defiance than she intended.

"Manny, I assure you—" Link started to say, his voice reflecting his anger.

"You are my little brother, Manny, whether you want to admit it or not. I have another place to stay if you don't want me here." Tori turned toward the door.

"Wait. What did the sign say that was painted on the side of Pop's wagon?"

Tori smiled and turned back toward Manny. "It said, 'Reverend Nathan L. Drumm, spreading the word of God, saving souls for Jesus, baptisms daily.'"

For just a moment Manny's face reflected shock. "Tori?" he said almost plaintively.

"Yes, Little Brother?"

A huge smile spread across Manny's face, and he opened his arms wide. "I'll be damned. You are my sister!"

The two embraced for a long moment.

"Now that that's settled, what do you want to do, Tori? Stay here or go back to Pearl's?"

"You stayed at Pearl's?"

"Yes, I did. They all seem to know you very well."

"You met Lucy, then. She's quite a girl, and when I get this union stuff all settled, I'm going to ask her to marry me." Manny smiled broadly. "Hey, are you a . . . ?"

"No, I'm not. But Pearl did help me get a job. I'm going to work for Mollie O'Bryan and I start tomorrow."

"Mollie O'Bryan." Manny rubbed his chin. "That's good. That's real good. You can stay here for as long as you want."

Link had a sinking sensation in the pit of his stomach. He had a sick feeling that Manny intended to use Tori in the exact way he had just accused the mine owners of doing. If she became an informant for the union . . . no, he couldn't think about that. This was Tori. His Tori.

"I'll get your bags," Link said.

Tori nodded, not trusting herself to speak.

"I'll follow you out," Manny said.

Link wanted to take Tori in his arms, to tell her he wouldn't leave her in this pigsty, but he couldn't. Not now. She had found her brother, and he would have to give her time to work it out.

Outside, Manny said, "Link, I hope I didn't offend you in there, but in this climate, a body can't be too cautious. It was John who put the idea in my mind the owners might be sending in a spy 'cause I never dreamed Tori would ever leave New York."

"Your sister is an extraordinary woman. I've only known her a short time and I haven't pried, but I have a feeling she's been through a rough time. I have to tell you, I care about her. Don't you dare put her in a position where she can get hurt, do you understand me?"

"I do, and thanks for bringing her to me."

Link nodded and the two men shook hands. Link reached into the buggy, got Tori's valise, and handed it to Manny. Then Link climbed in and drove off. He hoped he was doing the right thing.

Tori waited anxiously until Manny came back with her grip. What did one say to a brother one didn't know?

"You can't believe how surprised I am to see you," Manny said when he returned. "The last I heard from Mama, she said Aunt Frances told her you were a big star on Broadway—had taken some sort of stage name. Is that true?"

"I'm here, so I guess it's not true any longer."

"And I'm glad you came, but how long do you think you'll stay?"

"I don't have any idea." She looked around at the condition of Manny's cabin. "It will depend on a lot of things. My job, what happens with . . ." She stopped because the next word she was thinking was *Link*.

"You can stay here for a while, but you may not like it, it being so crowded and all. The only problem is you'll not find a place of your own. With the collapse of the silver market every out-of-work foreigner is pouring in from Aspen or Leadville, looking for a job."

"I could go back to Pearl's."

"Would you want Mama to know that?"

"Would you want Mama to know you want to marry one of Pearl's girls?"

Manny laughed. "I guess we're two of a kind. Does Mama know you've come out here?"

Tori looked down. "I've not heard directly from Mama or Pop since the day they sent me to live with Aunt Frances and Uncle Harold."

"What do you mean? They didn't send you away—you left."

"Manny—I was twelve years old. Does a twelve-year-old decide for herself she's running away from home?"

"Some do. Lucy was fourteen when she started working full-time. You were lucky. I suppose you got to go to school?"

"Yes, Aunt Frances was very good to me."

"Look at me. The only education I got was what Mama could teach me, and believe me, there's more to the world than what the Bible says."

"You seem to have done all right. Link says you are highly thought of in the community, and the man I met at the Union Hall said you had gone to see the governor."

"That's true. Governor Waite's a big Populist, and a lot of people around here don't like him, but we know he'll back whatever the union wants. Tori, if you stay around here—with me—you're going to hear things you're not going to like at first, but remember, we're fighting for a cause. Somebody's got to stand up to these cheap bastards. They're makin' tons of money, and it's all comin' off the backs of hardworkin' men."

Tori listened to what Manny was saying, but she

thought back to what she had heard from Link—that of over a thousand claims, only sixty were making money. There was more to this issue than either side was considering. She started to comment, but thought better of it.

"Tori, it's great seeing you again. And you are welcome to stay as long as you wish. Consider the house yours. You can have the bedroom. It's not New York, but it has a bed. I've got a pole run across the end where you can put your clothes. When you get your first paycheck, you can buy some wire coat hangers down at Robert's Store."

"I have money."

"If you're not broke, why in the hell did you come here?"

"I came to see my brother. I thought he'd be glad to see me."

"Aw, Sis, I didn't mean that the way it sounded." Manny came over and put his arms around her. "It's just that it's been so long, at least ten years."

"It's been fourteen."

Tori took her brother at his word. He told her to consider the house hers, so she began doing things to make it more livable. The first thing she did was put up some open shelves to hold the cooking pots and dishes. Then she bought a coal-fired cookstove, an icebox, and a copy of *Mrs. Shillaber's Cook-Book: A Practical Guide for Housekeepers*, in case she decided to learn to cook.

For Manny's two upholstered chairs, Addie Fitzgerald gave Tori some figured-chintz slipcovers, which brightened the gloomy room. Pearl had a discarded rag rug that she said Tori could have, and though to Tori's eye it did not match the slipcovers, it was better than the bare boards, so she took it with gratitude. The only things left to buy were window coverings and new bed linens.

That done, Tori turned to the cookbook and found the recipe for Beefsteak Smothered with Onions. Following the directions, she seasoned the onions with salt, pepper, and butter, seared a couple of venison steaks, and laid them in the frying pan with the onions. Covering the pan, she set it just off the burner plate to simmer.

When Manny came home, he looked around in surprise. "What have you done?"

Tori was concerned. Had she overstepped her place? "I—I'm sorry. If you don't like it, I can—"

"No, I think it's great! This place looks almost like a home." Manny laughed.

"I hoped you would like it. I have a couple more things I want to get."

Manny sniffed audibly. "I don't know what I'm smelling, but it smells delicious!"

"It's venison and onions. I have to confess that I'm not much of a cook, but I thought I'd like to try. You'll be my guinea pig."

"It's delicious," Manny said after the first taste.

"I'm glad you like it."

"But don't bother to cook anymore for me. You may have noticed that I don't have much of a kitchen." Manny looked around. "That is, I didn't have one before now. I usually eat all of my meals either at the Union Hall or someplace else, because that's where I get most of my business done."

"I'm sorry. I don't mean to try and change the way you live."

"Don't apologize, Sis." Manny reached across the table to put his hand on hers. "I must confess, I do like what you have done with the house."

"That's the second time you've called me Sis. It's been a long time since I've heard that. You don't have any idea how good it sounds."

"Tori, you said Mama and Pop sent you away. Why?"

Tori was silent for a moment,

"If you'd rather not say, I'll understand. It's just that for a long time I thought maybe it was something I had done that made you leave."

"Do you remember when we did a revival outside Sikeston, Missouri?"

"How would you expect me to remember that? We put that tent up hundreds of times. There's no way I could remember one specific town."

"Sikeston is where it happened. I was twelve years old, and Pop caught me holding hands with a boy. Holding hands, mind you, that's all. He whipped my bare skin until welts came." Tori paused for a moment before she continued. "It was after that that Aunt Frances came and took me away."

"I'm sorry. I asked Mama and Pop when you would be coming back, and the only thing they ever said was that you had chosen to live a life outside the Lord."

Unexpectedly Tori laughed. "Well, that I have done."

"Haven't we both?" Manny joined in the laughter. "Wait here, I want to show you something."

"What?"

"Just wait. You'll recognize it. At least, I think you will."

Manny got up from the table and headed toward his room. After a couple of minutes he returned and held out a small black leather-bound book. "Do you remember this?"

Tori took the book, then felt her eyes well with tears. "You kept this?"

"Yes."

Opening the New Testament, she saw, on the frontispiece, her name written in her mother's hand. Midway through the book she found a frayed scrap of paper.

> *Brother let me shake your hand*
> *Spread God's name throughout the land,*
> *He will rid you from your sin,*
> *Save the souls of women and men*

Reading those words, she was, for just a moment, a child again, standing in the tent in front of a group of men and women, reciting those very lines.

"When Pop and I came back that day, you were gone," Manny said. "Pop burned all your clothes, everything, but I took your New Testament because I always believed there would be a time when I'd be able to give it back to you."

"It took me a long time to realize that Mama must have sent for Aunt Frances just to get me away from

Pop," Tori said. "I don't know how someone who professes to be a man of God could have been so harsh."

"Tori, I had no idea. There was never any explanation as to why you were gone, and your name was seldom mentioned again."

Working for Mollie O'Bryan proved easier for Tori to adjust to than to her living conditions with Manny. She found the work interesting and began to learn the QWERTY system for typing.

It was now almost two weeks since Link had left her with Manny, and she was disappointed that she hadn't seen Link. When she heard the doorbell ring, she was genuinely pleased to see him enter the office.

"Link," she said with a big smile. "Where have you been?"

"Did you miss me?" He sat on the edge of the desk Mollie had set up for Tori.

"I did. I even went by your office, but it was all locked up."

"I should have told you. When I got back to the office the other day, I found I had some urgent business in Denver, so I caught the afternoon stage. But if you missed me that much, I won't let that happen again." He leaned down and gave Tori a light kiss.

"Don't do that," Tori said as she looked around despite knowing that Mollie was not in her office.

"Why not? I know you like it." Then Link kissed her again.

"Because I'm trying to be professional. Mollie

is the most competent businesswoman I've ever known, and I'm trying to be like her."

"You don't think Mr. Miller ever kisses her?"

"Of course not! He's married," Tori said emphatically.

"You just pay close attention and just see if you don't think the dapper young Charley Miller doesn't think Miss Mollie is pretty special."

"Link, I believe they are business associates."

"And you don't think business associates ever engage in any hanky-panky?"

Tori had no answer. Was her affair with Lyle anything more than hanky-panky between business associates?

"How are you and Manny getting along?" Link asked.

"It's almost like I have the house to myself. Manny leaves early in the morning for whatever it is that he does at the Union Hall, and he doesn't come back until quite late, if he comes home at all."

"He does stay in Cripple Creek, though, doesn't he?"

"I don't ask, but if I really needed to find him, I have a feeling Lucy Dawes could tell me where he is."

Link threw back his head and laughed. "Would you ever have thought a preacher's kid could be so lusty?"

"Two things." Tori cocked her head saucily. "First, who told you he was a preacher's kid, and second, which preacher's kid are you talking about?"

Link's eyes opened wide. "Victoria Drumm, I do believe you are flirting with me."

"I am not. I asked you a question. Who told you our father was a preacher?"

"Let me think." Link put his finger to his chin and squinted his eyes. "'Reverend Nathan L. Drumm, spreading the word of God, saving souls for Jesus, baptisms daily.' Somebody said that, but I don't remember who."

"Oh." Tori's hand flew to her mouth. "I guess I did say that, didn't I? Yes, he was a preacher. Does that bother you?"

"No, of course not. But getting back to Manny, I attended a meeting with some of the mine owners this morning, and I'm afraid trouble is coming. Has Manny said anything about it?"

"No, he doesn't say much when he's at home, but I think Mollie is concerned. She says if the miners go out on strike and shut down the mines, there won't be much business for us, but that's not going to happen, is it?"

"We'll just have to wait and see, but this notice might be the catalyst that brings it all to a head." Link pulled out a piece of paper and laid it on Tori's desk. The notice said that the Pharmacist, the Isabella, the Victor, and seven other mines were joining the Strong, the Portland, and the Independence in moving to a ten-hour day for three dollars.

"Those owners are awful," Tori said, thinking of the five dollars a day she was making sitting behind a desk. "I wouldn't do that backbreaking work for ten hours and only get three dollars a day."

Link had been sitting on the side of the desk, and with a strange expression on his face, he stood.

"Oh, Link, did I say something I shouldn't have said?"

"No, you're probably right, but right now I'm one of the owners you're talking about. My trip to Denver was to buy back some of the leases that I've sold, and until I can find someone ready to part with his money, it's my name on the dotted line. It's not a position I want to be in, but it is where I am right now. And even though the mines I own are speculative, with no working miners, the decision has been made to present a united front. Everyone is going to a ten-hour workday, and there's nothing I can do about it."

Tori thought about what Link had just told her. Was that information Manny would like to know? She was sure that it was, but if she told him, would she be betraying Link's trust in her? And she wasn't just thinking of Link's trust with regard to their relationship, but also in her professional position working with Mollie.

But the information was sure to come out soon, and she did have an obligation to her brother.

"What?" Manny asked that evening when he came back to the house. "The Pharmacist is going to increase their shifts to ten hours?"

"Yes," Tori said.

"How do you know that?"

"Link stopped by the office today and showed me the paper."

"Damn, are you sure it's the Pharmacist? That's always been an eight-hour mine, and from the beginning Aiden Jones has been good to us. I can't believe he's going in the opposite direction. Are there any more mine owners who will be posting that notice?"

"There are the others." Tori began ticking off the list.

"John asked me which side you were on. I think this answers that question." Manny smiled broadly.

After he left, Tori began to have second thoughts. Should she have told him?

That night, Manny invited John Calderwood and a few other men up to his cabin for a meeting.

"Is it true, Tori? Are the eight-hour mines really going to a ten-hour day?" Calderwood asked.

"I can only tell you what I saw," Tori said. "Several of the owners are posting a notice saying they're all going on the same schedule and that it will be a ten-hour day."

"Pardon my French, miss, but those bastards can't do that. I've got kids to feed," Junius Johnson said.

"The strike up at Coeur d'Alene taught us a lot. They had to give in because of just what you're saying. They got hungry," Calderwood said. "But we aren't going to let that happen. Any miner who keeps working is going to contribute to those who go out."

"That's right," Manny said, "and I've been contacting local businesses. Lots of 'em are willing to give us credit."

"I've been checkin' around, and I've decided if we make a stand, Altman is the best place to do it. The town's almost all union, and they've got lots of boardinghouses. And besides, Jack Smith has promised to give us free beer until he runs out," Calderwood said.

"Boardinghouses?" Tori asked. "Are you saying you would move up there?"

"Only as a last resort, ma'am," Calderwood said. "I've put together a proposal that I want to take to the eight-hour mines. If they'll stay with that schedule, they'll keep working."

"And if they don't?"

"Then I'd say they brought this on themselves. If the stockholders don't get any dividends for a while, the owners will pay bloody hell. No, they'll meet our demands. I can tell you, we'll get our eight-hour day."

Before she went to sleep that night, Tori wrote another letter to Miriam Leslie.

> *Dear Mrs. Leslie,*
>
> *I am very happy to tell you that I am no longer domiciled in a brothel. Actually, I spent only one night there, and the woman who runs it, as well as the ladies who were there, were very nice to me. It was a pleasant and interesting experience.*
>
> *Much has happened since my last letter to you. I am now living with my brother, who has gone out of his way to make accommodations for my stay. He has turned his bedroom over to me and has moved into a small room that was once a storeroom, or*

perhaps a pantry. If it was a pantry, though, it never served that purpose, because he never eats at home. I have offered to cook meals for him, but he says that he gets too much business taken care of during the meals, nearly all of which he eats at the Union Hall. Manny is an official in something called the Western Federation of Miners, Free Coinage Number 19.

There is, at present, great unrest here. The miners work for ten hours a day, under the most grueling and backbreaking conditions. For this, they are paid three dollars per day. The miners are requesting an eight-hour day for the same three dollars, but the mine owners are resisting. And for me, this has become somewhat of a personal problem.

I find myself more and more attracted to Link Buchannan. And while it would not be the same situation as before, because Link isn't married, there is a problem. With regard to the unrest here, my brother is on one side, that of the miners, and Link is on the other side, that of the mine owners. I don't know where this is all going, but I do seem to be caught in the middle.

With kindest regards,
Tori Drumm

TEN

The next morning, Link and Speck were riding in from Wilson Creek, having just met with Winfield Stratton at the Independence.

"Is Stratton going to an eight-hour day or will he stick with ten?" Link asked.

"It's hard to tell about that old bird. With his carpenter background, he tends to sympathize with the miners," Speck said. "So if I had to lay money on him, I'd say he goes it alone."

"You're probably right. I'm sure he won't be at the meeting the union asked for this afternoon, and to be honest, I wish I didn't have to go."

"You can't fool me, Buchannan, you don't want to go because of Manny Drumm."

"That's crazy. You know Manny's not that important. He's just Calderwood's horse holder."

"Maybe. But he's also Tori's brother, and that does put you in a rather precarious position."

"I can handle it," Link said.

"For your sake, I hope you can."

As the two friends rode side by side, returning to town, Link thought about what Speck had just said. What would he do if the town chose up sides and Tori was on one side and he was on the other?

He decided right then he would try his damnedest to stay in the middle of this issue. After all, he might be a mine owner today, but his claims weren't active and he hadn't earned a nickel yet. He certainly wasn't investing any of his own money to sink a shaft or to hire a single miner, so why should he get involved? As soon as he could get his claims capitalized, they would belong to new owners and the length of the workday wouldn't be his problem.

"'Pack . . . my . . . box . . . with . . . five . . . dozen . . . liquor . . . jugs. Heavy . . . boxes . . . perform . . . quick . . . waltzes . . . and . . . jigs.' There, that's the last one," Tori said as she rolled the paper out of the typewriter and handed the page of pangrams to Mollie.

"I should have known typing would be a snap for you. Anyone who can memorize the way you can would have no problem looking at the keys on the machine and then remembering where they are. Just keep typing 'The quick brown fox jumps over the lazy dog,' and before you know it, you'll be a better typist than I am."

"Thank you." Tori beamed under Mollie's praise.

Just then the door opened and a youthful man came in. He had a mustache, but instead of adding a bit of panache, it made Tori think of a boy trying to look more grown-up.

"Good morning, ladies."

Tori watched Mollie swoon for this man. If Mollie were an actress in a melodrama, she could not have done any better.

"I'm pleased to meet you, Mr. Miller," Tori said when neither Mollie nor the man said anything.

Both turned to Tori with disbelieving looks on their faces.

"How did you know me? We've never met," Miller said.

Tori shrugged. "I guess . . . I guess I recognized your voice. You rang for Mollie several times and I've taken your call."

Mollie shook her head. "Don't ask, Charles. This woman has talents you wouldn't believe."

"That's amazing. Three words and you knew it was me."

"Tori, I have something I'd like to ask you to do. I've been told that there's to be a meeting at the Union Hall this afternoon. Ordinarily I wouldn't ask you to go to a place like that, but since your brother's there, I think you'll be safe. Take your tablet and write down as much as you can remember," Mollie said, then turned her attention to Charles Miller.

"Yes!" Miller said. "That will be very helpful to us."

"Good, then that's settled," Mollie said, not waiting for Tori's answer. "You can just go now. I don't want you to be late."

"What time is the meeting?"

"Oh," Mollie said. "It's at one thirty."

Tori looked at the clock that hung on the wall. It

was eleven—two and a half hours before the meeting. "All right."

Where was she going to go for that long? At first she started to go around to Link's office, but she thought better of it. The only other friend she had in town was Pearl de Vere, so she headed toward Myers Avenue.

"Tori, how good of you to stop by," Addie Fitzgerald said when Tori came through the back door. "I think I hear noises coming from upstairs, so you're just in time for breakfast."

"Wonderful." Tori took a seat on a high stool. She watched as Addie prepared each girl a plate. First a slice of bread that had been buttered and browned on a griddle pan, then a mixture of chopped beef and flour, and finally a poached egg on top.

"If you'd like to help me, carry some of these plates into the dining room. I'll have Hugh ring the bell," Addie said.

When Tori came through the swinging door from the butler's pantry, Pearl looked up and saw her.

"Tori! Have you come back to us?"

"Only for breakfast. I love my job."

"I've heard you're good."

Just then all the girls started coming down the steps, all dressed in clothing that could have been found on any other woman in Cripple Creek. None of them had on any of the garish makeup that some of the other professional women wore at all times.

When Lucy saw Tori, she hugged her. "Manny tells me you've done so much to his cabin. I can't wait to see it."

"Come anytime. I'm afraid I don't see that much of Manny and I could use the company."

"Is that right? I thought you were having company every night," Pearl said. "None of the girls have seen hide nor hair of Link Buchannan since, I don't know, long before Christmas, and we all just surmised he didn't want to see us anymore. That he was busy."

Tori laughed to cover her embarrassment. First of all, she didn't want to know that Link had been such a regular visitor, and second, they just assumed he was spending his time with her.

"He's been in Denver, but he got back yesterday."

"Then that explains it," Pearl said. "I guess Manny's been telling you about the ruckus that's brewing."

"I know a little bit about the grievances, and it sounds like both the owners and the miners have legitimate issues," Tori said.

"You've got the right attitude. Keep an open mind, but you're in a particularly bad spot."

"Why do you say that?"

"It's like straddling a creek. You've got one foot in the miners' camp and one foot in the owners' camp. Right now, it doesn't make any difference because it's only a narrow gap. But if all this talk about miners' strikes and owners' shutdowns really happens and all hell breaks loose, then that creek you're straddling is going to turn into a raging river, and you're going to have to jump to one side or the other. Do you choose your brother or your man?"

Tori didn't know how to answer Pearl. My brother or my man?

She hadn't thought of Link as *my man*, but she knew she liked the sound of it when Pearl said it. The time was going to come when the question of their relationship would be put to the test. She was going to have to tell him about her past. If he could respect Pearl, and Tori knew he did, then there was hope that he could accept her the way she was. Until then, the idea of Link's being her man would remain a pleasant fantasy.

When Link got back to town, he stabled Major at the livery under the opera house. Just as he was leaving, he saw Pearl de Vere's phaeton coming down Myers Avenue at breakneck speed. Stepping out into the street, he raised his hand, but Pearl continued. It was then that he recognized her passenger.

"Tori!" he yelled, and Tori, while holding on to her hat, waved and yelled back. "Where in the hell could those two be going?" he asked aloud.

Pearl stopped in front of the Colorado Trading and Transfer Company.

"Go find Bert Carleton, and tell him I said to give you the best price for your coal," Pearl said. "And give Bert a good look. If things don't work out for you with Link, Bert's a good man."

"Pearl," Tori said shaking her head, "you're incorrigible."

"You better listen to me. If you can't get love, it's all about money, and believe me, this man right here is going to wind up with more money than all the

prospectors who plunder the hills. You can't separate the gold from the tellurium without a reduction
plant, and you can't have a reduction plant without fuel. Now you look around you. Where's this
fuel going to come from—no trees, no nothing, and
who has a monopoly on bringing in the coal?" Pearl
pointed toward the building. "I'm telling you, Carleton's going to be rich."

"Then why aren't you going after him?"

"You didn't listen. I said if you can't get love, then
you go after the money. I've got both." A broad smile
crossed Pearl's face. "When you've got your coal
loaded, you come over here and get me."

Tori watched as Pearl, wearing the finest dress to
be found in Colorado, ran across the muddy street
to a sawmill. A man saw her coming and, hurrying toward her, embraced her, and the two shared
a long, endearing kiss. Tori looked up at the sign:
CHARLES B. FLYNN, LUMBER FOR ALL YOUR NEEDS.

Who was Pearl de Vere? A businesswoman, a
philosopher, a friend, a woman in love?

Tori shook her head as she entered the shed.

When Link and half a dozen other mine owners
reached the Union Hall at one thirty that afternoon,
David Moffat held up his hand and stopped them
just before they entered the building.

"Men, the only thing this union has over us is
solidarity. When we walk in here, we represent all
the mine owners, the rich and the poor. Now, we
agreed back at Speck's office—it's a ten-hour day
or we shut down. Is everybody still in agreement?"

There was a round of ayes, though Link said nothing.

"What about you, Buchannan? I didn't hear your response."

"David, I don't have one miner working for me. I shouldn't have a vote."

"But Speck says you control three claims out at Beaver Creek. If somebody hits a vein, then you'll need to work your claims. So can I count on you to support us?"

"I won't oppose you," Link said, not wanting to be confrontational.

"I suppose that will have to be good enough." Moffat motioned toward the front door. "Gentlemen, shall we?"

Inside the hall, several tables had been pulled together and covered with a long roll of red-checked oilcloth, giving the illusion of one long table. Chairs were arranged around the table so that the representatives of the miners were on one side and the mine owners the other. A second table held a large coffee percolator, which gave aromatic evidence that the coffee was ready to serve.

At John Calderwood's invitation the owners took their seats on one side of the table. The miners, equal in number, sat across from them. "Gentlemen, thank you for agreeing to meet with us," Calderwood said. "If you don't mind, a few more of our members want to be present for this conversation. Are there any objections to their being here?"

"We know what you're going to say. Bring them in," James Hagerman said.

"Thank you. Will the sergeant at arms open the doors?"

A man rose and opened a door toward the back of the Union Hall, and men began filing in, one behind the other, and making a serpentine line, they packed the room.

Several of the mine owners began to roll their eyes at one another, suggesting that perhaps they should leave.

Just then the front door opened, and a woman entered among all the men. Manny saw her first.

"Tori, you can't be in here!"

"Is it a closed meeting?" Tori asked.

"Well, no," Manny said, "but it's just for men."

"I have only been in the great state of Colorado for a short time, but I believe the esteemed governor, whom you, Mr. Drumm, have met personally, worked tirelessly with the women's suffrage movement, the Farmers' Alliance, and the Knights of Labor to give women their enfranchisement. Do you intend to deny me the right to be here?"

"All right, you can be here, but sit down and don't say one word."

"Thank you." Tori sat at the end, and as she stared down the table, she saw Link grinning at her with a wide supportive smile. She gave him a quick nod before taking out a tablet and a pencil.

"Now that we've settled this family spat, shall we begin again?" Calderwood asked with a smile, trying to disarm the tension. "What we want is uniformity in our wages and hours. It's not right that some of our miners earn two dollars and fifty cents a day, while others earn three dollars a day, all for the same work. Nor is it right that one man works eight hours, while another works ten, but both men get the same wage."

"Does it make any difference to you that the amount of gold that comes out of the ground varies greatly from mine to mine?" Speck asked.

"But, Speck," Manny chimed in, "you can't tell me that when Aiden Jones threw his hat in the air and staked his claim where it fell, he was a rich man. And yet the Pharmacist has paid three dollars for an eight-hour day from the very beginning. All we're asking is that all the mines adopt that same formula. If the Pharmacist can do that and make a profit, doesn't it stand to reason that the other mines can as well?"

"Like I said, not all mines are the same," Speck said.

"Of course not," Manny said. "I think I read just a few days ago where the C.O.D.—that's your mine, I believe—just paid out twenty thousand in dividends at four cents a share. Don't you think that somewhere in that twenty thousand dollars you could have found three dollars for a miner?"

"Gentlemen, gentlemen, we're not here to address specific grievances," Calderwood said. "I began this presentation by saying that we wanted uniformity in wages and hours. Now, I'm going to say we demand it, and in order to enforce that demand, let me tell you what we have planned. This union, and by that I mean these men"—he gestured to the more than two hundred men assembled—"will strike all those mines that don't conform to our demands. If the mines that have always worked eight-hour shifts will continue at three dollars, they will not be struck."

"Mr. Calderwood," Moffat said, "is this your attempt at compromise? Compromise means that we work out some arrangement where each of us gives a little in order to meet in the middle. What you've just proposed is not a compromise. To use your own words, it's a *demand*. Well, let me tell you, this group isn't like Aspen." Moffat's eyes narrowed to slits. "We'll not be intimidated by the likes of you."

"Let me make sure you understand me, Moffat," Calderwood said. "If you bastards don't accept this offer, we'll shut you down tomorrow."

"I'll save you the trouble," Moffat said. "You don't have to call your men out because tomorrow there will be a lockout. All the mines will be closed. See how effective your damned strike is then."

"You're bluffing," Calderwood said.

"Then call it," Sam Strong said. "I think our pockets are deeper than yours."

"That may be, but I have the ear of the governor."

"Do you mean Waite? The laughingstock of the country?" Lennox asked.

"I do. We have the ear of Governor Waite, and he has the ear of Samuel Gompers, who was just reelected president of the American Federation of Labor, and if that's not good enough for you, he has the ear of President Cleveland. Now, you son of a bitch, you call my bluff."

With one motion of Calderwood's hand, the sergeant at arms opened the door and the rank and file moved out, leaving the owners and Tori sitting at the table.

"Now what?" William Lennox asked.

"I think we've just run into a buzz saw," Link said as he looked toward a stunned Tori.

Link was chuckling after they returned from the meeting and he joined Speck in his office.

"What's the joke?"

"Did you see how Tori stood up for herself when she came in?" Link asked. "She's quite a girl."

"What do you think? A grand tour on the Continent? A private railcar? Or should I just invest the money?"

"What money? What are you talking about?"

"The five thousand dollars I'm going to win when you marry Tori."

Link laughed. "What's happened to Sally? I've not seen her around here for a while."

"She's been up at Florissant, but she'll be back. She's bringing down more horses to train. And anyway, Richard was in town for the holidays. I don't know why, but my brother doesn't exactly like Sally."

"So you wanted to keep them separated, huh?"

"Sometimes that's best. Say, did you hear how Manny lit into me about the dividends for the C.O.D.?" Speck asked.

"I did, but he had the numbers right, didn't he?"

"Of course. If we want to get people to invest, we have to give them a good return. Which reminds me: What are you going to do about the Strong Mine? Are you going to buy into it?"

"Sam wants me to take over a third of the mine, but that's a little more than I want to handle right now. With the news getting out that Cripple Creek has labor problems, some people may want to just hang back and wait it out," Link said.

"I'd hate to be in business with Sam. He's such a damned hothead, but then again, if the mine's got a good vein, it may be worth it. Maybe you'd better go look it over before you make up your mind to walk away from it."

"You're probably right," Link said. "Bert Carleton probably rues the day he didn't inspect the Independence when Stratton offered it to him for five hundred dollars. Now Stratton's the millionaire and Carleton's the coal man."

"Well, if you're going out anyway . . ."

"All right, I get it. What do you want me to do?"

"If you're going to the Strong, could you go over to Beaver Park and look around? I need to know if they've laid out the racetrack yet."

"Speck, they've just laid out the lots."

"I know, I know, but when Charles and I start selling Gillette, we want people to know the town's got everything a man could want. Racetracks—casinos—brothels—saloons."

Link laughed. "All the important things, right?"

"Absolutely."

"All right, I'll go, but I think I'll ask Tori to go with me."

"Are you going to take her to the Strong, too?"

"Why not?"

Speck hesitated. "If you're going to have her with you, take your pistol."

❦

Returning to his office, Link took Speck's advice, taking out the Colt .44 that he kept in the bottom drawer of his desk. Opening the guard, he spun the cylinder to satisfy himself that every chamber contained a cartridge. He slipped the pistol into his holster, then stepped next door to Mollie's office.

"Mollie, I need to hire Tori for the afternoon. Speck wants me to ride up to Beaver Park and look around, and we need a woman's eye."

"That's the perfect spot for a town. It's flat, it's got water, but most of all, it's a beautiful site," Mollie said. "Aren't your mines close to Beaver Creek?"

"My claims, Mollie. My claims. No gold."

"Yet," Mollie said. "Tori, have you had a chance to get up in the hills?"

"I came down Tenderfoot Hill when I arrived, but I really didn't have the chance to look around."

"Sort of scary in a coach, isn't it?"

Tori recalled just how frightened she was when the coach started down the steep grade. Then, even as she recalled that plummeting ride, she remembered also how she had been surprised by a kiss. The kiss had been neither intrusive nor imposing, but it did accomplish its purpose.

"Not so much. I managed to get . . . distracted," Tori said as she smiled at Link.

"Then you need to go. You can ride a horse, can't you?"

"It's been a long time, but I know how," Tori said.

As Link and Tori were preparing to go out to Gillette, Calderwood was addressing a meeting of miners, both union and nonunion:

"Just over half of you have joined the union. But I'm here to tell all of you why you should join. If you're not working an eight-hour day, we're striking that mine."

"Maybe the union is goin' to strike," one of the men said, "but like you said, that's only half of us. Speakin' for myself, I'll tell you right here and now, I ain't got no intention in hell of goin' out on strike. I got a wife an' kids to support, an' I can't be goin' for who knows how long without I have some kind of income."

"It won't make any difference whether you belong to the union or not, you won't be working," Calderwood said.

"What makes you say that?"

"Because a strike can't be effective without everyone participating in it. That means that once I call the union workers out, nobody will be allowed to work. We'll have guards on all the mines, and we'll prevent any scab from going to work."

"That ain't right!" the nonunion worker said angrily. "There ain't nothin' a'tall right about that!"

"Consider this, friend," Calderwood said. "Once the mine owners meet the demands of the union—and believe me, they will meet our demands—then everyone will benefit. Do you think it's right if you get the benefit but don't make any sacrifice?"

"Besides," Manny added, "it's likely we're going to be locked out anyway, so we'll just see who has the backbone to stick it out—us or them."

"Hell, that's easy to answer," one of the miners said. "The mine owners ain't likely to go hungry if the mines ain't workin'."

"Neither will you, if you belong to the union," Calderwood said. "Manny's been working on this since November. He's got almost twenty thousand dollars we can count on. In addition to what the members have set aside, several businesses have agreed to lend us money, and Hickey Coleman over at the Green Bee Grocery told us he won't cut off any striking man's credit. Both the unions from over in San Juan County and from Butte have offered to help us, so if we're frugal, that should keep you from starving, and if you're in a boardinghouse, most of them have agreed to let you stay for free."

"We'll take care of you if you're a member, so I'll be signing up anybody who wants to join," Manny said as he moved to a table near the door.

Two union members, R. J. Lyons and Nichols Tully, were watching those who were standing in line waiting to join.

"There ain't enough of 'em signin' up," Lyons said. "That means them scabs'll be workin' while we're strikin', and when it's all over, they get the same as we'uns. That just ain't fair."

"We need to do somethin'—somethin' so's they knows we're serious," Nichols Tully said.

"Do somethin' like what?"

"I've got me an idea, if you got the nerve to go along with it."

"Well, I reckon I got 'bout as much nerve as you do," Lyons replied.

"Good. Come with me."

ELEVEN

Oh, it's beautiful here," Tori said when they reached the town site. She took in the panoramic view of the snow-covered Rockies and then turned to look toward the distant blue hills. "It's absolutely breathtaking."

She was panting hard from the exertion. "I mean it—it literally takes my breath away."

Link laughed. "It's not the scenery, it's the altitude. The air's thinner up here."

"But it's just as high for you as it is for me, and you aren't gasping for breath."

"That's because I'm acclimated to it." Link helped Tori down from her horse. "This manly chest is the result." He teased as he pounded on his chest. "The lungs and chest really do expand and you take in more air. You just wait—it'll happen to you if you stay here for a while."

Tori grinned. "You mean I'll have a manly chest?"

Link looked pointedly at her breasts. "Oh, no. When your chest expands, there won't be anything manly about it."

Link's face was just inches away, and he hooked his finger under her chin, lifting her face so that he could look into her eyes, which now seemed to be smoldering pools of liquid. Lowering his head, he pressed his lips to hers, and more than kissing her lips, he caressed them.

The kiss was different. Tori felt light-headed—not from altitude, but from passion. When Link stopped the kiss, she wanted more, and her heart began to race. She clasped his face in her hands and drew him to her, this time brushing her mouth over his in a kiss that surely told him she was his for the taking.

Link's chest began to rise and fall.

"Are you getting acclimated?" Tori asked as she kissed him again.

"Oh, yes, I think I was acclimated the first time I saw you." He pulled her to him.

Tori became the aggressor as she moved her hips against him, feeling the bulge in his trousers, awakening in her a desire that had long been denied. She wanted to throw off her coat and make a bed right here in the open country.

"Tori," Link said barely above a whisper.

When she looked at him, he was shaking his head with longing in his eyes. "Not here, not yet." He kissed her, and when he pulled back, he ran his fingertip across her lips, causing her to tremble. "I want to take you more than you know, but it won't be on hard, frozen ground."

He kissed her again, a deep and possessive kiss, then, lifting her up, helped her back onto the side-saddle. "Let's ride."

⭒

It was still light when they reached Cripple Creek, and Tori thought they would head for the livery, but they didn't.

"Would you like to see inside a mine?" Link asked.

"Yes, I think I would." Gold mines so dominated the town, and her work, that she welcomed the opportunity to finally see one.

"It's the Strong Mine and it's up on Battle Mountain, so you're going to have a hard time breathing again." He smiled a lazy smile, and Tori returned it. "It won't take us too long, and then we can find someplace warm. Maybe it's time you came to visit my house." Link raised his eyebrows in invitation.

Tori felt a swirl of excitement in the pit of her stomach. He was asking her to his house, to a warm bed and privacy. This was what she wanted, wasn't it?

But then she felt a twinge of anxiety. She was still withholding her past from him. She had to trust that when he said, "You're mine," he would want her no matter what she might have done.

Reaching the Strong Mine, they found the shaft house was empty.

"I wish the superintendent was here," Link said, "but since he isn't, I guess we're on our own. Come on, let's go on down and have a look."

Link led Tori down into the darkened mine, which had a lingering smell of turned earth and stale air. He lit an oil-wick lantern, then grabbed a pickax.

"This is as good a place as any to start," Link said

after a walk of about five minutes. The irregular sides of the shaft reflected back a wavering golden glow from the lantern. He started chipping at the exposed vein, breaking thumbnail-size pieces of rock away from the wall. He was examining them when he stopped to listen.

"Link, someone's coming," Tori said.

"I heard it, too," Link whispered. He held his hand out toward Tori as a signal to say nothing more.

"Where are we going to plant this stuff?" one voice asked.

"Right here at the bend. We've got enough dynamite to bring down half the mountain," a second voice said. The man laughed. "It'll be a long time before any scabs set foot in this mine again."

Link extinguished his lamp. "Grab onto my coat and stay behind me," he whispered.

In the pitch-blackness, they inched forward, moving toward the sound. They didn't go far before they could see a dim, wavering orange gleam reflecting off the wall at the bend.

Tori heard Link pull his pistol and she held her breath in a welter of fear and excitement.

When they reached the bend, Link stopped, signaling that she should stay in the shadows. He looked around the corner, confident that he couldn't be seen against the darkness that was behind him. In the dim light, he saw two men tying dynamite sticks into bundles.

"Be sure you make the fuse plenty long," one of the men said. "I don't want to be in here when the roof comes crashing down."

"I've got five feet. That ought to be enough."

The men were so involved in planting the charges that Link, with pistol in hand, was able to walk up to them before they saw him.

"Boys, I don't think you want to be doing that." Link's voice was cold and calm, but it was accented by the clicking sound of the hammer of the pistol being cocked.

"What the hell are you doin' here, Buchannan?" one of the two men asked in surprise.

"Apparently I'm preventing you from blowing up this mine," Link said. "Tori? Come out here and pick up the lantern, would you?"

The two men were surprised to see a woman step out into the light.

"All right, Lyons, Tully, let's go." Link motioned toward the front of the mine with his pistol.

When they reached the entrance, Lyons and Tully started toward their horses.

"Put the dynamite back in the saddlebags," Link ordered.

The men did so, then started to mount.

"No, bring me the reins," Link said. "I'll lead them. We'll ride, you'll walk. You boys are going to jail."

"There ain't nothin' a'tall right about you makin' us walk all the way back," Tully complained.

"There's nothing right about blowing up a mine, either." Link took two ropes and looped them around Lyons's and Tully's necks.

"Hey, what if we trip and fall?" Tully complained. "We could break our necks."

"Yeah, you could, couldn't you?" Link replied
with a devious smile.

A shimmer of sunlight was bouncing off the roofs
and sides of the buildings on Bennett Avenue by
the time Link and Tori got the two sullen men back
to town. They made a strange sight with Tully and
Lyons walking at the end of a long rope while their
riderless mounts were tied behind Link's horse.

"What you got there? What's goin' on?" someone
shouted from the door of McClosky's store. "How
come you got them two men on a rope?"

Link made no reply. When they passed the Newport Saloon, Sam Strong was standing out front
conversing.

"Buchannan!" Strong shouted. "What are you
doing with my men?"

"They work for you, do they?"

"You're damn right they do, and you've got no
right to prod them down the street like a couple of
steers."

"You tell 'im, Mr. Strong," Lyons said.

"Where do you think you're takin' 'em?" Strong
asked.

"Why don't you just come along and find out?"
Link replied.

Link rode straight to the jail, where Peter Eales,
the deputy assigned to Cripple Creek, met them just
outside the door.

"What do we have here?" Deputy Eales asked.

"These are my men," Sam Strong said as he
approached. "That's Nichols Tully and this is R. J.

Lyons, and they're hardworking miners—hain't done nothin' wrong."

"If that's the case, why'd you bring 'em to me, Link?" the deputy asked.

"I was in the Strong Mine when I came across these two men."

"What was you doing in my mine?" Strong asked.

"You're wanting me to buy into it, aren't you? I like to see something before I buy it," Link replied. "And besides, you told me to look it over."

"I did, but that don't explain what you're doin' with my men."

"I caught your men planting dynamite. They were about to blow the mine."

"What?" Strong asked. "Lyons, is that true?"

"I don't know what he's talkin' about," Lyons replied.

Link stepped over to a horse belonging to one of the two men, then pulled out four bundles of dynamite, five sticks in each bundle.

"Twenty sticks of dynamite? That'd bring down half the mountain," Deputy Eales said.

Link chuckled. "Funny you would suggest that, because that's exactly what they were planning."

"We wasn't plannin' on doin' nothin' of the sort. All you got is his word on it," Tully said.

"And my word," Tori added as she stepped forward.

"You were there, ma'am?" Deputy Eales asked.

"I was."

"Then that's enough for me, boys," Eales said. "I've got a cell all ready for you."

"If this is true, you're both fired, right here and now," Strong said.

"That's just fine, 'cause this is just the beginnin' of what you rich sons of bitches have got comin' to you," Tully said with a snarl.

"In here," Eales said as, with gun in hand, he waved the two toward the door of the jail. "Link, I'll need you and the lady to come in and give me a full report."

Several days after the incident in the mine, Tori and Mollie were in Mollie's office, playing checkers.

"The miners say they are on strike, the mine owners say it isn't a strike, it's a lockout, but no matter what you call it, the mines have been shut down," Mollie said. "What does Manny say? Is there any chance of the miners ending their strike?"

"Manny has been gone so much lately that it has been a while since we have spoken about it. But I doubt the miners will end it soon."

"The mine owners aren't moving either. It's like a couple of bulls staring each other down. And the problem is it isn't just the miners who are suffering. Every business in town is beginning to feel the effect."

"To tell the truth, Mollie, I don't even know why you're keeping me on," Tori said. "There's no work to do now, and I'm just costing you money."

"Ha! A triple jump! And crown me!" Mollie placed her checker in the last row and took off the three that she had jumped.

"Oh, I'm terrible at this game. I should pay more attention."

The doorbell jangled as Link entered the office. Noticing that they were playing checkers, he stepped over to examine the board.

"Mollie seems to be winning again."

"Doesn't she always?" Tori replied.

Mollie chuckled. "That's the answer to your question, Tori. I keep you on because I like to have someone I can beat."

Tori laughed.

"Well, I have some work for Tori to do," Link said. "That is, if you'll let me have her for the rest of the day."

"Sure, go ahead," Mollie said. "And if she gets done with your work, see if you can teach her to be a little better at checkers. I enjoy beating her, but it's almost too easy."

"Oooh, Mollie, have you never learned the art of gracious victory?" Tori teased.

"I tell you what, I'll spend the rest of the afternoon working on my humility." Mollie laughed and shooed Link and Tori away.

When they stepped outside, Tori headed for Link's office.

Link caught her hand. "No, not there."

"The Tutt and Penrose Building? You've moved into your new office?"

"This morning. Come, let me show it to you."

"That's my office up there, the two windows on the left, just above the restaurant," Link said, when they reached the new building. The words TUTT AND PENROSE, 1894 were chiseled in stone across the top. He led her up to the second floor, then down a hallway to a door with letters painted on the frosted glass:

LINCOLN BUCHANNAN, MINE BROKER
TELEPHONE NUMBER 37

Just across the hallway, Tori read:

TUTT & PENROSE
REAL ESTATE, MINES, AND STOCKS
INSURANCE, LOANS, AND INVESTMENTS
TELEPHONE NUMBER 36

"I'm surprised Charles and Speck let you put your office in their building," Tori said.

"Why wouldn't they want me?"

"Don't your businesses sort of compete with one another?"

"No, not really. Speck and Charles sell mostly real estate and stocks, while I find investors for mines. So when you think about it, my business sort of supports theirs."

When Link opened the door, Tori could see that this office was much larger than his old one. "Oh my, this would be the envy of any office in New York."

The room was painted a creamy white to contrast with the large oak desk that stood in front of two book cabinets. Near the windows, a brown leather sofa and two fauteuils formed a grouping around a red Persian carpet.

"This is your desk." Link showed her to a table off to one side that had a screw chair similar to the one that was in Mollie's office.

"My desk?"

"Yes. I think I need you to work for me full-time. Try it out and see if you like it."

Tori sat down at the table and moved back and forth in the chair.

"I don't know, Link. What would you have to keep me busy?"

"Close your eyes. I have a surprise for you."

Tori thought about Link's offer. Could she work for him full-time? Yes, why not? Mollie didn't need her right now, not with the strike. And she could think of nothing more wonderful than to spend all her time with Link.

She heard the storage-closet door open and close, then Link's footsteps as he crossed the floor. She then heard him put something on the table where she was sitting.

"Open your eyes."

Tori did so, then gasped in surprise. "A typewriter?"

"Not just any typewriter. This is a Remington Standard. I'm told they are the finest made."

Tori reached out to put her fingers on the keys.

"Do you like it?"

"I love it!"

"Then type something." Link got some paper from his desk.

Tori rolled two sheets of paper around the platen and began typing so quickly the words fairly flew from her fingers.

"What in the world did you just type?" Link asked, bending down to read. "'The quick brown fox jumps over the lazy dog.'" His brows furrowed in confusion.

"It's something Mollie taught me. It uses every letter of the alphabet, so you have to hit every key."

She could feel the soft sigh of his breath on her ear as he stood behind her, and her entire body began to tingle. Tori turned to look at him and saw the hint of fire in the depth of his hazel eyes.

Link touched her face with the tips of his fingers, and that touch made her cheek erotically sensitive. He moved toward her slowly, tentatively gauging her response, ready if necessary to withdraw, but she offered no resistance. Their eyes held each other's until their breaths merged, and the proximity of their lips was such that the kiss that followed was inevitable.

If his approach had been hesitant, there was nothing cautious about the kiss that followed. It was slow, hot, and deliberate. The kiss had a definite tang, a flavor created by the joining of their lips and tongues, a taste that was unique in all the world because it could only be created by the two of them. When their lips separated, Tori stood up and Link looked at her with an expression that suggested he might be concerned that he had taken advantage of her.

But he needn't have been troubled. Eager for more, she pushed up against him, molding her body to his, feeling her breasts mash against his hard chest, feeling the bulging evidence of his own need pressing against her. Then, pulling away from him, Tori walked over to the door and locked it. That done, without speaking or even making a conscious invitation, she moved to the sofa.

Smiling broadly, almost triumphantly, Link kissed

her again, this time deepening the kiss so that their tongues tangled, tasted, and teased one another.

His lips left her mouth, only to move down her throat, and realizing what he was doing, she lifted her chin and put her hands behind his head to pull him closer. Tori was on fire, eagerly anticipating each move. Never had every square inch of her skin been so responsive; never had her breasts throbbed and hungered so to be suckled; never had that most sensitive part of her been flooded with such need. She was shuddering with excitement, dizzy with desire.

She knew it wasn't right to be this acquiescent; she should show some resistance. She made one last grasp for restraint. "We shouldn't be doing this—here—in your office."

"We shouldn't be doing this? Or we just shouldn't be doing it in my office?"

"Yes," Tori replied, without being more specific.

With a chuckle buried deep in his throat, Link eased her down onto the sofa, and she responded easily, eagerly. Then, when she was stretched out full length, he lay down with her.

"There's not enough room for both of us like this," Tori said.

"Sure there is," Link insisted, "if we lie close together."

He continued to cover her with kisses, the kisses slow as his lips moved over hers.

Then Link began to unbutton the back of her dress. When the buttons were all open, he pulled the dress down over her shoulders, and without his urging, she withdrew her arms from the sleeves, leaving her top exposed except for the camisole, which did more to display than to cover.

Link stopped and gazed into Tori's face with a look of barely contained desire.

"What is it?" she asked, concerned by his expression.

"Tori, I told you once that I don't want you to ever be disquieted by something that I might do or say. If this is such a time, if you are uncomfortable with this, please just tell me and I'll stop."

In response, Tori drew his face to hers, kissing him again.

Quickly and eagerly he untied the ribbons on the camisole, and when her breasts were free, he cupped them, looking at them with obvious appreciation. He began to rub his thumbs over her nipples, causing them to rise into hard little buds. The sensations that this sent through her body seemed unbearable, and she put her hand behind his head, pulling it down, urging him to take a nipple into his mouth.

"Which one?" he teased, looking at them as they stuck out like small fingers projecting from the tops of the perfectly formed mounds of flesh.

"Either one, just do it!" Tori said between clenched teeth.

Link's laugh was muffled as he drew a nipple into his mouth and began to suckle.

Tori couldn't understand what was happening to her. Never before in her life, not even when it was the first time and it had still been new to her, had she ever sensed anything like this. Compared to this, her previous experiences had been furtive and almost clinical. The sexual encounters had been quick, as if they had to be got over with for fear of discovery, more times than not leaving Tori unfulfilled.

She felt as if she could take no more, and she laid her head on the back of the leather sofa, her breathing coming in ragged and audible gasps.

"Shall I go on?" he asked.

"Yes, oh, please, yes!"

He lowered his head to her other breast and began the same ministration, going ever so slowly, causing her to writhe about as she thrust her breast farther up, begging him to take more of it into his mouth. He went from one breast to the other, never rushing.

By now the fluids from her most private part were flowing from her body.

Without being told, she lifted her hips, and reacting quickly to the offer, Link removed her dress and petticoat.

That left only her underwear. He carefully untied the string but didn't remove her underwear. Instead he put his hand underneath the cloth and began to knead his fingers through her mound of hair.

"Take them off, please, take them off," Tori pleaded, her voice strained with passion. She pushing her underwear down, allowing Link to pull them the rest of the way off.

Now Tori was totally naked, and she writhed under his skillful manipulations of her body, aware that more was to come, knowing it would be much more than anything she had ever before felt. She began to strain and push upward, then, grabbing his hand, she pressed it harder against herself until he eased a finger into her cavity, moving it deeper, forward and upward, feeling her convulse around him.

Suddenly eddies of pleasure began coursing through her body as wave after wave came over her, and she cried out in surprise and wonder. Link continued with his ministrations until she had ridden out the last cascading wave of pleasure, then, pulling his hand away, he put his arm around her shoulders and drew her closer to him. They sat together for a long moment without speaking as, slowly, Tori began to wind down. Then, as if just aware that she was naked, she felt the cool air of the room on her skin, and she shivered.

"Are you cold?"

"A little."

Link walked over to the storage closet and removed a blanket. Returning to the sofa, he wrapped it around her so that she was completely covered from her shoulders to her feet.

"Did you? I mean, you didn't . . ." Tori said hesitantly.

"Don't worry about me." Link planted a kiss on her lips that Tori could only think of as loving.

What had he just done? Link asked himself. This wasn't one of the girls from Myers Avenue. This was Tori Drumm, an undefiled young woman who had put herself in his care. He was responsible for her, not only for her physical safety, but also for her innocence.

Tori perceived a change in him, a separation, and she wondered why. Had he discovered that she wasn't a virgin? The probing of his finger had certainly been thorough enough.

"What's wrong? Did I do something that . . . ?"

"No, Tori, you did nothing wrong. Nothing at all."

"Link," she said in a weak and tremulous voice. "I have something I need to say."

At that moment someone tried to open the door. "Link? Link, are you in there?" It was Speck's voice.

"Yes, come on in," Link responded, knowing full well that the door was locked. Even as he was calling out to him, he was grabbing Tori's dress, underwear, and shoes.

"I can't come in, the door's locked."

"Oh, how did that happen? All right, just a minute."

Link shoved the clothes into the closet. "Keep the blanket around you," he said quietly. "I'll say I gave it to you when you got a chill."

Tori nodded, and Link went over to unlock the door.

"What are you doing with the door locked?" Speck asked.

"I don't know. Tori, did you lock the door?"

"I must have," Tori said. "I wasn't thinking."

"Oh, I didn't know you had company."

"She's not company, she's working for me." Link pointed to the typewriter.

"What's she doing all wrapped up in a blanket?"

"She took a chill. What do you need?"

"Nothing, really. I was just going to visit for a while. But I'll let you get back to"—Speck glanced over at Tori again—"whatever it was you are doing."

"I appreciate that," Link said.

"Good day to you, Miss Drumm," Speck said with a nod of his head.

"Good day, Mr. Penrose," Tori replied.

Tori was sitting here totally naked in a room with two men, one of whom knew her condition and one who didn't. It was one of the most sexually arousing sensations she had ever experienced.

TWELVE

As Tori lay in bed in her small room at Manny's cabin two weeks later, she could not get out of her mind what happened in Link's office. She had been ready to tell him all her secrets, and had Speck not arrived when he did, she would have exposed her past to him in the hope that it would do nothing to change his opinion of her.

But what exactly *was* his opinion of her? They had almost had sex that afternoon. He had been wonderfully tender and considerate of her, and his erotic caresses had lifted her to the stars. If she hadn't known before, by the time that afternoon was over, she was certain that she loved him.

But did he love her? He hadn't told her that he loved her.

She was sure that he did—he seemed to show it in every way possible—but never, not once since she had known him, had he said, "I love you."

And now Link was gone. He had left town the next day and had spent several days in Colorado

Springs. She knew he had a legitimate reason to be there, but that knowledge didn't do much to alleviate her anxiety.

One month later, several of the mine owners were gathered in the lobby of the Palace Hotel.

"This nonsense has got to stop," Will Lennox said. "Isn't there something we can do legally? When a man wants to do an honest day's work and then some union bully comes along and threatens to do bodily harm—why, that's not right."

"There is something that could be done," Link said, "but it would mean getting Judge Becker involved."

"I know Judge Becker," Ed De La Vergne said. "What's your idea?"

"The judge could issue an injunction against anyone caught interfering with those who want to work. It would force Sheriff Bowers to send in more deputies. With all that's happening, Peter Eales can't handle it by himself."

"I think that's a good idea," Speck said. "We'll do everything nice and legal."

"I'll go see the judge today," De La Vergne said. "We'll show Calderwood and his union he can't run roughshod over us and get away with it."

Before the end of that very day the injunction was issued, and Pearl de Vere stopped by Mollie's office with a broadside that one of her clients had left behind.

"Have you seen one of these?" Pearl put a piece of paper on Tori's desk.

"'By judicial order of the court of El Paso County,'" Tori read aloud, "'it is unlawful for anyone to prevent, impede, or contravene the access to the place of work of anyone who is gainfully employed by the mine and seeks entrée only to ply his avocation. Judge H. R. Becker.'"

"What does that mean?" Mollie asked.

"I hope it means the strike is over," Pearl said. "If women were in charge, we'd have had this thing over a week after it started.

"Just look what it's done to the town," Mollie said. "Businesses are closing right and left, and heaven knows no one needs a stenographer right now."

"But what's really sad is what it has done to the people," Tori said. "The men who belong to the union are getting some assistance, but think of the men who aren't union. Even the saloons don't seem to have as much business."

"You're telling me that," Pearl said. "A couple of my girls are considering moving on, and believe me, I understand. I left Denver because of what the government did to the price of silver, but Cripple Creek is ruining itself."

"I wish there was something we could do to help," Tori said.

"We ought to do something to raise money for the miners," Pearl said.

"You mean the strikers?" Tori asked.

"No, I mean all of the miners. They're all hurting, and maybe if we could think of something, they would remember what Cripple Creek was like before this all started. We have our problems, sure, but everybody used to take care of one another. Maybe we could just have a dance or something."

"Before I came here, I lived in Lake City," Mollie said. "I remember when the town needed a pumper for the volunteer fire department, and we put on a play."

"Where would we get the money to bring a troupe in here?" Pearl asked.

"No, no, the play I'm talking about was put on by the people of Lake City." Mollie laughed. "I was even in it."

"A play might be fun, but who could we get to write it? And who would take charge of it if someone could do it?" Pearl asked.

"We could do *A Young Woman's Travail*," Tori said.

Both Mollie and Pearl looked over at Tori in surprise.

"What is *A Young Woman's Travail*?" Pearl asked.

"It's a play that was on Broadway last year. And it so happens that I have a copy of the script. I could type up enough copies to give to all the people who would need one if we decided to use it."

"How many will we need?" Pearl asked.

"Fifteen should take care of it," Tori said. "That will provide scripts for the production crew, as well as extras in case one gets lost."

"Won't that be a lot of work?" Pearl asked.

"Not with our new mimeograph machine," Mollie said with a smile. "You'll only have to put it on a stencil."

"Yes, of course," Tori said. "I hadn't thought of the mimeograph."

"Are you sure you can do this?" Pearl asked.

"Not type it, but put on somebody else's play. Don't you have to pay someone before you can use their work?"

"That's true, there are stage rights," Tori said, "but generally that's done if it is a commercial production for profit. And we won't be doing that."

"Anyway, who's going to know?" Mollie asked. "I say we do it."

"I'd be willing to direct it, but we'll need to find actors and actresses to fill all the roles," Tori said.

"You'll direct it? Do know how to do that?" Mollie asked.

"Yes." Tori was so adamant in her response that neither Mollie nor Pearl challenged her.

"I think this is going to be fun," Pearl said. "Do you think I could be in it?"

"Just a minute and we'll see. I'll type out a few lines for you to read." Tori sat down at the typewriter.

"You know the lines by heart?" Pearl asked.

"Of course she would know them. Don't you remember the little memory demonstration she gave us when I hired her?"

"Why did I even ask?" Pearl shook her head.

Tori rolled paper into the typewriter and began to type. After a moment she pulled out the sheet and handed it to Pearl. "Read this. And dramatize."

"Dramatize?"

"Yes, put everything you've got into it. Really act."

Pearl cleared her throat, then began to read. "'David, do not speak to me of such things. Are you of the impression that I am a prude? Well, I have something of the moralist in me, that is true. My mother was stern to me, and she taught me the difference between right and wrong. She accorded no compromise, nor will I.'"

"Oh, my!" Mollie said. "That was very good, Pearl!"

"Mollie's right, you are good." Tori said. "I think you'll make a great Lily Fontaine. And I know who would make a perfect David Dudley."

"Who?" Pearl asked.

"Now, just who do you think?" Mollie asked, rolling her eyes. Then to Tori: "Do you think he'll do it?"

"I think I can talk him into it."

"Ha," Pearl said. "I have a feeling you can talk Link into doing just about anything."

Tori walked up the street to the Tutt and Penrose Building. When she reached Link's office, she tapped lightly and, pushing the door open, stepped inside.

Link was sitting behind his desk when she entered. Looking up, he smiled when he saw her. "Well, what a pleasant surprise."

"Link, I need your help."

"You know I'll do anything you ask."

"I'm glad you said that, because that is exactly what I told Mollie and Pearl. We're going to do something to help raise money for the miners."

"You mean the strikers?" Link said the word *strikers* with an edge.

"Yes, but not just them. We want to help all the miners. Pearl says that some of the stores may stop giving credit, and then what are they going to do?"

"That's what the mine owners are counting on."

"What? You mean you want the men to suffer? You want the whole town to suffer more than it already is?"

"I didn't say it's what I'm counting on. I said it's what the mine owners are counting on. They think if they hold out long enough, and the miners get desperate, they'll be forced to go back to work, and this whole thing will be over."

"What do you want? And don't you dare say that because you don't employ anybody, you don't have a voice. What do you want to happen?"

"I think the miners deserve a decent wage for reasonable hours," Link said. "And I certainly don't want to see them starving in the streets."

"Then does that mean we can count on you to help us with the benefit?"

"It depends on what the benefit is. What are you planning?"

"We're going to put on a play, and we've chosen *A Young Woman's Travail*. We already have the lead actress, but we need others to make up the rest of the cast."

Link smiled. "You'll do a great job. You even look like a leading lady."

"I'm not going to be in it. It will be Pearl."

"Pearl?"

"Yes. Why? Do you think that's a mistake?"

"No, I think she's a good choice. If she's the star, you'll make a lot of money. You've ridden in her open carriage, you've seen how everybody stops to look when she rides by."

"I want you to be in it."

"Whoa, not so fast there," Link said. "You want me to be in a play?"

"Yes. You just said you'd do anything to help me."

"Well, yes, but I was thinking more along the lines of . . . well, just helping out when you had something specific to do."

"I do have something specific for you to do. I want you to be in this play."

"What makes you think I could even do it?"

"Because you're intelligent, you're handsome, and, like Pearl, you're very outgoing."

Link smiled and ran his hand through his hair. "I'm a handsome man, huh? It's my streaks of gray. That's what you like, isn't it?"

Tori laughed as she handed him a sheet of paper. "Here, read this. And do it like it's something you're actually saying."

Link looked at the paper Tori handed him, then he put it down to deliver the line. "'The truth is seldom spoken without some deception, and it is often quite provocative. How very tedious life would be, if that were not so.'"

"Oh, you did that quite well. And you delivered the line without having to read it."

"It wasn't very long, so it wasn't hard to remember. But you told me to say the line as if I were speaking, and that's impossible."

"Why do you say that?"

"Who talks like that?"

"David Dudley does. And so will you when you play the role. Please tell me you'll do it. You know it's for a good cause."

"Even if I said I would, wouldn't the director have to choose me?"

"She just did."

"You? You're the director?"

"Yes. Don't you think I can do it?"

"Tori, I've learned you can do anything you put your mind to." Link chuckled. "But I hope you appreciate that I'm willing to make a fool of myself just for you."

"Oh, I do appreciate it, Link. I do."

"But I'm not going to do it by myself. Is there a role for Speck? If he's in it, too, he won't be teasing me."

"Sure, if you think he'll do it, I can find a role for him."

"I can get him to do it. And I'll also see that he gets the Grand Opera House for your venue."

"Oh, I don't think we'll be able to afford that."

"Leave it to Speck. He'll get it for free."

Tori returned to Mollie's office with the news that Link had not only agreed to act in the play but had promised to bring Speck into it as well.

"That's wonderful," Mollie said as she handed a letter to Tori. "This came today."

"Oh, good, it must be from my old neighbor." Tori took the letter and began to read.

Dear Tori,
    What a joy it is to get your post and to
know that our friendship continues, albeit
by long distance. I am thrilled to learn

*that you no longer find it necessary to
reside in a brothel, though, when next we
meet, you simply must tell me all about
it. (I've always thought I would like to do
that!)*

*I gather that there may be more than
a platonic relationship between this Mr.
Buchannan and you. If that is what you
want, then I hope it is true, and I wish you
all the best.*

*I continue to stay busy and the magazine
is back to making a profit, in spite of the
economy. I've stopped having my salons for
a while. Most of my friends, like you, my
dear, have fled the city.*

*I'm looking forward to the time when
"Sabrina" will once again make her
appearance in Gotham. She was much too
good of an actress to be gone forever. Think
about it before you put her aside completely.
We all miss her.*

*Please do take care of yourself. Your
friendship is much too dear to me.*

    Affectionately,
    Miriam

When Tori looked up from reading her letter, she
saw Mollie setting empty crates on the floor.

"What are you doing?" Tori asked.

"Moving."

"To a new office?"

"Yes. I want you to work in the back room. Get

rid of things you don't think we'll need and label everything else. Bert Carleton's men will be here in about an hour to move the furniture. Do you think you'll be finished?"

"I'll try," Tori said.

"I'll be over at Speck Penrose's office if you need me."

"All right."

Tori watched Mollie leave before she realized that she hadn't even asked where they were going. She wondered if something had come up to cause Mollie to have to move. Tori knew that Mollie's business was down, but there had been no mention of moving before now.

Tori began going through all the documents Mollie had in storage, organizing them in a way that would allow her to know where everything was when she needed it.

Tori found herself thinking about the letter she had received from Miriam—and, by extension, about herself.

Was Sabrina, or even Tori, ever going back to Gotham?

No, she had burned all the bridges that led to New York. But that didn't mean she wouldn't leave Cripple Creek. There wasn't much of a bond between Manny and her, but how could there be? They hadn't seen each other for so long, and she had done nothing to maintain a relationship. She could have written, probably should have, but never did.

If she did leave, where would she go? Chicago? Denver? San Francisco? Thanks to Mollie she would have no trouble finding employment. She was now an accomplished "typewriter," which, because of its uniqueness, was quite marketable. And with the strike and the deteriorating conditions here, why stay in Cripple Creek?

But even as she asked herself that question, she knew the answer. One thing held her here, more firmly than all other considerations. Link Buchannan.

Less than an hour later a wagon pulled up in front and two men came in.

"Mr. Carleton sent us over here to load some furniture. We're supposed to see Miss O'Bryan."

"She asked me to tell you that you may go ahead and load everything into the wagon."

"Do you know where we're goin' with this stuff?"

"No, I don't, but I expect Miss O'Bryan will be back by the time you've loaded."

Mollie wasn't back, and Tori went over to the Tutt and Penrose Building to find her. Tori heard Mollie's laughter as she walked down the second-floor hallway toward Speck's office.

"All loaded already?" Mollie asked when she saw Tori.

"Yes, the wagon is out front. Where shall I tell them to go?"

"What do you mean where to go? They're here." Mollie smiled broadly. "Come on down to the other end of the hallway and I'll show you our new office."

"Here? Our office is going to be here in the Tutt and Penrose Building?"

"Do you have a problem with that?" Speck asked.

"Oh, no. I'll like it very much."

Speck and Mollie looked at one another conspiratorially.

"We thought you would," Mollie said.

Link returned to his office late in the day. In a single-handed effort to try to find some compromise with the union, he had met with every mine owner in town and had even called several in Colorado Springs. Only Winfield Stratton and Jimmie Burns had agreed to his proposal.

Tired and discouraged, he sat on the sofa and, leaning his head back, closed his eyes. What did one have to do to stop all this before an actual labor war broke out?

"Are you taking a nap?"

The words were softly spoken, but Link instantly recognized the voice. Opening his eyes, he saw Tori standing in the open door.

Link smiled but didn't raise his head. "No, no, please, come in; I was just sitting here, feeling sorry for myself."

"Feeling sorry for yourself? Why?"

"I guess I'm not much of a negotiator. I only got two owners who are willing to even offer a compromise."

"I'm sorry. At least you tried."

Link chuckled. "I tried?"

"Yes."

"What if something had come up, and Paul Revere hadn't been able to warn the Americans that the British were coming—that all he did was try? Do you think Longfellow would have written a poem about him? What kind of poem do you think it would have been?

"'Listen, my children, and you shall hear of Paul Revere's midnight ride. His horse lost a shoe, and he knew not what to do, but at least he tried.'"

Tori laughed out loud. "Link, that's awful! Don't ever try to write your own poetry."

"What if I'm that bad as an actor for your play?"

"You won't be because I'm going to teach you, and now we'll be seeing each other even more."

"How's that going to happen?"

"Come with me." She took Link's hand and pulled until he stood.

"Where are we going?"

"You'll see."

When they stepped into the hall, a sign painter was putting the finishing touches on the frosted-glass door at the back of the building.

Link read, "'Mary E. O'Bryan, Stenographer. Victoria Drumm, Typewriter.' Did you know you were moving here and you didn't tell me?"

"No, I had no idea. I just found out when we got here, but I'm glad." Tori opened the door and they walked in.

The room was filled with the crates Tori had packed, and Link helped move them out of the way while Mollie directed the placement of the furniture. At last she had the office arranged the way she wanted.

"Tori, while Link is here to help you put the rest of the stuff away, I think I'm going to go now. Don't stay too long, and don't work too hard. Oh, and here's your key. Good night," Mollie said, and left.

"That was nice of Mollie," Link said.

"You mean giving me a key?"

"No, I mean leaving us alone. Do you think her sofa is as comfortable as mine?"

Tori giggled when she thought about what had happened in Link's office. "Mollie doesn't have a blanket."

"But I do, and my office is just down the hall. Why don't you lock up and let's go down there?"

As soon as they stepped into Link's office, he took Tori in his arms and kissed her. She wrapped her arms around him and was prepared for more, then Link started moving them toward the couch.

Just then they heard the unmistakable click of Speck's riding boots marching down the hall.

Link broke off the kiss and moved to his chair.

"Link?" Speck called before he opened the door without knocking. "Tori. I thought I'd find you here. Welcome to the building, and I hope you'll not find it too chilly. I'm thinking I'll provide blankets for every office, just in case."

Tori's face flushed, but she didn't avert her gaze. "That would be nice."

"What have you got there?" Link asked, seeing that Speck was carrying a bottle of wine and two goblets.

"Romanée-Conti, the oldest and perhaps the finest wine in the world. But no expense is too great for my friends." Speck placed the glasses on Link's desk and poured the wine.

"Oh, my goodness," Tori said. "That has to be very expensive."

"It is, and if I've played my cards right, it will cost your friend here five thousand dollars."

"What?" Tori gasped.

Link's face split into a wide smile, then he lifted the wine and held the glass toward Speck in a toast. "And it will be worth every penny."

"Ha! I knew it!" Speck said. "Yes, sir, I knew it! No more talk about the Amazon now, huh?" He laughed out loud, then left the office.

"Link, what in the world was that all about?"

"It was just Speck being Speck."

Tori wasn't sure what had just happened, but she had a feeling it had something to do with Link and her. And she was pleased.

THIRTEEN

In the newspaper a few days later the citizens of Cripple Creek saw, prominently displayed on the first page and in between all the stories of the strike, an announcement of an upcoming theatrical production.

CALL FOR LOCAL THESPIANS

A Young Woman's Travail is to be produced in Cripple Creek in the near future. The play enjoyed a long and most successful run in New York last year. Proceeds from the play will be distributed to the most needy of our citizens, the wives and children of the miners who are now unemployed because of the strike.

Organizers say that they will use only local talent for the actors and company. All who are interested in auditioning for the play are asked to present themselves for such a purpose at the Grand Opera House at seven o'clock of the

*evening next Wednesday. There, readings will
be conducted in order that the players may be
selected, and rehearsals begun.*

The nine cast members consisted of four men and
five women. Tori was pleased to see that the casting
call was well received, as many more than she would
actually need showed up. One of the women was
considerably taller than the others and big busted.
Tori smiled as she thought of how Miriam Leslie
would refer to her. "Statuesque," Miriam would say.

"Well, I see the Amazon is here," Link said under
his breath.

"The Amazon?"

"The tall lady is Sally Halthusen. Her father owns
a horse ranch near here, and Sally breaks and sells
horses. She also has her cap set for Speck."

"Oh! That's what he meant when he said no more
talk of the Amazon, isn't it? I wondered what that
was about. Well, she's quite an attractive woman,"
Tori said. "I'm sure Speck thinks so as well."

"He is somewhat taken with her," Link agreed.
"But I don't think it's going anywhere. Speck's father
doesn't approve of her, and for all Speck's bravado,
he has never quite declared his independence from
Dr. Penrose."

In addition to Sally Halthusen, Lucy Dawes, Pearl
de Vere, and Mollie O'Bryan were there, as well as
six other young women, nearly all of whom worked
on Myers Avenue.

Grant Crumley, proprietor of the Newport
Saloon, had come for a part, as had Peter Eales.

The remaining male aspirants were all unemployed miners.

"Ladies and gentlemen, I thank you so much for coming. Miss Dawes, if you would, read Julie's first line."

The young woman looked at the script, then read, "'Oh, these are such lovely flowers. Miss Fontaine does keep a beautiful garden.'"

"Read it again, but pretend that you are watering a garden," Tori said. "You will have to get used to reading and acting at the same time."

Peter Eales, the deputy sheriff, was the next to read. "'Think not that you can act with im . . . impu . . .'"

"Impunity," Tori said.

"Well, I ain't never heard that word. What does it mean?"

"Acting with impunity means acting without fear of punishment."

After listening to all of them, Tori selected the cast. In addition to Pearl, she chose Sally, Lucy, Mollie, and Maxine for the women's roles. Link, Speck, Peter Eales, and George Campbell filled out the four men's parts.

George, Tori realized with a smile, was the disembodied voice she had heard calling Maxine a "sweet girl" on Tori's first night in Cripple Creek.

"I'll walk you home," Link offered, after the play was cast.

"You don't have to."

"I want to. Besides, you live only a block and a half from my house."

It was cold, but not bitterly so, as they walked.

From behind them they could hear the discordant jangle of a couple of saloon pianos.

"So your father is a preacher?" Link asked.

The question was completely unexpected, and Tori looked over at him. "Do you mean you still remember that? That was a long time ago."

"I don't forget things about you, Tori. And seeing the church reminded me."

"Yes, he is a preacher all right, but the church has nothing to do with it."

"What do you mean? How can a church have nothing to do with a preacher?"

"My father is a preacher without a church. He travels around giving his sermons in what he calls a tent cathedral."

"Oh, like a revival," Link said with a smile.

"Not exactly. My father . . ." Tori paused, then took a deep breath. "My father is convinced that he has been chosen by God as his personal vindicator, charged with rooting out sinners everywhere. And when I was twelve years old and made the mistake of holding hands with a boy, I became one of those sinners. He sent me off to New York to live with my aunt and uncle."

"How did your aunt and uncle treat you?"

"They had no children, so they treated me as if I were their own. I had a good life with them."

"I'm glad that you did. But I'm more glad that you are here now."

"Yes. I am here now."

"Tori, there is something I have been wanting to ask you, and given the way our . . . relationship . . . is progressing, it's something I need to ask."

Tori grew tense as she anticipated the question.

"Are you married? Are you running away from a husband?"

Tori laughed in relief. "No. I'm not married, nor have I ever been married. Why did you ask if I'm running away from a husband?"

Link smiled broadly, then reached out to put his arm around her shoulders, pulling her a bit closer to him. "That's good. That's very good. I don't relish the thought of running into a jealous husband waving a gun."

"Good point."

When they reached the house, they found it dark.

"Looks like Manny isn't home," Link said.

"He's been working long hours ever since the strike started. Thanks for walking me home."

"I would feel better if you would let me see you safely inside."

"That's not necessary."

"I don't want to scare you, Tori, but Manny's right in the middle of all this, and there might be someone out to get him."

"Oh. I hadn't thought of that."

"So, if you don't mind, I would feel better if you would let me come inside, just to check things out."

"All right."

Link went inside with Tori and, turning on the lights, examined the house to make certain no one was there.

"It seems to be all clear," he said, coming back after checking the bedroom. They were standing together when the front door opened, surprising both of them.

Stepping inside, Manny challenged, "What are you doing in my house?"

"He walked me home, then he saw me safely inside," Tori said.

"Oh," Manny said. "Yes, that's probably a good idea. Thanks."

"I was glad to do it."

The three stood in awkward silence for a moment, then Link said, "Well, I guess I had better go. Good night."

Tori watched Link leave, wishing that her brother hadn't shown up when he did. She wanted to kiss Link good-night, but knew that she couldn't do that in front of Manny. On the other hand, what if a simple good-night kiss had developed into something more and Manny had come home a few minutes later? That considered, she decided it was probably a good thing her brother had arrived when he did.

"Sis, about Link Buchannan," Manny said hesitantly.

"About Link? What about him?"

"Is there anything going on between you two?"

"Well, we work together. Why are you asking?"

"I'm asking because you're my sister and I feel responsible for you. I think you should know that Link Buchannan has quite a reputation. He and his friend Penrose are two of the biggest womanizers in town. I don't want you to get mixed up with him, that's all."

Tori smiled at her brother. "Manny, I appreciate your concern, but I've been looking out for myself for some time now. I know how to avoid getting hurt." Thanks to Lyle Ketterman, she thought.

"Oh, by the way, this will be my last night here for a while," Manny said.

"Where are you going?"

"Altman. Right now, that seems to be the center of everything, and I'm moving up there first thing in the morning. I hope you'll be all right staying by yourself here in the house."

"I'll be fine. But I'm a little worried about you. Please be careful, Manny. We've just found each other again, and I wouldn't want to see something happen to my little brother."

"I'll be careful," Manny promised.

"If you'd like, I'll fix breakfast for you in the morning?"

"I appreciate that, but I'll be gone before you even wake up."

For the first month after the move into the new office, Mollie did less and less business, and Tori wondered how Mollie could afford to keep her. Then Link began providing more and more work to Mollie, and he replaced the typewriter table with another desk, which he brought in exclusively for Tori's use. He explained that his load had actually increased because he had to work harder than ever to try to move mines that weren't producing.

Tori wasn't entirely convinced that was the case. She believed he was helping Mollie by providing her with business. But such an arrangement also meant that she and Link were spending more time together, and she enjoyed that.

Link had gone to Colorado Springs again, and he asked Tori if she would take care of his office while he was away. There were no telephone calls, nor people coming by, so she had to look for things to do. She set up a filing system for Link's properties and was surprised to see that he held positions in almost two hundred claims, most of which were purely speculative. When that task was finished, she drew a chart of the stage of the Grand Opera House and began working out blocking for *A Young Woman's Travail*.

When she was finished, she thought she would write a letter to Miriam, but instead of using pen and ink, she decided to show off her newfound skill and type the letter. She smiled when she thought of Miriam's reaction.

> *Dear Mrs. Leslie,*
> *Much has happened since last I wrote. As the miners were threatening, they now have gone out on strike, and that is taking its toll on Cripple Creek. My boss is barely hanging on to her business, but my friend Link Buchannan has come to her rescue, so to speak. I work most of the time for him right now, but I believe he is just finding jobs for me. (I don't mind, because I do enjoy his company.)*
> *In your letter you asked if "Sabrina" would ever make another appearance in Gotham. Right now, my answer is an unequivocal no, but here in Cripple Creek, she is making a comeback—not as an actress, but as a director! We are putting on*

A Young Woman's Travail *to raise money to give to the miners who are out of work while the strike is on. Wouldn't Bob Walker throw a tantrum if he knew an amateur could take over his position?*

The rehearsals are going well. Pearl de Vere, the "madam" at whose brothel I stayed, is playing the role of Lily Fontaine, and she is doing a remarkable job. You would like Pearl. She is a personable woman who has a good head for business. Her "house" is the envy of all the other houses in town. Listen to me—I sound as if I know all the madams personally, but I get my information from Link and his friend Spenser Penrose.

And that brings me to the role of David Dudley. Yes, the leading male role will be played by Link. I had to twist his arm a bit, but at last he agreed.

I'm glad he will be kissing my friend Pearl because I think I might be jealous if he were kissing anyone else.

Does that seem strange that I'm not jealous of her? She is indeed a paradox. Not long ago she introduced me to a man—not a man of means, mind you, but a man who runs a sawmill. She told me how much she loves him and that she plans to marry him.

I must say that, for the first time in my life, I'm beginning to think about what it would be like to be married. No one has mentioned this, but if someone ever did,

*I need to know how I feel about it. I'm
counting on you with all your experiences to
offer your advice.*

I look forward to hearing from you.
As always, your friend,
Tori

At the next rehearsal, Tori was pleased with the progress. Most of the actors were learning their lines, and the stage crew was building sets that, while not up to New York standards, were adequate for an amateur production.

Maxine, who had the role of Julie, walked to the front corner of the stage and began dusting a table. She spoke her lines directly to Tori.

"How is it that Simon McGraw thinks he can win Miss Fontaine's hand by such evil threats? Does he not know that honey can ensnare more flies than vinegar?"

"No, Maxine, never break the fourth wall," Tori called from her position in front of the stage.

Maxine had a confused look on her face. "What did you say? I didn't break anything, Tori."

"You did." Tori moved toward the stage. "When our sets are in place, you will have a wall here, here, and here." Tori motioned with her hand parallel to the front of the stage. "But as you can see, there's nothing here but the front of the stage—that part that is between you and the audience. That is called the fourth wall. The audience suspends all reality except for what they see on the stage. If you look toward the audience—if you acknowledge their presence, like you just did with me—that's called breaking the fourth wall, and it destroys their perception of reality."

"Oh," Maxine said with a smile. "I see that now."

"All right, do it again, take it from when you come over to dust the table."

As Tori continued to put the cast through their paces, she realized two things: one, that she missed the theater, and two, this production, even though it was local, satisfied that need. She thought about instructing Maxine and the others and realized how rewarding it would be to actually teach drama.

Play rehearsal continued until almost midnight, when Speck pointed out the time to her.

"I want you to know that never in my life have I been up this late without a drink in my hand," Speck said.

"Oh, heavens," Tori replied, checking the watch that lay beside her. "I'm sorry. I had no idea it was getting so late. Can everyone meet tomorrow night at seven?"

All agreed that they could, and with an exchange of good-byes, they left the theater.

Bundled up against the night air, Link and Tori walked down the stairs of the opera house, past the livery, and out onto the street. Normally, at this time of night, Myers Avenue would be filled with activity. Tonight it was uncharacteristically quiet and dark.

"Did Manny go with the others up to Altman?" Link asked.

"Yes," Tori said, letting out a long sigh. "I wish I could understand what all of this is about."

"The rumor is that, because Bull Hill overlooks Altman and tops several important mines, it will be the easiest place for the miners to defend."

"Do you think it will actually come to a showdown?"

"I hope not," Link said. "But on the other hand, just look around us. Who would have thought the saloons and even the cribs would be shut down?"

"Pearl said she doesn't think Mindy's coming back. She had a baby, and she's decided to stay in New Orleans with her family, and now Nell has left for Cincinnati. She says she's going to try to get a job on a riverboat."

"I don't understand the miners. There's unemployment all over the country, but here they were offered a nine-hour day, and they turned it down. When they give up women and whiskey, I guess the strike really is about principle."

"That's what Manny says."

"What does he think about you doing this play?"

"As far as I know, he doesn't even know I'm doing it. He would probably think all the money should go just to the union, but Pearl and Mollie are adamant that it go to anyone who needs it, and I agree. I just hope we make enough to do some good."

"I believe you are going to do quite well."

"Why do you say that?"

"Because Winfield Stratton has practically bought out the house and is passing tickets out all over town. Think about it, Tori. How long has it been since there has been anything to offer the slightest bit of entertainment? Because of the situation there has been nothing here since January, and it's all doom and gloom. This town is desperately in need of some diversion."

"That, I believe, we can give them. I'm really pleased with how well everyone is doing."

"Tori, how is it that you know so much about the theater?"

"What do you mean?"

"You obviously know your way around. You're very comfortable giving directions, and some of the terms you use—*blocking, downstage left, upstage right*—and all this business tonight about the 'fourth wall.' How do you know all that?"

Tori let out a big sigh. "I told you I lived in New York. My uncle owned a theater, and I worked in and around it for fourteen years."

Link chuckled. "That would explain things."

Tori was relieved that her explanation was enough for him.

When they reached Manny's street, somewhere in the distance they heard a baby crying.

"It seems strange, hearing a baby. We're so caught up in all the talk of strikes and the chaos it brings, it's hard to think about people living normal lives," Tori said.

"I would agree with you, but is there such a thing as normal in a place like this? We all know the gold can't last forever, so everybody's trying to take what they can get while they can get it. That's me, Speck, Manny, Calderwood—the whole bunch. Someday, we'll all be gone from here."

"I don't want to think about that. I've only been here a short time, and yet the friends I've made are some of the best I've ever had. You, Mollie, Pearl, even Speck. I've never had such genuine friends."

Reaching Manny's house a few minutes later, Tori unlocked the door, then Link went inside, turned on the light, and brought her in.

"It's chilly in here," Tori said.

"I'll light the fire."

When the kindling took hold, Link joined Tori on the sofa. Soon the room, and then the entire house, was comfortably warm.

"How would you like a cup of hot chocolate?" Tori asked.

"That would taste good."

As Tori began to make the hot chocolate, she could almost hear her father's voice. *Satan uses chocolate to reach children the way he uses whiskey to reach adults. It is decadence.*

Now the idea of sharing a cup of hot chocolate with this man, late at night with just the two of them, elevated the occasion from one of pleasure to an outright sensual experience.

"Link, when we were walking home, you asked me how I knew so much about the theater. My answer was true, as far as it went, but I feel that I must tell you the whole truth. My uncle does own a theater, but it's more than that. I am also, or perhaps I should say I was, an actress on Broadway. My professional name was Sabrina Chadwick, and I was quite successful. Then last year I made a fool of myself by walking offstage in the middle of a performance."

"There must have been a compelling reason for

you to do something like that." Link's voice was
gentle and unchallenging.

"There was. Or at least, I thought so. I had been
betrayed by the man I was having an affair with."

Tori stopped talking, waiting for a response from
Link, but the only response he gave was to lean over
and kiss her lightly on the lips.

"Any man who would betray you is a fool."

"I'm not a virgin, Link."

"I love you, Tori."

The words brought tears to her eyes. "It doesn't
bother you than I'm not a virgin?"

"Does it bother you that I'm not a virgin?"

"No, of course not."

"Then why should it bother me?"

Link rose from the table and pulled her to him,
wrapping his arms around her, holding her ten-
derly. She leaned against him until she felt the tension leave her. The barrier that she had thought was
between them, that she had erected, was gone.

"Link?"

"Yes?"

"I love you. You don't know how long I have
wanted to say those words, how afraid I was to say
them."

"Are you still afraid?"

"No, not anymore."

Tori lifted her head and he kissed her again, deepening the embrace as he pulled her more tightly
against him. Then, gently, he tugged her head back
to break the kiss. She stared up at him with eyes
filled with wonder and as deep as her soul. Her lips
were still parted from the kiss.

Lifting her in his strong arms, he carried her the short distance to the bedroom, then lowered her gently to the mattress. As Tori lay there, she stared up at him with eyes that were hazy beneath half-lowered lashes. Her breasts rose and fell with each breath she took, and her skin was flushed. Her tongue darted out to lick her lips, leaving them shining.

Link kissed her, teasing her lower lip with his teeth until a little moan of ecstasy sounded deep in her throat. Tori had never before been so intensely aroused, and she could tell—not only by the way Link was examining her, but also by the fire gleaming in his eyes—that his ardor fully matched her own.

She felt him trace her eyebrows, then the lines of her mouth, until finally his hand moved lower, and his fingers dipped into the hollow of her collarbone. She knew that he could feel her pulse there, beating as rapidly as the wings of a hummingbird.

Not content to be only the recipient, Tori reached up to his shirt, then began unfastening it, button by button, until it hung open. She pushed it off his shoulders, then he shrugged out of it and dropped it on the floor by the bed. He took her hand and pressed her palm against his bare chest. She needed no further guidance as she slid her fingers down the length of his torso in a light erotic glide. She felt his stomach tighten as her fingers came to rest just above his belt line.

She began to explore him, stroking over the tight muscles of his belly, pleased with herself when she heard him groan. Next, she undid the belt buckle, then started opening the buttons of his trousers.

"Wait," he said, and for a moment she thought he was going to stop, but all he did was remove his boots and socks. With those out of the way, it was easy enough for him to slip out of his trousers, then his drawers, and she was rewarded with the sight of his perfect symmetry: broad shoulders, expansive chest, powerful arms, ribbed abdomen, and the symbol of his manhood, thrusting potently toward her.

Tori sat up on the bed, then turned her back to him so he could unbutton her dress. She sat there quietly, enjoying the sensation of being undressed by him. The only help she offered was in turning her body or lifting as necessary until finally she lay back on the bed as naked as he.

Again they kissed, and she breathed the scent of him as she felt his hand trail across her smooth skin. There was no wonder or mystery in this kiss; it was a kiss shared by lovers who knew what they wanted and were anxious to give what they could.

Now Tori grew bolder as she sent her hand on an exploratory journey, down across his hard, muscled body until she wrapped her fingers around that most male part of him, a huge thing that seemed to throb with a pulse of its own. She had thought she couldn't be surprised—after all, she had been here before—but she hadn't expected anything of this heat and size.

Link continued to kiss her and move his hands over her body, stoking the flames. Tori could easily believe that she was putting out as much heat as the little coal stove in the other room. She knew that this was the moment she had been looking for and fantasizing about for several weeks now. She knew that this time there would be no holding back, no interruption. This time they would complete what had, until now, only been promised.

Tori began moving on the bed, repositioning herself in a way that would tell Link that not only she was ready but she was eager for him. Link moved over her then, and Tori experienced a flood of sensation as she felt him slide in through her moist cleft. He started to move his hips again, pulling out, pushing in, his breathing coming in audible gasps.

She had thought she was experienced, but she might as well have been a virgin compared to what she was feeling now. She clung to him as he worked his magic inside her, thrusting up with her hips to match his pace.

Link was giving her what she needed, but more than that, he was giving her what she craved but dared not ask for. His tongue, both gentle and demanding, hesitant and aggressive, dipped in and out of her mouth, matching the thrust and withdrawal of his shaft. There was nothing in her past she could call upon to measure what she was feeling; it was if she were caught in an ice storm while, at the same time, being consumed by flames.

The strokes grew stronger, faster, and her reaction to them started a maelstrom of sensations deep inside. These grew, heightened, then spun out of control, bursting through her like a simultaneous bolt of lightning and a booming thunderclap.

Never before had she experienced a climax like that one, and even as the shuddering release of the first one passed, another one rose up from somewhere deep, deep inside.

Link had come to the edge many times but through sheer willpower had pulled himself back, delaying it, not only to enable him to hang on to the intense, almost excruciating sensation, but to allow Tori to experience all that she could. Then, feeling her moist chamber clutching at him, throbbing and massaging that part that connected him to her, he let himself go, groaning in ecstasy as he emptied himself. Then, totally satiated, he pulled out and cradled her head on his shoulder, his arm wrapped around her, feeling the heat gradually receding from both of them.

In her mind's eye, Tori could see a feather slowly drifting down, only to meet an updraft that would cause the feather to rise a bit before resuming its slow descent.

Afterward they lay together on the bed, Link on his back and Tori on her side, propping herself up on one elbow, looking down at him. Her breasts swung like pendulums, and a nipple trailed across the muscle on Link's forearm, sending tiny currents of pleasure coursing through her. She ran her hand lightly across his chest, curling his chest hair around the ends of her fingers.

"Tori, do you mind if I stay here? I think I would like to feel you beside me all night long."

Tori draped her leg over his. "You just try and get away." She put her head on Link's shoulder and he wrapped his arm around her.

They were silent for a long while, and Tori thought Link had gone to sleep.

"Tori?"

"Yes."

"I love you."

"I love you, too, Link. I love you so much it frightens me."

FOURTEEN

When Tori went to work the next day, she could hardly contain her smile.

"What happened?" Mollie asked.

"What do you mean, what happened?"

"I don't know . . .there's something different about you this morning. And if I had to guess, I would say it has to do with Link."

"Oh, really?" Tori laughed.

"I picked up a letter for you at the post office this morning. It's over there on your desk."

When Tori saw the envelope and recognized the neat penmanship, she smiled.

Dear Tori,

I was quite pleased to hear about your latest endeavor, and how exciting that you are directing A Young Woman's Travail. *I would say that I hope it is going well, but I have no doubt but that it is.*

You asked me for a few words of guidance

about marriage. Given my experience, I hardly feel qualified to advise you, other than to say don't be frightened of love because some previous experience may have turned out badly. What if, after two failed marriages, I had not chosen to marry Mr. Leslie, rest his soul? How different my life would have been. All I can say is go where your heart leads you. You will know when it is right. By the way, my divorce from Mr. Wilde is now final.

Continuing along that line, I have a bit of gossip that may be of interest to you. I feel I am not speaking out of turn, as the decree has been published in the Times. *Bella Chase has filed for a bill of divorcement from Lyle Ketterman. The scuttlebutt is that when Bella left, so did the Chase money. It appears that Lyle is most distraught, though whether because he has lost Bella or whether because he has lost her money is left to the imagination.*

A Young Woman's Travail *has shuttered on Broadway, and Lyle, in an attempt to be relevant, has taken the show on the road. It is said that it has played before nearly empty theaters in Louisville and St. Louis.*

I am happy to report, though, that your uncle has not been hurt by the closing of the play. Time to Go, *which had a successful run at the Empire, has now moved to the Freeman, where it continues its success.*

*Do keep corresponding; I love hearing
from you and look forward to that happy
occasion when we will meet again. And
perhaps you will introduce me to your Mr.
Buchannan.
     Your dear friend,
     Miriam*

Tori frowned at the news. Six months ago Lyle's
impending divorce would have been welcomed.
Now she was totally indifferent to it.

"Bad news in the letter?" Mollie asked, noticing
Tori's change of expression.

"No, just news. I wouldn't say it's bad."

"I'm to go see Addie for a fitting this afternoon,"
Mollie said. "I can't wait to see what she designs
for me."

"Yes, Mrs. Fitzgerald did an outstanding job with
Pearl's costumes. She is so talented."

"Do you think we'll be ready in time?"

"I'm certain we will."

At the other end of the building Link was in
Spec's office when the telephone rang and Speck
answered it.

"You don't say. No, I hadn't heard about it. Thanks
for telling me."

"What is it?" Link asked.

"Sheriff Bowers got a phone call from the
superintendent of the Victor Mine. It seems that
a gang of Altman miners are about to destroy the
Victor."

"Is Bowers going to do anything about it?"

"He's sent out six armed deputies. But, and get this, Peter is leading the group."

"Peter? Peter Eales?"

"Yes. I wish he had sent someone else. What happens to our play if something happens to Eales?" Speck asked.

"Damn, Speck, I would hope you would be more concerned with what happens to Eales than you are with what would happen to the play!"

"Well, yes, I'm worried about him, too."

Of the six men in the wagon who'd responded to Charles Keith's call, only Peter Eales was a permanent deputy. All the others had temporarily been deputized for this special purpose.

Just after sundown the horses strained to pull the wagon up the steep grade of Bull Hill, and it lurched and jerked from side to side through the deep ruts and over the rocks. As the wagon passed through a ravine with a thick growth of bushes on both sides, several men suddenly emerged from the shadows.

"Hold it! Stop the team! Put up your hands!" a voice called out to them.

"What the hell?" one of the deputies shouted. He fired into the darkness and one of the men returned fire.

"Ahhh! I'm hit! I'm hit!" another deputy called out in pain.

"Throw down your guns!" one of the assailants called.

"Better do it, boys," Eales said. "They've got us outnumbered, and we're sitting ducks in this wagon."

The deputies all tossed their guns out, and the ambushers moved toward them.

"Landry, what are you doing here?" Eales asked. "You just can't stay out of trouble, can you?"

"I might've known it would be you, Eales," Landry replied. "How about you boys climbin' on down from up there?"

"Landry, you got no right to be stoppin' us like this. We're officers of the law, come to protect the Victor Mine."

"So are we," Landry replied, "and any protection the Victor Mine needs, the Altman police will provide, not a bunch of El Paso County deputies."

"Well, even if you are Altman police, you've got no jurisdiction out here. You're in the county, and I'm the county law."

"Ain't you heard? This ain't El Paso County anymore. We seceded and now we're the Independent Kingdom of Bull Hill," Landry said. "Tie 'em up."

"What do you think you're going to do with us?" Eales asked.

"In my mind, you've come to make trouble, so we're going to treat you like we would any other bunch of outlaws."

"My God, you ain't a'goin to hang us, are you?" one of the other deputies asked, his voice cracking with fear.

"Not unless we have to," Landry sneered. "Right

now, we're marchin' you into town, where our authorities will deal with you."

"What are you sayin'?" Eales asked. "We aren't outlaws! We are the law. I've been the deputy sheriff in Cripple Creek for more'n a year now."

"I know that. Don't you think I remember when you wasn't nothin' but a down-on-your-luck prospector? Now you're a down-on-your-luck deputy, but you ain't our law. Mayor Dean and Marshal Daly are our law." Landry chuckled. "Daly got word that you men was comin' up here. That's how come we was able to be out here, waitin' on you. Come on, now, let's get into town."

"I need a doctor," one of the deputies said. "I got a ball in the shoulder."

"I'm sure Mayor Dean'll get somebody to take just real good care of you," Landry said.

"You'll see," Eales said. "As soon as we get to town, your marshal or whoever's in charge will let us go, and I'd say it's more'n likely you boys will be in big trouble."

Sheriff Bowers had just gone to bed when he got another telephone call from Charles Keith, the superintendent out at the Victor.

"What do you mean, callin' me in the middle of the night like this?" Bowers grumbled, clearly showing his irritation.

"They took 'em, Sheriff. They shot one of 'em, and they took the rest," Keith replied.

"Who took who?"

"A bunch of them miners that was here to cause

trouble, that's who. They say they've been deputized by Marshal Daly in Altman. I think that's where they took 'em."

"Who was shot? One of my deputies?"

"Yes. I don't know which one, and I don't know how bad he's been shot neither. You better come quick, Sheriff. There ain't no tellin' what's goin' to happen next."

Play rehearsal was just coming to an end when Jimmie Burns burst through the doors. "I hate to barge in, folks, but we've got us an emergency on our hands."

Link moved toward the front of the stage. "What's happened, Jimmie?"

"Sheriff Bowers sent some deputies out to guard the Victor, and on the way they were ambushed. Some of 'em was shot, and the rest was captured."

"Shot? Was anybody killed?" Link asked.

Burns shook his head. "I don't know. All Charley Keith reported was that some of 'em was shot. Now Sheriff Bowers is deputizin' near 'bout ever' man in town. Go get mounted and get yourself armed. We're all meetin' in front of the jail within half an hour."

"Meeting to do what?" Speck asked.

"As far as I know, we're formin' a posse. I've got to go spread the word. You men get to the jail as quick as you can."

Link jumped down from the stage and walked over to Tori.

"You don't suppose Manny is involved, do you?" she asked, clearly agitated by the news.

"I doubt it," Link said. "More than likely it's nothing but a bunch of hotheads. And we both know Manny's not a hothead."

"Burns said some of the deputies were shot. Let's hope Peter is all right."

"I hope so, too, but we'll just have to wait and see."

"Do you think you'll be deputized?"

"I expect I will. If Sheriff Bowers thinks he needs a large show of force, I intend to be a part of it."

Link watched the play of emotions cross Tori's face, and he took her in his arms, giving her a reassuring hug. "Don't worry, they're not going to do anything—at least not tonight."

"Link," Tori said, her eyes dark and liquid, "I meant what I said last night."

"I know. That's why I know I'm coming home."

"I wish I could be as sure," Tori said, Link's confidence comforting her.

When Link and the others got to the jail, at least thirty men were already assembled, and more were arriving. About three dozen saddled horses stood at the hitching rail.

"Gentlemen, fall into some sort of group and hold up your right hand so I can swear you in as deputies," Sheriff Bowers said. "Once that's over with, those of you that's not mounted, find one of these horses you're comfortable on."

"Where are we a'goin', Sheriff?" one of the men asked.

"We're goin' up to Altman and get my deputies back."

Just as Sheriff Bowers's posse was about to get mounted, someone saw a wagon coming down Bennett Avenue.

"Sheriff, ain't them the deputies we're supposed to be rescuin'?"

The driver of the wagon, seeing all the assembled men, urged the team into a fast trot, and the wagon pulled up in front of the sheriff.

"What happened?" Eales asked.

"You tell me. We heard you were taken into custody and we were coming to rescue you," Sheriff Bowers said.

"They let us go. Perkins was shot and he needs to see the doc," Eales said, climbing down from the wagon. "I don't mind tellin' all of ya, these men mean business, and it ain't gonna end well."

"Well, come on in and we'll talk," Sheriff Bowers said. "Thanks, men, for turnin' out. I'm glad I didn't need you. Go on home."

"You mean you don't need us tonight," Speck said. "But now I have a need, and it's for a drink. Come on, Link."

Link, Speck, and at least a dozen other men from the impromptu army gathered at the Newport Saloon. The saloon had been closed during the excitement, but Grant Crumley was glad to reopen it.

"It's gettin' on close to two o'clock and that's awful late, but come on in, boys, if you are of a mind to," Crumley said, and the men filed in.

Most remained at the bar, but Link and Speck got their drinks, then moved to a table in the back corner.

Standing at the bar, Sam Strong said loudly enough for everyone to hear, "We missed our chance! While we had everyone together, we should have acted."

"What do you mean, 'acted'?" Deputy Foster asked. "We're here. Who did you need to rescue?"

Strong laughed without humor. "Rescue? Hell, Foster, do you think anybody gave a damn about rescuing you? What I'm talking about is that rat's nest of a Union Hall. While we had that many armed men, we should have attacked it."

"Strong, you're a damn fool," Grant Crumley said. "If you want a drink, shut up and order it. Otherwise, get the hell out of my saloon with that kind of talk."

"You can't talk to me like that." Strong put his hand on his jacket pocket.

Crumley reached down and brought up a double-barreled shotgun, which he laid across the bar. "Yeah, as a matter of fact, I can, and I think I just did. And if you try and pull that hogleg out of your pocket, I'll blow your damn fool head off. Now order a drink or get the hell out of here."

Strong looked around at the others and, seeing little support from anyone else, turned and stalked out.

"There's going to be real trouble between those two one of these days," Speck said. "As long as I've known them, there's been bad blood between them."

"Strong's not a very pleasant drunk," Link said. "But then, who is?"

"Sir, I resent that," Speck said with a broad smile as he downed his drink in one swallow. "I'm a most pleasant drunk."

"You never get drunk, Speck. You just get mellow."

"Mellow, yes, I like that. I get mellow."

Link took a sip of his drink. "What do you think's going to happen? Are we going to have an all-out shooting war?"

"My friend, we're already there. Just ask Mort Perkins."

"I'm glad they let the deputies go," Mollie said as she reported to the others. "They say Mr. Perkins was shot in the shoulder, but that was all."

"I hope Manny wasn't involved," Tori said

"From what I've been able to find out, it was Gorran Landry and a handful of men. No one said anything about Manny, so I'm sure he had nothing to do with it."

"Maybe, since it has come to this, and people realize how short everyone's tempers are, both sides will come to their senses and settle this thing," Tori suggested.

"I'm afraid not. It's just going to get worse. Sheriff Bowers has contacted the governor to ask him if he'll send in state troops."

"I have to say it puts producing our play in perspective. I'm beginning to feel a little foolish," Tori said.

"Well, don't feel that way. In the first place, we came up with the idea so we could raise money for the out-of-work miners, and those folks still need it. But now it has become more than just the money the play will raise; it might also help bring the people of the town together." Mollie laughed. "And there's one other thing—if there are that many extra people in town, think how much bigger our audience could be."

"That's why you're my friend, Mollie. You can always see the sunny side of things."

"Listen, it's too late for you to go home tonight, and I wouldn't feel good about you walking there alone. Why don't you come down to the Palace and stay with me in my suite?"

"Thanks, that's very nice of you. I accept."

The next morning the residents of Cripple Creek were awakened by the sounds of Gatling guns and artillery pieces rolling through the streets. The Chaffee Light Artillery had taken the train from Colorado Springs to Midland, then marched all night over the mountains, arriving in Cripple Creek as the sun rose.

In addition to the artillery, there were three hundred other men from the Colorado state militia. The soldiers were trooping in with company guidons indicating they were from Company A of Colorado Springs, Company C of Pueblo, and Companies B,

E, and K of Denver. Soon a dozen or more campfires burned as the soldiers, under the command of General Thomas Tarsney and General E. J. Brooks, bivouacked in the streets.

Link picked his way through the crowd, which was made up of the soldiers as well as the citizens of the town, including a large number of unemployed miners, who had turned out to watch all the activity.

"What you soldier boys doin' here?" Link heard someone call. The man was wearing a hat with a WFM patch sewn onto it. "You plannin' on goin' to war against us?"

"Why don't you shoot off one of them big guns?" another asked. "I sure would like to see one of them things go off."

Stepping into the Tutt and Penrose Building a few minutes later, Link hurried up to the second floor. He quickly glanced toward Mollie's office, wondering if Tori was there, but decided he would check a little later. When he reached his own office, he hesitated before opening the door, choosing instead to look in on Speck Penrose.

"What's going on out there? Are we under martial law?" Speck asked.

"No, but I wouldn't put it past General Tarsney to invoke that if it strikes his fancy."

"I've been thinking that might not be such a bad thing," Speck suggested. "I don't see how we're going to get through all this without some violence breaking out. Having martial law might put a damper on how serious it would be."

"I'd say be careful what you ask for. If there's martial law, wouldn't that mean the military controls everything that comes in and out of Cripple Creek?"

"I suppose so. What are you getting at?"

"How's your supply of brandy?"

"Ooooh," Speck said. "I'd better take care of that."

FIFTEEN

Good morning, ladies," Link said, walking into Mollie's office and finding both Mollie and Tori looking out the window onto the street.

"Link, what's going on? Why is the army here?" Mollie asked.

"It isn't the real army; it's the state militia," Link said.

"Well, they certainly look like the army. They're wearing uniforms, and they have cannons."

"Don't worry, we're not likely to have an artillery barrage. Sheriff Bowers asked the governor to send them here to keep the peace," Link said.

"I think the sheriff is going to wind up regretting calling on this governor," Mollie said. "The last thing the mine owners need is to have him involved."

"I agree," Link said.

"What's wrong with Governor Waite?" Tori asked.

"He's a Populist who's declared war on, and I quote, 'the producing classes, who profit upon the backs of labor.' Now, just how dumb is that? In the entire history of the world, production has always been based upon a combination of the producing classes and labor."

"I wonder how long the soldiers will stay," Mollie said.

"I don't have the slightest idea," Link said, joining Tori and Mollie at the window.

"But didn't you meet with the general this morning?" Tori asked. "At least, that's what Speck said."

"I met with him all right, but about the only thing I learned is that he is an overblown bag of wind."

From down on the street they heard a bugle being played, and they saw a group of soldiers moving into a precise formation with lines of uniformed men standing at attention.

"What are they doing now?" Tori asked.

"It looks to me like they're just putting on a show."

"Ahh. Like our play," Mollie said with a smile.

"You might say that," Link said. "Oh, by the way, I saw Peter Eales. He's none the worse for his adventure, and he wants you to know that he has every intention of being in the play."

"Assuming there is a play," Tori said.

"Of course there's going to be a play. I worked too hard learning my lines, and besides, why shouldn't there be one?"

"I just wonder if, in the midst of all this turmoil, having a play might not be considered frivolous."

"Nonsense. I think that makes the play even more important, no matter how much money it raises."

"That's exactly what I told Tori," Mollie said. "Now, I don't want to hear another word about this more foolish nonsense. Why, would you deny the world the opportunity to see me act?"

"The world?" Link asked with a chuckle.

"Well, maybe not the world, but at least Cripple Creek." Mollie struck a pose and spoke a line from the play. "'I fear that Simon McGraw looks upon Miss Fontaine as his plaything, the slave of his pleasure, a pretty toy to be exhibited that others might envy him his ownership. He has no real love for her.'"

"That's exceptional, Mollie. Now, tell me, Tori, how could we possibly deny the world this talent?" Link asked with a teasing laugh.

"No, nor even Cripple Creek," Tori replied, joining in the laughter.

The door opened, and turning toward it, Tori saw her brother. "Manny!" she said in surprise.

"Hello, Sis . . . Mollie . . . Link."

"What are you doing here?" Tori asked. "I thought you were in Altman."

"I am—that is, I'll be going back there. General Tarsney is meeting with John over at the Palace, and John wants to send a record of this meeting to the WFM headquarters. I said I'd come and see if you could come up and take notes and then put the report together for him. We can't pay you, of course, but I said you'd probably do it for me."

"Well, that's up to Mollie."

"Of course you can go," Mollie said.

"All right, I'll just get my pad and pencil," Tori said.

"And I'd better get back to my office," Link said.

Tori followed her brother to the Palace Hotel.

There, she saw John Calderwood sitting at a table in the corner of the room. She also saw a rotund man in uniform sitting across from him.

"That's General Tarsney," Manny said under his breath. "He's from the governor's office.

Calderwood and Tarsney stood as Tori and Manny approached.

"Miss Drumm, this is General Tarsney, and he's come to help us get this thing settled," John Calderwood said.

"General Tarsney." Tori greeted him with a smile.

"Miss Drumm is Manny's sister, and I've asked her to keep a record of our meeting," Calderwood said.

"Well, shall we get started, then?" Tarsney pointed to a chair. "After you, miss."

Tori sat in the chair the general had indicated, then raised her tablet and, with pencil poised in hand, prepared to take notes.

"What kind of mess have you created here, Calderwood?" Tarsney asked as an opening salvo.

"General, with all due respect, I beg to differ. We are merely exercising our constitutional right to strike."

"Are you familiar with a Supreme Court decision handed down in '88 that said any strike that represents a threat to the safety of the citizens can be declared unconstitutional?"

"I am familiar with that case," Calderwood said, "but I do not think we are anywhere near meeting those criteria."

"Then is my information false? I've been told that you've taken over the town of Altman, that you have . . . seceded . . . from the state of Colorado, and from the United States, that you have declared the town of Altman and its surroundings to be the Kingdom of Bull Hill, and that you have crowned yourself king."

Calderwood laughed. "You don't really believe that, do you?"

"Have you or have you not raised your own flag over Bull Hill, and are you or are you not requiring passports to be issued before anyone can enter? You might remember a similar experiment conducted about thirty years ago, and we all know how that turned out. Have you forgotten that bloody war, Mr. Calderwood?"

"I wasn't a participant in that conflict, General, having been in my Scottish homeland. But I have read of your civil war. Please don't misunderstand my actions; we've no intentions of firing on Fort Sumter. This conflict is not about politics—it's strictly a business move. My aim is to force the mine owners to meet our demands and give my union members a decent wage for a day's work."

"Did you or did you not detain six deputies who were acting in the pursuit of their duty?" General Tarsney asked, taking out his pipe and lighting it.

"If you are talking about Eales and those idiots with him, that was a misunderstanding, pure and simple," Manny interjected.

"What kind of misunderstanding?"

"We got word that a group of men were coming to Altman to cause trouble," Calderwood explained. "It wasn't our union miners who took them. It was police deputies from Altman. And as soon as we discovered they were legitimate deputies, we released them."

General Tarsney pulled his pipe from his mouth and examined the gleaming bowl for a moment. "Here is where we stand. I believe Sheriff Bowers is going to get warrants to arrest you and some of the other organizers."

"What do you mean he's going to arrest us? We've done nothing wrong!" Calderwood said.

"I don't know the charge. It may be something as innocuous as disturbing the peace," Tarsney replied. "The point is, he will have warrants, and I'm advising you—I'm telling you—not to offer any resistance to the arrest."

"Wait a minute. You're saying submit to an arrest? What happens to the strike if we're put in jail?"

"I know a good lawyer that would defend you," Tarsney replied.

Calderwood smiled. "Would that lawyer also happen to be the adjutant general of the state of Colorado?"

"He just might be," Tarsney said, returning the smile.

Calderwood nodded his head in understanding. "You tell Sheriff Bowers to come for us if he must, General, and you have my word, they'll be no trouble."

"Good. We are through here." General Tarsney stood and, without saying good-bye, left the hotel.

"Wow, who would have thought we'd get that kind of support from the state of Colorado?" Manny asked. "Sis, maybe you'd better not say anything about what you heard here."

"That's good advice, Miss Drumm. I think I'd like two copies of your report—one for us, and if you would, send another one to the Western Federation of Miners' headquarters in Butte, Montana. Can you do that?"

"How shall I get your copy to you?" Tori asked.

"Just leave it at the house, and I'll pick it up the next time I'm in town," Manny said.

"All right." Tori reached across the table and put her hand on Manny's arm. "You're my little brother and I'm worried about you. Don't let anything happen to you."

Manny leaned over and planted a kiss on Tori's forehead. "Don't worry, I'm not going to do anything foolish."

"Promise me that."

Calderwood laughed. "Come on, little brother. We need to get back up the hill."

Link was busy at his desk, trying to concentrate on his work, but he was wondering what Tori was doing. He heard someone at the door, and he looked up expectantly.

"Link, do you have a minute?" Sheriff Bowers asked.

"Sure, come in and have a seat." Link moved to the seating area.

"You heard Tarsney say I have to attempt to arrest the union before the militia can get involved. I've been thinking, and I believe I could accomplish the same thing if I arrest Calderwood and Drumm and a handful of others."

"That makes sense."

"I'd like you to ride up with me when I do it."

"Would you have to deputize me?"

"No, I think it would be better if you went as a private citizen. I'm told you and Manny Drumm get along pretty well together. I think, at least I'm hoping, that having you along with me will keep me from getting shot."

"I don't know, Sheriff. If somebody starts shooting, a bullet can hit me just as well as it can hit you."

"I know I'm asking a lot of you, and after all, as I was told in such a haughty manner, this is my job and no one else's. If you don't want to go, I'll understand."

"No, that's all right. I'll go with you."

"I'm ready to go now," Bowers said. "Maybe you'd better strap on your pistol."

Link opened a drawer and withdrew his pistol. Then he put it away. "Sheriff, if I'm going up as a private citizen, don't you think it might be better if I'm not armed?"

"Yeah, I guess, now that you mention it, it probably would be better."

Link grabbed his hat, stepped into the hall, then stopped. "Let's look in on Speck a minute. Maybe somebody ought to know what we're doing."

"All right."

When Bowers told Speck what he was planning, Speck was troubled. "How many deputies do you plan on taking?"

"None."

"None? You're going to arrest Calderwood all by yourself?"

"Not exactly," Link said.

Speck glanced quickly toward Link in curiosity. "What do you mean 'not exactly'? Link, what's going on here?"

"I'm going, too."

"What? Why would you do a damn fool thing like that?"

"I asked him to," Sheriff Bowers said.

"No," Speck said. "I'm not going to let you do this."

"I have to go, Speck," Link said. "If there's any chance to defuse this thing before it gets worse, we have to take it."

"Maybe *he* has to take the chance, but that's what he's paid to do," Speck said, pointing to Bowers. "There's certainly nothing that says *you* have to go."

"I'm going, Speck."

"What does Tori think about it?"

"She doesn't know."

"Don't you think you should tell her?"

"No."

"No, and I don't blame you, because she could talk some sense into you." Speck rose from his chair. "Maybe I should go tell her right now."

"Please don't. If you're my friend, don't say one word to her about this."

"And what do I tell her if you two get plugged up there? That you said, 'Please . . . please don't tell her'?"

Link forced a smile. "Well, let's just hope that conversation doesn't come up."

Speck shook his head. "Sure. Let's hope."

As Link and Sheriff Bowers traveled by buckboard on the five-mile road between Cripple Creek and

Altman, Link was acutely aware of every hill, rock, and shrub. His skin felt as if it were being pricked by a thousand needles.

"You should have brought your pistol," Sheriff Bowers said.

"If they're going to kill us, one more pistol isn't going to make a difference. And seeing me unarmed might cause them to think about it before they start shooting."

"Yeah, but think what?"

"Maybe that they'll shoot you instead of me, since you're the only one armed."

"What?" Bowers, incredulous, turned to Link.

Link laughed. "Now you see why I didn't want to bring my gun."

They saw three miners walking down the road toward them. Bowers put his hand on his gun, but Link stopped him. "No. They aren't armed."

Bowers continued to drive the buckboard toward the three men.

"Sheriff, Buchannan," one of the miners called out. "Welcome to Bull Hill."

"I hope you folks have a pleasant visit," another man said.

"What was that all about?" Bowers asked as the miners passed and continued on down the hill.

"I don't know, but it certainly wasn't hostile."

They were met by several others before they reached Altman, and each offered friendly greetings. When they did get to the outskirts of Altman, Calderwood and Manny were standing there, obviously waiting for them.

"Hello, Sheriff, Mr. Buchannan," Calderwood said.

"Calderwood, I've come to arrest you," Sheriff Bowers said. "You, Manny Drumm, and I've got sixteen other names on this list here. I hope you don't give me any trouble."

"No trouble from us," Calderwood replied with a pleasant smile. "Come on inside and have a drink with us. We can discuss it."

"There's nothing to discuss," Bower said, growing more emboldened by Calderwood's demeanor.

"Don't tell me you're going to turn down my hospitality?"

"I . . . I guess we could have a drink."

Link and Sheriff Bowers followed Calderwood and Manny into the Smith and Peters' Saloon. They saw three tables pulled together with a couple of bottles of bourbon, some platters of boiled eggs, cooked sausages, and plates of sliced bread sitting in the middle. Several men were already sitting around the table.

"You two sit here," Calderwood said, offering two chairs in the middle of the table. "I expect these are the men whose names are on your list."

Sheriff Bowers was taken by complete surprise. "Yes, they are."

"Well, as you can see, they are all here."

"Am I to understand that you are offering no resistance at all?"

"None at all," Calderwood said. "After all, we want our strike to be legal in all respects."

"How's my sister?" Manny asked Link as he sat down beside him.

"She's fine." Link was as surprised as Bowers by the reception they had received.

"Good. Make sure you tell her how well I behaved. She worries about me."

"I'll do that," Link said.

For the next several minutes all the men ate, drank, and conversed amicably, and it was hard to believe the animosity had been going on for almost five months. Then Calderwood stood and lifted his glass in toast.

"Gentlemen, I drink to the eventual peaceful resolution of this labor grievance."

Once everyone drank, he put his glass down and looked across the table at Sheriff Bowers. "Very well, Sheriff. We're your prisoners. Take us away."

When Link returned to Cripple Creek, he stepped into Speck's office. "I'm back. And as you can see, there was no need for the conversation with Tori. There was . . ." Link stopped, looking around Speck's office, seeing no fewer than a dozen rubber hot-water bottles, all apparently full. "Speck, what in heaven's name are you doing with all those hot-water bottles?"

"Ah, to you they are hot-water bottles." Speck smiled and held up his index finger. "But to me, they are emergency reserves."

"Emergency reserves of what?"

"Brandy, my friend. And not just any brandy—Hennessy. If this labor war gets any more serious, I fear that my supply may be cut off. If that happens, I shall be able to survive the drought with my hot-water bottles."

Within two days of the arrest of Calderwood, Manny and the other sixteen all were freed, the release arranged by none other than Thomas J. Tarsney, the commandant of the militia and the adjutant general of the state of Colorado. In addition, the Kingdom of Bull Hill had reasserted itself as an independent principality. Now its borders were patrolled by armed guards, and entrance was allowed only to those who presented passports, issued by the "sovereign" nation of Bull Hill.

Despite the deteriorating situation between the miners and the mine owners, rehearsals for *A Young Woman's Travail* continued, and Tori announced they were ready. She ran off flyers, and they were posted all over town, advertising the production. At Pearl's suggestion, she left off the names of the actors and actresses.

GRAND OPERA HOUSE
Myers Avenue Above 2nd Street
BENEFIT PLAY
Starting 8:00 p.m. Nightly
Beginning May 21st through May 23rd
All Proceeds Go to Support
Out-of-Work Miners without Regard to
Affiliation
A YOUNG WOMAN'S TRAVAIL
Victoria Drumm, Director
Grant Crumley, Stage Manager
Cast Made Up of Local Citizens

On opening night, not a seat was empty in the theater, with those in support of the strike and those opposed in equal attendance. At least while everyone was in the theater, comity and accord prevailed.

"Oh, Tori, it's going to be a huge success." Mollie said excitedly. "Do you have any idea how many people are here?"

"Don't count the house," Tori warned.

Mollie smiled. "I know, I know, don't count the house, don't whistle backstage, don't wish anyone bad luck, and don't say the word *Macbeth*."

Tori laughed. "Well, you just said it, so I hope that's nothing but one of the many theatrical superstitions. Where's Pearl? Has anyone seen her?"

"She's here. As far as I know, she's still in the dressing room."

"Maybe I should check on her."

"Tori, you want the houselights down before or after the curtain opens?" Crumley asked as Tori walked by.

"Before. Have you seen Pearl?"

"Not for a while."

Tori hurried back to the dressing room, tapped lightly, then stepped inside. "Pearl, are you about ready, curtain goes up in—"

Pearl was curled up in the corner.

"Pearl, what's wrong?"

"I can't do this," Pearl said in a whisper. "I can't go out there in front of all those people. I can't."

"Sure you can, Pearl. I've seen you around people. You relate very well, you are self-assured. And you have done a wonderful job in rehearsal. Don't worry about it, you'll be great, I know you will."

"No, I can't. Please, Tori, I just can't. I'm sorry."

Tori thought about it. What if Pearl froze up and just walked off the stage? Tori knew firsthand what a disaster that could be.

"All right, Pearl, I'm certainly not going to make you do it."

"I've ruined the whole thing."

"No you haven't. I'll take your part tonight. I'll wear your dress, and you help me with the makeup."

"But you can't do this. You haven't rehearsed."

"I've watched you. That's enough."

Half an hour later the curtain went up and the audience saw Lucy onstage, sprinkling flowers with a watering can.

"Oh, these are such lovely flowers. Miss Fontaine does keep a beautiful garden."

"Damn, that's Lucy Dawes. Look at her up there, big as life," someone said in a shout. Tori was waiting in the wings, and when she heard the remark, she thought for a moment that the play would get away from her. But she needn't have feared. She was pleased to hear a cascade of shushing noises, and she smiled. That meant that the audience was into the play, more interested in the characters than the actors and actresses portraying them.

Tori swept out onto the stage. "Julie, thank you. You are doing such a wonderful job."

Lucy looked up in surprise at seeing Tori where she expected to see Pearl, but she recovered quickly.

An hour and thirty minutes later the play ended to a standing ovation. During the curtain call the applause was loudest. After the play the cast and company gathered for a late dinner at the Third Street Dining Hall. There, Tori was the center of attention, not only from those who worked with the play, but from others in the restaurant.

"I must say, Tori," James Hagerman said. "I've seen dozens of plays in my lifetime, and I can honestly say I've never seen anyone who was any better than you were tonight. And now I'm told you didn't even rehearse."

"She didn't," Pearl said. "I was supposed to play the role of Lily, but I had such a case of stage fright, I couldn't go on. I thought I had ruined it for everyone, but as it turned out, I think it was good I didn't go on. We would never have known what a brilliant actress Tori is."

"You're all being too kind," Tori said as, with a glance toward Link, she let him know that she didn't want him to tell her secret.

Tori was in her element tonight. Not only had she genuinely enjoyed acting in the play, but even this, the postperformance dinner, was part of the theater scene that she had missed. Her biggest surprise was when a messenger delivered her a big bouquet of flowers.

"Oh, my!"

"You have Link to thank for that," Mollie said.

"Not true," Link said quickly. "Everyone in the cast and company contributed to it."

"Yes, but it was your idea."

When they left the restaurant that night, Link hired a cab to take them to Manny's house.

"You can go on, Junior, I'll walk home from here," Link said, paying the driver.

"Yes, sir, Mr. Link." Junior smiled broadly as he drove away.

"You walk home with me," Link said.

"Oh?"

"I know Manny's in Altman, but I wouldn't want him to come home unexpectedly and find me here. And I know for sure, nobody's going to come in unexpectedly at my house."

"Link Buchannan, do you think Lily Fontaine, or even Sabrina Chadwick, is bold enough to come to your house at this hour of the night?"

"You misunderstand me, madam. I don't want the boldness of either Lily Fontaine or Sabrina Chadwick. I want the loving acquiescence of Tori Drumm."

"Oh." Tori smiled widely. "Well, if you put it that way, I'd be more than happy to go home with you."

SIXTEEN

It started to rain on their way home, a gentle rain at first, but gradually increasing until it was coming down quite hard by the time they reached Link's house.

Link lived in a shingled cottage with a red tin roof, part of which protruded out over the front porch, thus affording them some protection from the rain as he unlocked the door.

"I sure chose a fine time for us to take a walk," Link said.

"It's all right, we weren't out in it too long. And I like the rain."

"I like it better when I'm inside looking out at it." They stepped inside quickly, then he turned on the light.

This was Tori's first time in Link's house, and she couldn't help but compare this small cottage with his house in Colorado Springs. The one large room served as a combination sitting room, dining room, and kitchen. Unlike Manny's kitchen when she first saw it, Link's kitchen was neat, with no dirty dishes, pots, or pans.

A narrow set of stairs led up to what Tori could see was an open loft. She knew without having to ask that the loft was his bedroom.

"There's a bathroom back there if you want to dry off."

"Thanks, I believe I would like to do just that."

The rain began falling even more intensely, drumming loudly against the tin roof. A flash of lightning was followed a few seconds later by a roar of thunder.

"It's a good thing we got here when we did," Link said.

When Tori went into the bathroom, she saw a neat stack of folded towels, and she took one and began toweling off after she undressed. She looked at her wet clothes, thinking she would have to put them back on, then noticed a flannel shirt hanging from a hook on the back of the door. She removed the shirt from the hook and held it to her cheek. She could smell the faint, and erotic, scent of him. On impulse, she put the shirt on. It was long enough that its hem hit her midthigh.

Link was standing with his back to the bathroom door, staring through the window at the rain, when Tori came back into the room.

"Link, I hope you don't mind that I borrowed your shirt."

Something about the sound of her voice, low, husky, and erotic, aroused Link's senses even before he turned. When he saw her, naked except for his shirt, he gasped, feeling an immediate sexual charge.

Tori's breath quickened, and for a moment she wondered if, perhaps, she had been too bold. She reached up and ran her fingers through her hair, cool and still damp against her skin.

"My shirt has never looked better," Link answered in a hoarse murmur.

Tori was unable to respond. She could only watch with shortened breath and drumming heart as he moved across the room toward her. Her arm was so heavy that she found it impossible to remove her hand from her hair.

With a smile that sent her pulse racing, Link took her hand in his and brought it to his lips. Tori was not prepared for the tumult of desire that this simple kiss sent surging through her. Her lips were quivering, whether from excitement or from the wet-induced cold, she didn't know.

"You're shivering," Link said.

"Yes."

He moved his hand to her chin and tilted her head up. His finger traced the outline of her lips, and she watched as he brought his mouth down toward hers, stopping a mere inch away. She closed her eyes and pursed her lips, expecting to meet his, but instead his mouth found the smooth underside of her chin, then went down to her throat. He slowly began licking away the few droplets of water that she had missed, tracing each rivulet to its end. The feeling of his tongue on her was both oddly soft and rough.

Link lifted his mouth away from her throat, then wound his hand into her hair, drawing her closer to him. He loosened the buttons on the shirt she was wearing, causing it to gape open. Tori shuddered in the night air. Then, unashamedly, and without the slightest embarrassment, she removed the shirt and let it drop to the floor behind her. Before he could react, she walked over to and then climbed the narrow stairway.

Upstairs was more of a sleeping loft than a bedroom, the loft being furnished only with a bed and a table. Tori didn't lie on the bed but rather lay on a bearskin rug that was butted up against the edge of the loft. Lying here, on her stomach, sensually aware of feel of the fur against her naked skin, she looked down at Link, who was now removing his own wet clothes.

When he, too, was completely naked, she enjoyed the sight as much now as she had the first time she'd seen him, viewing with pleasure his muscular arms, his broad shoulders and chest, his flat and ribbed abdomen. But even more arousing was the sight of his thick erection, protruding at a slightly elevated angle. She expected him to come upstairs to join her, but instead he picked up his wet clothes, and the shirt she'd been wearing, and took them into the bathroom.

Tori smiled at his penchant for neatness, even now.

A few seconds later, as Link climbed the stairs, he saw Tori lying on her stomach on the bearskin. The gentle curve of her back, the rise of her buttocks, and the sweep of her legs intensely aroused him. She started to get up.

"No," he said, holding his hand out toward her. "You stay there, I'll join you."

Tori lay back down, and with a gentle pressure from his hand on her shoulder, he indicated that he wanted her to stay on her stomach. Then, lying down beside her, he began kissing her and laving her with his tongue, first behind each ear, then on the back of her neck, before he followed the slight indention of her spine down to the very hollow of her back.

He kissed her in that well, then he kissed and ran his tongue over the rise of her butt cheeks, on down her thighs, to the backs of her knees, and finally her ankles. By the time he reached her ankles Tori was so enflamed that she couldn't imagine how he could possibly do that without her skin burning his lips and his tongue.

Then and only then did Link roll her onto her back. Again he made the journey over her body with lips and tongue, starting now at her ankles and working his way back, pausing at that most sensitive place, then at her belly button, and finally ending by going from nipple to nipple.

Her hands were on the back of his head, guiding him in his ministrations until, gently, he spread her legs and moved over her. They kissed again before the final invasion, a kiss that went beyond passion to exploration and wonder. It was a lover's kiss, exciting because it was unique, but comfortable because this was not new to them: they had shared kisses and more before tonight, so they had an unspoken understanding of what each expected from the other.

When the time was right, Link made that final

connection, and she felt the fullness of him in her well-lubricated tunnel, each inch of his entry eliciting the most delightful sensations. When he was fully inserted, he began to pull back, the movement again sending tremors of ecstasy through her. There was no rush; he gave her what she desired and needed, and she returned in kind.

As his heavy shaft invaded and withdrew, so, too, did his tongue in her mouth, both gentle and rough, tentative and demanding, enticing and frightening. Tori sought it all eagerly, lost in the sensations that were overcoming her. It didn't seem possible, but it was better this time than it had been before, and as they continued to make love, all thought and awareness of anything beyond themselves ceased. There was only pleasure, the feel of his tongue against hers, the rake of her fingernails across his back, and the muscular hardness of his body, molded so completely against hers.

Outside, the rain continued, beating against the tin roof like orchestral timpani with rhythmic percussion—harmonic bass notes from the larger drops, and delicate trills and melodious tinkling from the water that dripped off the eaves. Its ballad built and swelled, joining its sweet refrain to the song of Tori's racing blood.

Then the goal she had been chasing, the goal that had teased her with a tender torment, burst over her again and again, showing no signs of ending or even slowing. Were these powerful sensations ever going to stop? She wanted them to go on and on, but knew that they couldn't; her body simply could not take any more!

Then she felt Link jerking in pleasure, filling her with the hot, wet evidence of his own release. She rode with him, matching him in wave after wave of shuddering gratification, as if they were in a private cocoon, caught up in a burst of ecstasy that made them one.

When the last ripples of pleasure had subsided, he pulled himself from her. After that they lay together, her head on his shoulder, his arm around her, his hand resting on her naked buttock as her leg curled over his body.

It was still raining, and Tori was almost surprised by that. So intense had the last several minutes been that even the sound of the rain had been unable to penetrate her consciousness.

The next morning Link and Tori had breakfast at the Third Street Dining Hall, and as they sat across the table from each other, Link could scarcely keep his eyes off her. The night before had been the most incredible night of his life, a night of erotic exploration combined with long periods of relaxed, loving togetherness.

A couple approached their table.

"Miss Drumm, I want you to know how much my wife and I enjoyed the play last night," a man said. "You were absolutely wonderful."

"Thank you," Tori replied with a gracious smile.

Several others dropped by their table to express the same sentiment.

"Do you think any of those people realized I was also in the play?" Link asked with a teasing smile.

"Oh, were you, dear?" Tori replied in an assumed haughty voice as she touched her hair.

Link laughed. "I'd better get you up to the office before Mollie starts making assumptions."

"What do you mean 'starts making assumptions'?" Tori smiled.

Half an hour later Link and Speck were standing at Link's office window, looking down on Bennett Avenue. Winfield Scott Boynton was on the corner just below him, making a speech and firing up the citizens of the town. Link raised the window to hear Stratton more clearly.

"Citizens! If you have the blood of 1776 in your veins, in the name of God, in the name of your country, in the name of your homes, your wives, and your children, I ask you to stand by law and order that the government of the people, by the people, and for the people shall not perish from the earth!"

"Grand speech, isn't it?" Speck asked.

"Oh, yes, especially the 'government of the people, by the people, and for the people shall not perish from the earth' part," Link said. "It seems to me like Abraham Lincoln might have already used those words."

"Ah, what's a little plagiarism when it's for a good cause? Anyway, I don't think Lincoln will mind. I'm told Boynton's speech will appear in the *Crusher* today."

"Boynton's a politician, and I've never known a politician to pass up the opportunity to take advantage of any situation that will get his name in the paper."

"Things sure are getting in a mess," Speck said.

"Yes, they really are."

"Good morning," Tori said from the open door to Link's office.

Link turned to her, greeting her with a broad smile. "Hello, Tori. Come on over here and listen to this fine speech."

"I would love to, but my brother wants to talk to you."

"Manny? He's here? Did he come in last night?" Link asked.

"No," Tori said, barely suppressing a giggle as she imagined what Link was thinking. "He's on the telephone, down at Mollie's office."

"Oh, I'll come speak to him, then."

"Well, I would hope you would," Tori replied.

Link followed Tori down the hall, walking rather quickly. As they stepped inside, Link heard Mollie say, "Here he is now, Manny, just a moment."

Link took the phone. "Link Buchannan."

"Link, what's going on down there? We got word an army's being raised to attack us. If that's true, I want you to call it off."

"Manny, you've reached out to the wrong man. Whatever's going on is beyond my control. To tell you the truth, right now I think half the town is convinced that your union is going to come down the hill and attack us."

"I guess I can understand that. We've got a couple of hotheads up here who are trying to get us to do just that."

"Is it Junius Johnson and Jack Smith?"

Manny laughed. "I guess nothin's a secret, is it? But that's not why I called."

"What do you need?"

"I know you care for my sister."

"That's true."

"Link, I'd like to ask you to do me a favor. Will you?"

"Sure, if I can."

Manny hesitated. "I want you to look out for my sister."

"Of course I'll do that, but, Manny, is something—"

"Don't say anything. She's worried enough as it is. But I think things are starting to simmer up here, and anything could happen."

"I understand," Link said. "Would you like to speak to your sister?"

Link handed the receiver to Tori and stepped away.

Mollie said, "According to Manny, those people in Altman are getting restless. He says they're ready to attack us. Do you believe that?"

"Anything can happen, and all the fools speechifying around here isn't making it any better. You should hear what Boynton's been spewing on the street corner."

"I saw the crowd gathering. Were you down there?" Mollie asked.

"No, you can hear it all from my window."

"I want to hear what they have to say. When Tori gets off the telephone, we're coming down."

A few minutes later, when the women walked in, Speck and Link were standing at the open window.

"Who's speaking now?" Mollie asked as she and Tori approached the window.

"Judge Colburn," Link said, "and he's about as crazy as Boynton. Just listen to this hogwash:"

"It is my belief that we should telephone President Cleveland and ask that he send the United States Army out here to quell this insurrection. John Calderwood has declared the independence of Bull Hill. Now, I ask you, how is that any different from when the rebellious Southern states seceded from the Union? I think we should impeach Governor Davis Waite, lynch John Calderwood, and hang Adjutant General Thomas Tarsney. I'm calling upon every able-bodied man and boy to wrest Bull Hill from the insurrectionists before they despoil our fair womanhood and slit the throats of our little children!"

Colburn's speech was met with cheers and applause.

"And now I want to introduce you to one of our fairest young ladies of Cripple Creek, who is prepared to do her part: Miss Susan Dunbar."

"Who is that?" Tori asked.

"She's the biggest troublemaker in the whole town," Mollie said. "When I started my business, she said it wasn't right for a woman to be alone in the presence of a man, and then she tried to get all of Myers Avenue shut down. Have you noticed that Pearl and her girls can only go into the stores on Bennett Avenue on Wednesday morning? Well, that's Susan Dunbar's meddling."

"Ladies!" Miss Dunbar shouted in a high, shrill voice. "I am, today, forming the Ladies' Auxiliary

Corps. I ask that all the fair ladies—the *decent* ladies—of the district convince your husbands and your sons to take up arms in our defense. And, to support that effort, join the Ladies' Auxiliary Corps and be ready to roll bandages, fill canteens, bind the wounds of those injured in battle, and give comfort to the dying!"

"For heaven's sake, if you listen to those fools, the grapeshot is already flying," Speck said.

"This is exactly what foments trouble," Link said, turning away from the window in disgust.

"Oh, Link, do you think so?" Tori asked, concerned.

"I don't know. Maybe cooler heads will prevail."

"I wouldn't count on it," Speck said. "If you ask me, Bowers is as big a hothead as Jack Smith or Junius Johnson."

Tori recognized the two names. In an atmosphere of increasing separation between the two sides, there were, from time to time, points of agreement. Manny thought that Sheriff Bowers, the titular head of the "citizens' army," and Smith and Johnson, the leaders of the "miners' army," were all three hotheads. Link and Speck shared that thought.

The next day, an article ran in the *Crusher* that validated everyone's opinion about Bowers.

CITIZENS' ARMY RAISED
WILL REPEL ATTACK BY MINERS

Special to the Crusher—*May 23, 1894—In an interview with this newspaper Sheriff Bowers made the following comments: "I propose that the law shall be obeyed in El Paso County as long as I am the sheriff. It is an outrage that armed bodies of men should go about, intimidating men, ruining the camp, and half beating to death those who do not do as they think they ought to do.*

"I have raised an army of 1,200 deputies and put them under command of Commissioner Winfield Scott Boynton. I will see to it that the law is enforced in Cripple Creek."

The 1,200 armed deputies, under Boynton, have proceeded to the Hayden Divide.

Wednesday, May 23, was the last showing of *A Young Woman's Travail*. It had been performed before a full house every night, due in no small part to the presence of so many extra people in town, and also because word had gotten around that Victoria Drumm was an outstanding actress.

Alongside the *Crusher* article that told of Sheriff Bowers's plans to effectively declare war on the striking miners, there was a glowing article about the miners' benefit performance.

PLAY HUGE SUCCESS

PROCEEDS TO RELIEVE SUFFERING OF THE NEEDY

This writer has been privileged to see many touring plays in which the finest actresses of the New York theater have appeared. And I can easily say, without fear of contradiction, that Miss Victoria Drumm's stage presence, as well as the

*way she delivers her lines, is not to be exceeded
by anyone. If you have not seen this wonderful
production, tonight is your last opportunity, and
I wholeheartedly encourage you to do so.*

After the final performance of the play, the cast
and company and their guests gathered for a late
dinner at the Third Street Dining Hall.

Mollie O'Bryan rose to address the gathering.
"Ladies and gentlemen, I've been keeping a careful
tab of our numbers—how many people paid, and
how much our expenses were—and I have to admit,
I had no idea this little endeavor would be so successful."

"Where's Crumley?" George Campbell called out.
"Has anyone seen him? Our stage manager hasn't
run off with the money, has he?"

The others laughed.

"Now, George, how's Mollie goin' to tell us if you
don't sit there and be quiet?" Eales asked.

"Go ahead, Mollie, let's hear it," Speck said.

"Well, I will continue." Mollie's smile showed
that she was taking it all in good cheer. "For the
three performances, we had a total attendance of
six thousand people, including several who came at
least two or more times. From that six thousand, we
raised a total of fifteen hundred dollars. Our total
expenses—"

"Here it comes," Sally Halthusen said. "The
expenses will eat up half the money."

"Because of generous benefactors, our total
expenses were . . . are you ready? . . . zero!"

There was a round of applause as everyone oohed and aahed.

As the meal continued, those around the table began trading stories and laughing about funny things that had happened during the production of the play.

"What about when Lucy was watering the garden, but there was no water in the watering can?" Campbell asked. "The expression on her face was so funny."

"Grant, you're the stage manager, you should have made certain the can was filled," Maxine said. "Poor Lucy."

"The can was filled," Crumley insisted. "And if I ever find out who emptied it, I . . ." He stared at Campbell.

"You have to admit, it was funny," Campbell said.

Others had stories to tell, but Link, who was sitting next to Tori, took her hand in his. "You're the reason for all this, you know. The paper was right. You were brilliant."

"It wasn't just me. Mollie, Lucy, you, Speck— everyone did a good job."

"That's because you brought out the best in us."

"Thank you. But we also have to thank the 'benefactors.'" Tori cocked her head knowingly. "I just wonder who they could have been?"

Link shrugged his shoulders. "Your guess is as good as mine."

When Link and Tori left the restaurant after the meal, they made no effort to hide that they were leaving together.

Speck came outside with them. "When do I get my five thousand dollars?"

"I've got it all set aside," Link said, "and I hope you win."

"Ha!" Speck hit the palm of his hand with his closed fist. "I knew it!"

This time when Link hailed a cab, he had the driver deliver them to his house.

Not until they were inside did Tori ask the question that had been puzzling her. "All right, what sort of bet do you and Speck have?"

"Are you talking about the five thousand dollars?" Link smiled. "Speck and I bet on who would be the first one to get married. At the time, I thought it was a sure thing. He had Sally, and I had nobody. Now he's convinced he's going to win."

"You said you hoped he would win."

Link nodded.

"In order for him to win, you need . . ."

"A bride?"

"Well, yes. I would think that's pretty important." Tori broke into a wide, open smile.

"Do you know of anybody who would marry me?" Link asked as he drew her into his arms and began raining kisses on her neck.

"I do." Tori threw her head back to give him better access.

"I do? Isn't that what the groom is supposed to say?" Link stopped kissing her and looked into her eyes, which were now shining brightly. "Tori, will you marry me?"

"Yes, yes, yes. I love you, Link." Tori smothered

him with kisses as Link gathered her in his arms
and carried her up the stairs.

Link was awakened the next morning by bars of
morning sunlight streaming in through the gable
window. Tori was asleep in the bed beside him,
and he reached over to lay his hand on her, enjoying the touch of soft flesh, the sharp edge of her
pelvic bone, and the cushioning effect of the nest
of hair.

As he lay here, the room quiet except for the
measured rhythm of her breathing, he began making plans for their wedding. Should they get married in Colorado Springs? Or here in Cripple Creek?
His business was here, so he needed to live here,
but this house was not what he wanted for Tori. The
next question was: Should he build a new one or
purchase something ready for Tori to decorate with
her special touch?

Even before the rhythm of her breathing changed,
even before he felt the change in her body, Link was
aware that Tori had awakened. That awareness was
validated when she put her hand on his and drew it
tighter against herself.

After a few kisses and knowing caresses, Link
moved easily and unhurriedly over her, molding his
naked body to hers. Her legs were downy soft and
creamy white beneath his muscle-hardened ones,
and they began making love, their motion establish-
ing an easy rhythm. They mirrored each other move
for move, touching, loving, kissing, until she, and
then he, were engulfed in a maelstrom of pleasure.

Afterward Link and Tori lay together, their breathing slowly returning to normal.

"Will we start every day like this once we're married?" Tori asked.

"Every day."

"What if we have a house full of children?"

"What if we do?"

"We can't start every day like this, then."

"We'll have a bedroom with a door that locks," Link promised.

Tori laughed, then sat up. "I'm going to fix breakfast."

"Well, I would certainly hope so. That's the only reason I brought you home with me."

Half an hour later a fire was going in the stove and a pot of coffee was giving off a rich, welcome aroma. Tori was bent over the table, beating some sort of batter.

"You don't really have to do that, you know," Link said. "We could have breakfast at the Dining Hall again, and everyone could stop by the table to tell you how great you were in the play."

"I'm not doing this because I have to. I'm doing this because I want to. Do you know how long it's been since I made pancakes?"

"How long?"

Tori chuckled. "Well, I've never made them. But I watched Aunt Frances and Hulda make them. Are you brave enough to try them?"

"Have you not heard? I am a man of immutable valor. I'll eat your pancakes."

"Well, I would hope so!" Tori stuck her finger into the batter, then flipped some onto him, following that with a laughing embrace.

"Tori, my Tori. We're going to have so much fun together. I want to get married as soon as possible."

SEVENTEEN

It was early afternoon and Mollie had left the office, so Tori was all alone when the door opened. Looking up from her desk, she was surprised to see Charles Tutt. She smiled, stood, and started toward him.

"Mr. Tutt! What a delightful surprise to see you here. Have you seen Link yet?"

"No, I'm about to go down to see Speck now, then I'll say hello to Link. In the meantime I have a surprise for you."

"A surprise, for me?"

Charles stepped aside and Tori gasped.

"Hello, Tori."

"Lyle!" Tori said in a choked voice.

Link was just writing out a bank draft for five thousand dollars when he saw Charles Tutt step into Speck's office. Thinking this would be a good time to tell both of them that he was getting married, he decided to go get Tori so she could be with him when he paid off his debt. He was practically to her office when he heard Tori's voice through the open door.

"How did you find me? Why did you come here?"

A man replied, "I'm in Colorado Springs with a touring company, and lo and behold, I read that *A Young Woman's Travail*, my play, was being produced in Cripple Creek, of all places, and that Victoria Drumm was the director. Now, don't you think that was a coincidence—that Victoria Drumm, the woman who once professed her undying love for me, is directing my play without telling me?"

"The play was for a benefit. I should have known—"

"The play is not the point. Tori, I have wonderful news to tell you! Bella is gone—we're divorced, and now I can marry you, just like we always dreamed! I've written a new play with a part just for you. You'll reemerge as Victoria Ketterman and we'll capture the New York theater just as we did before, only this time we'll be man and wife."

"I was so in love with you—and you betrayed me!"

"My darling, you ran away before I could explain things to you. I didn't know if the baby was even mine, and when she lost it, I couldn't leave her. There was the play to think about, but now that I've found you, our fortunes will rise again. You have to come back with me. You were born to be on the stage, and even these country rubes recognize that."

"Lyle, why didn't you—"

"Enough talking."

Link had heard enough. Feeling a stabbing pain in his heart, he turned and walked away, going first to his office to get his gun and then down the stairs. In his mind he was formulating his next move. When he reached the street, he tore up the bank draft, letting the small pieces scatter in the wind.

"Are you mounted?" Sheriff Bowers asked when Link volunteered his service to the sheriff's army.

"I can be," Link answered in a clipped tone.

"Good, and I see you are armed." Bowers wrote something on a piece of paper and handed it to Link. "I've just appointed you captain. Go up to the Hayden Divide and show this to Boynton. Right now the army's camped there and Boynton's in command, but he can find a place for you."

"Right."

As Link turned to leave, Bowers called out to him, "Link?"

"Yes?"

"In all likelihood this is going to break out into a shooting war. Are you prepared for that?"

"I am."

"I can't and I won't marry you, Lyle," Tori said. Once she had twisted out of his embrace, she had managed to put her desk between them and was keeping it that way.

"Didn't you give up your career, disgrace yourself, and embarrass me just because you wanted to marry me?"

"That's what I thought I wanted then, but it's not what I want now."

"And why not?"

"Because I've found someone else."

"I suppose it's some poor schmuck who's made a penny or two out of this godforsaken place and all you can see is his money. Tori, you know and I know—these are not your people. You belong in New York, whether it be onstage or dining at Delmonico's. What can there possibly be for you here?"

"Love. There is love for me here."

The pleading expression left Lyle's face, replaced by anger. "We'll just find out how strong your resolve is after I speak with Charles Tutt."

"About what?"

"You'll see."

Spinning on his heel, Lyle strode out into the hallway and, not seeing Tutt where he had left him, called out loudly, "Tutt! Charles Tutt!"

Several doors opened along the hallway as the occupants looked out to see who was causing the commotion. Charles Tutt emerged from one of the doors.

Lyle pranced down the hall toward Tutt. "Come with me, dear. You'll want to hear this."

Frightened and confused, Tori followed along behind Lyle. When she got to Link's door, she opened it. Whatever Lyle might have to say, she wanted—no, she needed—Link to be with her.

Tori was disappointed that Link wasn't there, and when Lyle followed Charles into Speck's office, she went in behind him.

"Mr. Tutt," Lyle said. "Did you or did you not tell me that *A Young Woman's Travail* was performed in this city?"

"I'll answer that because I had a role," Speck said. "Tori played Lily Fontaine, and I've never seen anyone who could have done a better job."

"That isn't surprising," Lyle said. "Especially as Miss Drumm—or I should say Miss Sabrina Chadwick—portrayed that very role on Broadway for two hundred and sixty-five consecutive shows . . . until she humiliated herself, and the theater, by walking offstage in the middle of a performance."

"What?" Speck asked, and he and Charles shot a questioning glance toward Tori. "You're a Broadway star?"

Tori made no verbal response. The hanging of her head was answer enough.

"Not just any star—she was Sabrina Chadwick, and I made her who she was," Lyle said. "Now, how much money did the play make?"

"Fifteen hundred dollars, but Tori didn't make that. We gave all the money to a worthy cause."

"It was larceny, pure and simple. Victoria Drumm knows all about copyright protection, and she had no authority to produce my play. She stole it, and I intend to see to it that she is prosecuted to the fullest extent of the law."

"Mr. Ketterman," Charles said. "Suppose the entire fifteen hundred dollars went to you?"

"No!" Tori said. "That money isn't his. It belongs to the miners."

Charles held his hand out toward Tori, not harshly, but in a gentle request to say no more.

Lyle smiled. "I suppose, if the fifteen hundred dollars was paid to me, plus the two thousand eight hundred dollars I had to refund to the ticket holders after she walked out on me in that disastrous production in New York, then I could be convinced to forgo pressing charges against her. That would come to a total of . . ." Lyle tried to compute the amount.

Speck spoke up quickly. "Four thousand three hundred dollars."

"Yes, four thousand three hundred," Lyle repeated with a smile.

"If I have a letter drafted to the effect that you have authorized the production of your play in exchange for the total amount of its proceeds, and that you also hold Victoria Drumm blameless for lost proceeds from the aborted play, would you sign it?"

"Yes, I think I could be persuaded to do that."

"Very well. When you sign the letter, I'll give you my personal bank draft for the amount in question."

"Oh, Speck, I can't ask you to do that," Tori said.

"Think nothing of it, Tori. I believe I've been told I will soon come into enough money to more than cover the amount," Speck said as humor reached his eyes.

Tori smiled appreciatively. "Thank you. How can I ever repay you?"

"That's nothing for you to worry about now."

Lyle cleared his throat to remind Tori of the issue at hand. "How soon will I get my money?"

"I want you on the afternoon train back to Colorado Springs. In the meantime, I suggest that you wait in the Newport Saloon," Speck said. "I think we can make arrangements for free drinks while you wait. You'll have the letter and the bank draft within the hour."

Lyle smiled again and nodded. "Sir, it has been a pleasure doing business with you."

"Get out of this office before I personally throw you out," Charles Tutt said.

As soon as Ketterman left, Tori sat down at a typewriter and began composing the letter.

Charles went to the phone. "I'm going to call the opera house back in Colorado Springs. I'll make certain that no Ketterman production will be allowed there, and they will pass the word to other venues. Whatever his play is, it will not be seen in the West."

Speck chuckled. "It serves him right, the bastard."

"Have you seen Link?" Tori asked as she handed the document to Speck.

"I would imagine he's in his office," Speck said. "I know he was there earlier."

"No," Charles said, cupping his hand over the speaker as he waited for the operator. "I passed him in the hallway after I brought Ketterman to see you. I assumed he was coming to see you, since you and Mollie have the only occupied offices on that end of the hall."

"Oh, no," Tori said quietly.

"What is it?" Speck asked.

"Link must have heard everything." Tori ran from the room. "He won't understand. I've got to find him."

Link was not at his house, and with Speck's help, every saloon in town was searched, without success.

She also went to the dance halls, but no one had seen him anywhere.

"He's got to be here somewhere. He can't just have disappeared," Speck said. "Tori, you said he heard everything. What do you mean by that?"

"I'm sure he heard Lyle when Lyle was pleading with me to marry him."

"Should that worry Link?"

"No, not at all!" Tori said forcefully. "But he may have heard me say . . ."

"He may have heard you say what?"

"He may have heard me say that, at one time, I thought I loved Lyle, and I did want to marry him. And he may have even seen Lyle kiss me."

"Oh, I see."

"You see what? Speck, I don't like the way you said that. What do you mean, you see?"

"I've known Lincoln Buchannan for his entire life. He's as fine a man as I've ever known. He also has a great sense of honor and personal pride. If he overheard all that and saw you kissing that man, he may well think that you are still in love with Ketterman. And if he thought that for a moment, he would get out of the way rather than cause you any kind of trouble."

"No, oh, Speck, I don't want him out of the way! I love him! Where would he go? Do you have any idea?"

"Have you tried Pearl's place?"

"Oh, do you think he might go there?"

"It's a possibility. But, Tori, if he is, and he's with one of the girls, how would you feel about that?"

"I would feel nothing but joy in finding him, and I would pray that he would forgive me."

Speck shook his head. "Sounds to me like there's nothing to forgive."

"No, honey, he isn't here," Pearl said. "I've not seen him since the two of you lit out all lovey-dovey last night."

"Oh, Pearl, I've got to find him. I simply must! Please, help me."

"I'll do what I can, but if you haven't been able to find him, I'm not sure I can."

"Could you . . . I mean, do you know any of the other . . . ?"

Pearl smiled. "You don't have to say it, I know what you mean. All right, I'll search all the other houses and even the cribs for you. If he's in town, we'll find him."

"If he's in town." Tears streamed down Tori's cheeks. "That's what I most fear . . . that he's gone someplace and I'll never find him."

Up at the Hayden Divide, Boynton called for volunteers to board two railroad flatcars from David Moffat's newly completed railroad that had reached Cripple Creek from Cañon City.

"We're going to attack Bull Hill. We'll show those jackleg miners what they're up against," Boynton said.

"You might want to reconsider that," Link said.

"And why would that be?"

"Two carloads of men would make an awfully tempting target. I think we'd be better off if we advanced toward Bull Hill spread out in a line of attack."

"Well, you're not in command here. I am, and I

say we're going up on these flatcars. Now, you can join us or you can stay behind. It's your choice."

"I'm going, but I think you're making a big mistake."

"Come on, boys, let's show those striking sons of bitches they can't declare themselves a new country and get away with it," one of the deputies said.

Many of the deputies the sheriff had recruited to make up his army were ex-police and former firemen from Denver. They all had an ax to grind with Governor Waite because he had fired them over an earlier resistance to his militia. Now they were anxious to get back at the governor, and because they correctly perceived that Waite supported the strikers, they figured defeating the union at Bull Hill would accomplish their objective.

"All right, boys," Boynton said. "Let's get on board!"

Feeling uneasy about this whole operation, Link climbed onto the flatcar with the others, and the engineer of the dinkey train started toward Bull Hill.

They saw nothing suspicious as they approached, only a work gang on a wagon moving toward Battle Mountain.

"You've sent those men to do *what*?" Manny Drumm asked as he watched a wagon head down the hill from Altman.

"They're going up on Battle Mountain," Marshal Daly said. "Tully came up with the idea. Him and Lyons and Landry are gonna blow up the Strong Mine."

"Blow it up?"

"Why not? They've had a bone to chew with Sam Strong since the very beginning, and if we're gonna fight this thing, can you think of a better place to start?"

"You can't let them do that. Why didn't you stop them?"

"What authority do I have? I'm the Altman city marshal, that's all. I don't have no jurisdiction out there."

"That's crazy! Someone has to stop them!"

"Well, Calderwood ain't here, so guess who's in charge of the miners? If it gets stopped, it's up to you, son."

Manny reached the Strong Mine half an hour later and, dismounting, approached the shaft house. Just as he stepped inside, he was confronted by Landry.

"What are you doing here?" Landry asked, pointing his gun square at him.

"I've come to stop you. Where are Tully and Lyons?"

"We're over here, Drumm. We're finishin' up what we was startin' when Buchannan and your slut of a sister stopped us," Lyons said.

Turning toward the voice, Manny saw Tully planting dynamite charges around the boiler, the steam donkey, and the hoist mechanism, while Lyons was attaching the fuses.

"It didn't stop us for long. We got let out 'cause we didn't actually do anything. But we are now. We're fixin' to blow this mine all to hell," Tully added.

"What do you think blowing up a mine will accomplish?"

"It'll show them rich bastards they can't wait us out. They'll see with their own eyes what's fixin' to start," Lyons said.

"If you think I'm going to let you do that, you're out of your minds," Manny said. Pulling his pistol, he started toward the two men. "Now step away from that dynamite."

"No," Landry shouted. "You stop right there!"

Paying no attention to Landry's demand, Manny continued toward Tully and Lyons.

"I warned you!" Landry fired, and Manny felt a blow to his back. Spinning around as he was falling, he pulled the trigger of his own pistol, and just before passing out, he saw a black hole appear in the middle of Landry's forehead.

"What was that?" Link asked.

"I don't know. It sounded like a couple of gunshots," Boynton said.

"I'll tell you what it was! Them sons of bitches is shootin' at us!" another shouted.

"No, I don't think those shots were at us." Link said. "It sounded like they—"

Link was interrupted by the sound of a tremendous explosion. The blast blew the Strong Mine shaft house three hundred feet into the air. A second detonation sent the Strong's steam boiler racing up like a rocket.

"Look out!" someone shouted as the air was filled with fragments from the shaft house.

The deputies on the flatcars scrambled to take some sort of cover as steel cables, steel wheels, bits of framing, large pieces of fractured metal, and chunks of wood and concrete came raining down around them.

"Let's get the hell out of here!" Boynton shouted.

"Don't cry, honey," Pearl said as she tried to comfort Tori.

"He doesn't want anything to do with me," Tori said between sniffs.

"I don't believe that. I know Link, and I've known him since the day I arrived in Cripple Creek. He wouldn't just turn his back on you like that."

"Then where is he? Why can't I find him? Why didn't he tell me he was going? It's because he doesn't want anything to do with me, that's why."

"Didn't you say a moment ago that you had already told him you'd slept with a man?" Lucy asked.

Tori nodded.

"Did Link walk out on you when you told him that?" Lucy asked.

"No."

"That's because he's a good man, as decent a man as anyone I've ever known," Pearl said.

"That's just it," Tori said, breaking down in sobs. "He's a decent man, and he found out I'm an indecent woman."

At that moment the windows rattled and they felt the house shake as they heard the roar of a loud explosion.

"What was that?" Lucy asked. "There aren't any mines working now, and even if there was one, we've never heard an explosion that loud."

The three women stepped outside and, looking

around the hills, they saw a large column of smoke billowing up from Battle Mountain.

"What is that?" Tori asked. "What do you think happened?"

"I think someone just blew up a mine," Pearl said.

"Oh! Which one?" Lucy asked.

"I can't really say, but it looks like it's coming from the general direction of the Strong, or the Independence, or maybe the Portland," Pearl said. "And if I had to guess, I would say it's the Strong."

"You mean you think it was done on purpose?" Tori asked.

"I'm just guessing," Pearl said, "but I've heard a few things. All I can say is some folks really don't like Sam Strong."

The explosion knocked Link off the flatcar, and he rolled down the rocky berm, winding up at the bottom of a ravine. The fall was painful, and he had cuts and bruises, but as he lay there, carefully examining his body, he was sure that he had no serious injuries. Standing up, he saw that the train he had ridden up on was now backing down the hill as fast as gravity and the dinkey could make it go.

A moment later he saw an unattached flatcar freewheeling down the grade. At first he was confused by the sight, wondering where the car had come from; then, when the car reached a curve, it left the track and overturned. This caused an explosion almost as loud as the first one.

Link made his way back up to the tracks and stood there looking toward the flaming wreckage.

"Link Buchannan," a voice called out to him. "What are you doing here?"

Turning toward the sound of the voice, Link saw Marshal Daly. "I'm about to ask myself the same thing. What the hell made that car explode like that?"

"Ha. General Johnson loaded it with TNT and sent it down toward the deputies' camp. I expect you'd better come with me." Daly had a pistol in his hand and gestured with it to underscore his "invitation" for Link to join him.

"What do you want with me?"

"I'm goin' to put you in jail," Daly said.

"For what?"

"For . . ." Daly paused for a moment, trying to think of a charge. "For trespassin' without a passport."

"You're insane." Link sighed. "But I don't suppose you're any more insane than I am."

Like thinking Tori would give up the excitement of New York for the likes of me, Link thought.

"You're not goin' to give me any trouble, are you?"

"No. I can't think of any reason why I want to go back down there." Link nodded toward Cripple Creek.

"Well then, let's get on up the hill. I just can't believe those damn fools actually did blow up the Strong."

"Was it Lyons and Tully?"

"Yeah, them and Landry, too, but how did you know?"

"I caught them trying it once before."

"I kinda wish Manny had been able to stop 'em."

"Manny? Manny Drumm? What does he have to do with all this?"

"Calderwood's in Salt Lake City, so Manny's in charge of the union. When he found out what those three galoots had planned, he took a gun and went to the mine to stop them."

"Where is he now?"

"I don't know. I've not seen 'im since."

"You mean Manny might still be there? At the mine?"

"Could be, as far as I know."

"Marshal, look, I know I'm under arrest, and I'm not trying to pull something, but let's go up to the Strong and see if Manny's all right. I've got a bad feeling."

"Why do you care about Manny Drumm?"

"Because before all this started, he was my friend. And if he's still alive, I'll still consider him my friend."

"All right, it won't hurt to go look," Daly agreed.

When they reached the mine, several people were gathered around the rubble. Lyons and Tully were among them.

"We done it!" Tully said, smiling broadly. "We said we was goin' to do it, and we done it!"

"Tully, where's Manny Drumm?" Marshal Daly asked.

"In there," Tully answered.

"Is he dead?"

"I think so," Lyons said. "Him and Landry shot each other just before we set the charge."

"In where? Where did you see him?" Link asked.

Lyons glared at Link, then turned to Daly. "What the hell is he doin' up here? He's the enemy."

"Just answer the question. Where was Manny when you last saw him?" Daly asked.

"I told you, he was in the shaft house." Lyons giggled. "Or what was the shaft house. There ain't one no more."

"You mean you just left him in there when you set the charge?" Link asked.

"Why not? I told you, more'n likely him and Landry was both dead. Anyway, he got his own self kilt, comin' to try 'n' stop us like he done."

"Which he had no business doin' in the first place," Tully added.

"We think there's at least three other men trapped down there," another said.

"Who?" Daly asked.

"Sam McDonald, Charles Robinson, and Jack Vaughn."

"Damn, Tully, the least you coulda done was make sure the mine was vacant when you done this," Daly said.

"So, Daly, what's it going to be?" Link asked. "Are you going to take me to jail, or are we going to rescue those men?"

Daly thought for no longer than a couple of seconds, then he looked at the men gathered around him. "All right, boys, and that includes you two." Daly looked directly at Lyons and Tully. "Let's start clearin' away this rubble."

The engine with the two flatcars full of deputies hadn't stopped at the camp set up at Hayden Divide but, taking advantage of the newly completed rail-road, took everyone back into Cripple Creek.

"Them miners up there is crazy! They done blowed up a mine," one of the deputies said. "Then they loaded a car with TNT 'n' run it down the track right toward us. Why, if that car hadn't run off the track, there ain't no tellin' what it would have done."

Charles Tutt picked his way through the anxious and angry crowd along Bennett Avenue as he headed for the Tutt and Penrose Building. The streets were crowded with men, some of whom had drunk too much whiskey and were now armed with shotguns, rifles, pistols, and knives.

Susan Dunbar had tables filled with rolls of bandages lining the block in front of the building. A hand-lettered sign erected near the table read LADIES' AUXILIARY MEDICAL ASSISTANCE.

"Ladies, join in the fight!" she was calling.

A woman from Myers Avenue—not one of Pearl's girls but from one of the other parlors—approached the table. "I would like to help."

"We don't need the assistance of harlots!" Susan shouted. She pointed in the direction of Myers Avenue. "Go on back to whatever crib or whorehouse you came from, and leave the decent women to look after our men!"

The woman, with tears in her eyes, turned and started back toward Myers.

"Honey, if you would give it away for free, that would help lots of men," someone called to her, and his shout was met with ribald laughter.

"I thought Boynton was goin' to take care of this! Why don't he do somethin'?" someone asked.

"He tried, and he near 'bout got us all kilt," one of the deputies responded.

When Charles reached his building, he hurried upstairs and, seeing Link's door ajar, stepped inside.

"Link, have you seen what's—" Charles found Tori sitting on the sofa. "Tori, I didn't expect to find you here. Where's Link?"

"I don't know," Tori replied quietly.

"Oh, is something wrong? Has something happened to Link?"

"I wish I could tell you, but I really don't know where he is."

"Well, I'll check with Speck. He may know." With a nod Charles withdrew, closing the door behind him.

"What's going on across the hall?"

"You mean in Link's office?" Speck asked.

"Yeah, Tori's sitting over there acting like she's just lost her last friend. Has something happened to Link?"

"Nobody's seen him since yesterday, so we don't know."

"That's strange that he didn't tell anybody, or at least tell Tori. I was under the impression that Link was quite taken with her. Is that all off now?"

"It's hard to say, but whatever it is, it's complicated," Speck said, thinking that the better part of valor would be to say no more.

After a long, hard afternoon of pulling away debris, the workers at the Strong Mine discovered the body of a man under a donkey engine. The body was badly mangled and distorted, but they identified it as Gorran Landry.

"Too bad," Daly said, "but at least he didn't suffer none when the mine was blown up. Look, there's a bullet hole in his forehead."

"Didn't Lyons just tell us he was shot?" Link pointed out.

"Yeah. We'll probably be pullin' Manny Drumm out of this pile, too," Daly said. "He was a good kid, but this sure don't look good for him."

Daly pointed to huge pile of twisted steel and large chunks of broken concrete. "If he's under there, it don't seem to me like there's much point in goin' on."

"What about the other three that are missing? They could still be alive," Link said. "If it were you down there, wouldn't you want to think that your men would come after you?"

"You're right," Daly said. "Men, let's get to it. We've got more work to do."

Tori hadn't left Link's office all day. Now she sat in the darkened room illuminated only by the ambient light of the outside streetlamp. The door opened, and with a leap of hope she looked toward it, hoping to see Link enter. Instead, it was Mollie, backlit by the hall light.

"I thought you might be in here."

Tori didn't answer.

"Would you like to go downstairs and get a cup of tea with me? Or are you just going to sit here all night?"

"Oh, Mollie, how could this have happened? When Link asked me to marry him, I was never happier in my life, and now it's all over. Because of me. I've made such a mess of things."

"You don't really believe that, honey." Mollie sat beside Tori. "You haven't made a mess of anything."

"Yes I have. He knows what kind of woman I am, and now he doesn't want me."

"I don't believe that—not for a minute. Link loves you. Everybody around him knows that. He's not going to give you up just because you shared the bed of another man."

"Lyle wasn't just another man. He was another woman's husband, so that makes me a wanton of the worst kind. It's one kind of sin to fornicate, but it makes it worse if I'm an adulterer."

"Oh, Tori, my dear friend, none of us is perfect." Mollie reached over and took Tori's hand. "Do you know Charles Miller is married?"

"Oh, no, Mollie." Tori embraced her friend. "Why do we let ourselves get in . . ." Tori let out a deep sigh. "I thought my heart was broken when Lyle betrayed me. But until now, until this very moment, I had no idea what a broken heart really was."

While Link and the few men who stayed to help were still frantically searching for survivors at the Strong Mine, Junius Johnson, who had now begun calling himself General Johnson, had stepped up the confrontation with the remaining deputies just south of Victor. Commandeering a work train, Johnson sent his army of men to engage the "enemy," as he called the deputies, and the gunfire could be heard until just after midnight. Word was sent to Marshal Daly that two of the striking miners had been killed, and General Johnson needed every available man.

"Tell Junius we're not coming," Marshal Daly said. "About an hour ago, we heard what sounded like somebody yelling down below. These men have to believe we're still comin' for 'em."

"The general's not going to like it if you don't obey his orders," the messenger said.

"Hell, who told that little West Point dropout he was in charge? Get back to him and tell him what I said. Oh, and leave your wagon. If these men are hurt, we may need it."

The search continued, now with the light of several lanterns Daly had confiscated from the Independence.

At first, as Link worked, he told himself he was doing this for Tori, but then he reasoned that she wouldn't even know anything about it. By now she was long gone, on a train somewhere across the country, returning to New York with the man who could give her what she wanted, what she deserved.

He didn't see how she could possibly love this man, because Link had truly believed her when she had said she loved him.

But he had also watched how she'd reveled in the success of the play. He recognized that she was too talented an actress to walk away from the gift she had been given, and he couldn't hold it against her if she chose her career over him.

This was what his mind was telling him.

But it wasn't what was in his heart.

He had never before been in love, so he had never experienced the feelings he was having now. *Heartbreak* was just a word that other people—people he considered weak—would use. But now he understood what heartbreak was.

As he continued to search for Manny, he realized that this wasn't the first time he had experienced heartbreak. It hadn't been the pain of losing a lover, but the pain that had overwhelmed him when his sister had died. Then, when he added the belief that he was the cause of her death, the pain was compounded. That grief was the closest thing he had to compare with what he was going through now.

"I wish to hell you had never come here."

"What do you mean you wish I hadn't come here? It wasn't me that done this," the miner who was working beside him said.

Link realized then that he had spoken out loud. "I'm sorry. Pete, is it?"

"Yeah, Pete Mathis."

"I guess I was thinking about my friend Manny. I wish he hadn't come here, and I must've said it aloud."

"He was a good man. All the miners said that about him."

"Hey! We're breakin' through over here!" someone shouted. "Everyone, over here on this side!"

As many men moved over as could be accommodated by the small space, and within another fifteen minutes, they had a hole big enough to look through.

"It's Drumm!" someone shouted when they lowered the lantern.

They saw a couple of crossed beams that had pro-
tected a small cavity under all the rubble. Though
the shaft house with all its timbers and bracing had
fallen around the shaft, it hadn't actually collapsed
on Manny.

Link didn't know if that mattered, though. Manny
looked to be lifeless.

"There's an opening here where we can climb on
down into the mine," someone called.

"All right, see if you can find McDonald and the
others," Daly ordered.

Link hurried over to the hole and put his hand on
Manny's neck. He felt a faint pulse. "He's still alive!"
Link said excitedly. "Help me get him out of here!"

Carefully, Link and Daly cleared the remaining
debris that covered Manny and then carried him to
the waiting wagon.

"He's mostly dead," Daly said. "I'd say take him to
Altman, but the doc's probably with Junius."

"He needs more than a doctor, he needs a hospital," Link said. "We have to get him to Colorado
Springs for him to have even a fighting chance, and
I just hope he lives long enough for me to get him
there."

Link was thankful that David Moffat's railroad had
reached Cripple Creek, and while the route through
Florence was longer than going through Midland,
he could go the whole way by train. With one engine
pulling just one car, they made a fast trip to Colorado Springs.

Manny was unconscious for the whole trip, and
when they reached St. Francis Hospital, Dr Taylor

said, "He's lost a lot of blood. There's not much hope, but he's a young man. Maybe he'll pull through."

"Do you mean I've rushed him here, literally moving heaven and earth, and there's nothing that you can do about it?"

"Well, there's one thing, but it doesn't always work."

"If there's even a slim chance, shouldn't we do everything we can?"

"Have you ever heard of a blood transfusion?" Dr. Taylor asked.

"Yes. I even know of some successful ones back in Philadelphia."

"*Some* is the operative word there. I can't say I've had very good success with the procedure."

"Well, what's this man's prognosis if we don't try it?"

The doctor shook his head. "I don't give him much hope."

"What do you need to try a transfusion?"

"A willing donor."

"You have one." Link sat down and rolled up his sleeve.

Colorado Springs Gazette—Monday, June 11, 1894

THE SITUATION RESOLVED

SETTLEMENT OF THE TROUBLES ARRANGED

These are the terms of the compromise reached by the mine owners and the miners. The mine owners will offer wages of three dollars per day for an eight-hour day of labor. The union has withdrawn its demand that only union miners be employed.

Sheriff Bowers credits the performance of his deputy army for preventing union strikers from attacking Cripple Creek and bringing untold injuries to the innocent and loss of property to the businessmen. He says of his deputies, "They are the finest I've ever seen. It must be remembered that they were all volunteers, serving without contract, and could have quit at any time they wished. They did not quit but stayed until the situation was resolved."

Sheriff Bowers says that there will be a homecoming parade in Cripple Creek to celebrate the agreement, which will again make Cripple Creek the busiest and most prosperous gold camp in the country.

Link put the paper down and looked over at Manny, who was sitting beside him in the waiting room of the Colorado Springs depot.

"Well, it looks like we'll get back to town just in time for a big parade," Link said.

"What kind of parade?"

"I guess it's to welcome us back home."

Manny chuckled, then shook his head. "Calderwood was right. He said the mine owners would finally come around. What I'm wondering is why it took you all so long to do it."

"No you don't," Link said, holding up his hand. "Don't put me in with that batch. Unlike you, who did have a role in the calling of the strike, I had nothing to do with the stand taken by the mine owners. I was only an innocent bystander."

"You're right. And you and I shouldn't be fighting anyway. I've got your blood in me, and that pretty much makes us brothers, doesn't it?"

Link chuckled. "I think it does."

"I'm just sorry Tori's not here."

"You aren't the only one, brother."

"You know, Link, you should have fought for her. I've never met this jerk she ran off with, but I'd be willing to bet he isn't half as good a man as you are."

Link smiled. "I appreciate that, but sometimes you have to love someone enough to let them go. You didn't get to watch your sister, but she really is a brilliant actress. Her name will be every bit as well-known as Lily Langtry's or Sarah Bernhardt's. What could I have given her that would compete with that?"

"I can think of something."

"All aboard for Manitou Springs, Colorado City, Florissant, and . . . now Cripple Creek! Board!" someone shouted, and Link and Manny started toward the train.

"This'll be the first time either one of us has gotten to ride the Midland all the way to Cripple Creek," Manny said.

When the cab stopped in front of Pearl's place, Manny jumped out first. Running up the steps, he threw open the door and went inside.

"I'd say Mr. Drumm's in a mighty big hurry to see Miss Lucy," Junior said.

"You amaze me, Junior. You're better than the newspaper," Link said as he handed him the fare.

"I know somethin' else, but I'm not gonna tell you." Junior snapped the reins and the cab hurtled forward.

Pearl, Lucy, and Maxine were sitting in the parlor when Manny stepped through the door.

"Oh, my God! Manny!" Lucy gasped the words in complete shock.

"Aren't you happy to see me?"

None of the three women replied. They just continued to stare at him, their faces as white as sheets.

"What is it? What's wrong?"

"We thought you were dead," Lucy said, clasping her hands over her chest.

"Well, as you can see, that's not true," Link said as he walked in through the open door.

"Link!" Pearl squealed in delight. "Where have you been for the last two weeks?"

"Colorado Springs. I've been taking care of Manny."

"But you didn't tell anybody. We have telephones, you know."

"I didn't want to talk to anybody. When . . . when . . . when Manny's sister left . . . oh, hell, I just didn't want to be here, but I'm over it now. Have you heard from her?"

"Yes, I have," Pearl said.

"Link, what are you—" Lucy started, but Pearl held out her hand to stop her.

"I'll bet you two are hungry. Go on into the dining room and sit down. I'll have Addie bring you something to eat, and when you're finished, we can talk."

"Best offer I've had in a while," Manny said.

"Pearl, why didn't you let me tell him?" Lucy whispered after the two men left the parlor.

"Maxine, quick, get my phaeton and go get Tori. Tell her Manny is alive and that he's here. But don't mention Link. Let's just put them together and let nature take its course."

Link and Manny were the only two at the dining-room table, and they were enjoying the meal that had been put before them.

"Did you take that last biscuit?" Link asked.

"What last biscuit?"

"I wonder if Mrs. Fitzgerald has any more back in the kitchen." Link walked into the kitchen with easy familiarity and called, "Mrs. Fitzgerald!"

Manny waited until Link left the room, then, smiling, he lifted the biscuit from under the table.

"Manny? Oh, Manny, you're alive!" Tori said, stepping into the dining room.

"Tori!" Manny got up and went to her quickly. They embraced.

"Why didn't you call me?"

"I thought—that is, *we* thought—you had gone back East."

"'We' thought?"

"Yes, Link and I. He's been—"

"Link? Link is here?" Tori asked in a small, weak voice.

"Don't say I'm not a friend. I brought you another biscuit as well," Link said, stepping back into the dining room. "Here you—"

Link stopped in midsentence. "Tori?" As Tori's

had been, Link's voice was quiet, tentative, as if he couldn't believe what he was seeing.

"Tori!" he said again, this time shouting and dropping the two biscuits as he moved toward her with his arms spread wide.

With no hesitancy, no recriminations, no questions or challenges—with only pure joy—the two embraced, then kissed, a deep, loving kiss.

"Are they going to come up for air?" Pearl asked, she and Lucy having come into the room then.

"I don't know," Lucy said. "Do you think we should remind them that they have to breathe?"

"Seeing as Tori is my sister, I wonder if I should ask Link what are his intentions?"

"I'll tell you my intentions," Link said, finally interrupting the kiss, though not the embrace. "My intentions are to marry your sister. That is, if she'll have me."

"Yes, Link. Oh, yes, my darling."

Tori and Link were in bed in Link's loft. The room was redolent with the scent of sex, and they were lying together, naked skin against naked skin.

Link chuckled.

"What is it?"

"On the day I saw you and Ketterman kissing—"

"Wait. You didn't see us kissing—you saw him kissing me. There's a difference."

"Yes. But the reason I was coming to your office was because I had just written out a bank draft for Speck's five thousand dollars. I wanted you to be with me when I gave it to him."

"Where is it? We'll give it to him now."

"Now? Don't you think we should get dressed first?"

Link lifted himself up to rest on his elbow. He let the open palm of his free hand come down to gently brush against first one nipple, then the other, causing them to draw into tight little buds. It was not the passion-driven, absence-intensified sexual hunger that had brought them together earlier; this time it was a comfortable, shared possessiveness.

"On second thought, we can give him the money some other time," Tori said. "There's something else we need to do first." She reached over to grasp his shaft and was pleased that with only the lightest touch on her part it began to grow. "Or maybe I should say *again*." Tori mumbled the last word into Link's lips as he kissed her.

EPILOGUE

A large crowd was gathered in front of the Ambassador Hotel, standing behind the red felt ropes that were looped through shining brass stanchions. In addition, policemen were strategically placed along either side of the wide red carpet that led from the curb, helping to hold back the crowd as the Hollywood luminaries and their entourages arrived for the Academy Awards ceremonies.

Link and Tori were riding in the backseat of the chauffeured Packard that had picked them up at the Los Angeles airport, having just flown in from Denver. They were listening to Conrad Nagel on radio station KCEA.

"Tonight the Academy of Motion Picture Arts and Sciences will be presenting its highest awards. In alphabetical order, the nominees for Best Actor are Wallace Beery for his role in *The Champ*, Stan Hardegree in *The Night Rider*, Alfred Lunt in *The Guardsman*, and Fredric March in *Dr. Jekyll and Mr. Hyde*.

"The nominees for Best Actress are . . ."

"Here it comes," Tori said, reaching over to take the hand of her husband of thirty-seven years.

Link squeezed Tori's hand as they listened.

"Della Buchannan for *The Bridge Back*, Marie Dressler in *Emma*, Lynn Fontanne in *The Guardsman*, and Helen Hayes in *The Sin of Madelon Claudet*."

The car glided majestically to a halt in front of the hotel, and a uniformed doorman opened the back door for them. At sixty-three years old, Tori, dressed in an elegant white gown, still had the svelte figure that had once graced the New York stage. And Link, his hair now snow-white, made a distinguished escort in his tuxedo.

Though Link and Tori were not a famous couple, they were still glamorous, and the crowd applauded politely as they moved up the red carpet.

Just inside, they looked across the ballroom and saw their daughter dressed in a regal blue gown shimmering with sequins. A man was behind a microphone, and Della was standing beside him. When she saw her parents, she smiled and waved.

"Ladies and gentlemen, you have been listening to Della Buchannan, one of the nominees for Best Actress tonight, and now if I may, I am going to bring to the microphone the woman to whom Miss Buchannan credits her enormous success: her mother, Professor Victoria Buchannan. Mrs. Buchannan, if you would, please?"

Tori stepped up to the microphone.

"I understand you are an instructor of the dramatic arts at Colorado College. Was your daughter your best student?"

Tori smiled before she answered. "I have had

many talented students, but her father and I are particularly proud of Della."

"For those of you in our listening audience who may not be aware of it, in the nineties, Professor Buchannan was quite the star herself, appearing in such Broadway productions as *Sunday in the Park*, *A Summer Dwelling*, and the long-running *A Young Woman's Travail*.

"Tell me, Professor, from the view of one who has not only taught but acted, what is your opinion of your daughter's performance in *The Bridge Back*? Do you think she has a chance to win?"

"She's already won," Link chimed in.

"I beg your pardon?" the radio announcer asked, surprised by the comment. "Do you know something that we do not?"

"She won when she was born to the wonderful woman who is her mother."

"What a charming sentiment, sir. You have two lovely and talented women here," the announcer said. "Thank you for taking the time to chat with us. Oh, there's Mr. Beery. Sir, Wallace Beery, can you come to the microphone?"

Forgetting Della and her parents, the announcer turned his attention to Mr. Beery.

"Come on," Della said. "Gary Cooper has asked us to sit at his table."

After the awards ceremony, Gary Cooper and his fiancée, Veronica Balfe, joined Tori and Link and Della and her escort, Mark Worley, at dinner.

Della stood to speak. "History may record that Helen Hayes won for Best Actress. But I feel every bit a winner for being born to Lincoln and Victoria Buchannan." Della held out her glass of wine. "Mama, Papa, I love you more than I can say."

"Hear, hear," Gary Cooper said as the table applauded.

"Professor Buchannan, I wonder if I could ask you a question," Mark Worley said.

"Of course."

"One of the biggest mysteries in theater lore is . . . why did Sabrina Chadwick walk away from such a brilliant career?"

Tori looked over at Link and smiled. "Because sometimes you just know which way to go when you come to a fork in the road."

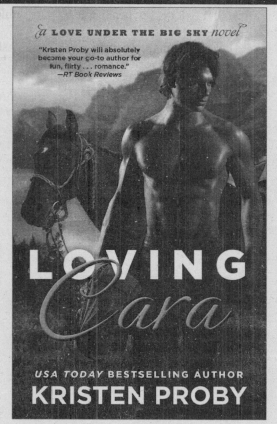